T0246055

A LETHAL
QUESTION

ALSO BY MARK RUBINSTEIN

A LETHAL QUESTION

A NOVEL

MARK RUBINSTEIN

OCEANVIEW  PUBLISHING

SARASOTA, FLORIDA

ISBN 978-1-60809-574-2

Published in the United States of America by Oceanview Publishing

Sarasota, Florida

www.oceanviewpub.com

10 9 8 7 6 5 4 3 2 1

For Linda

"Death–the last sleep? No, it is the final awakening."

—SIR WALTER SCOTT

"Our lives are written in disappearing ink."

—MICHELLE CLIFT

A LETHAL
QUESTION

CHAPTER 1

At noon on a splendid day near the end of April, Boris Levenko sits at an outdoor table at Nadia's, a restaurant facing the boardwalk in the Brighton Beach section of Brooklyn. As owner of the place, he always has his pick of the best table on the veranda.

Grigory Shokin and Oleg Ginzburg, his two senior aides, are with him. Grigory chortles and says in Russian, "I wonder which fool coined the expression 'Crime doesn't pay.'" Oleg laughs loudly.

"You must not speak in Russian or Ukrainian, Oleg," Boris commands. "English only."

Boris knows the truth of the matter: crime has paid handsomely for the Odessa mafia, but Boris is feeling somber these days. He's sick of all the *Yes Men* in his circle of Bratva brethren. Sure, they rule the streets of Brighton Beach, Coney Island, and Sheepshead Bay. And soon, they'll control much of the Bronx, because the Albanians are growing weaker by the day.

But Boris has grown tired of it all. At sixty years of age and as a pakhan in the Odessa mafia, he realizes this life of crime is a young man's pursuit. Now, he cherishes simple things like sitting in the open air and inhaling the scents of the Atlantic Ocean while waiting for the waitress to bring the borscht he ordered for all three men. The restaurant's food brings back memories of the dishes his mother so lovingly prepared when he was a child back in Ukraine. It's amazing how so simple a thing as an aroma can take you back in time and place so quickly.

Boris is aware that in contrast to his early ambitions—the strivings that drove him to eliminate potential rivals—he now takes pleasure in his family: his children's success, spending more time with his wife, Nadia—for whom the restaurant is named—and watching his grandchildren thrive. As Americans, they'll never struggle through the hardships he was forced to overcome.

"Boss," Grigory Shokin says in Russian, "we must deal with these Albanians. As your brigadier, I must order my soldiers to take action and—"

Boris raises his hand: an instant Stop sign. Though Boris loves the Russian language—he thinks its sound is somewhere between the roar of a walrus and a Brahms melody—he says, "English, Grigory . . . *English*. Not Russian or Ukrainian. We only speak English in public."

The lunchtime crowd is made up of older Russians, Georgians, Ukrainians, and Belarussians, all refugees from the former Soviet Union, who understand very little English. But Russian and Ukrainian are their mother tongues, so Boris discourages his men from using those languages in public settings.

Grigory resumes speaking in English, but Boris barely hears a word. Rather, he gazes at the gray waters of the Atlantic. He watches a seagull plunge-dive for fish. Amid the splash, the gull rises in the air with a small catch snared in its beak.

Yes, it's a dangerous world of hunters and prey. And in this world, he's used his skill, his personal *kharizma* to become a pakhan in the Bratva, the Brotherhood. But it's the success of his immediate family that provides his real happiness.

"So, Boris," Grigory continues in broken English, "these Albanians must learn a harsh lesson."

"They will at an appropriate time," Boris says.

"But, Boris," continues Grigory, "if we wait we could lose all Bronx operations. We must not sit like . . . how do you say . . . Like *truslivyye vory . . .*"

"Like *cowardly thieves,*" Boris says as he watches the elderly couples strolling past them on the boardwalk in the brilliant April sunlight. *Soon, I'll be one of those old-timers*, he thinks. *It all passes by so quickly.*

"Yes, cowards that they are, "Grigory says. "We must make move. We are more strong than they are."

But Boris Levenko doesn't want to think about mobsters and drug trafficking and money laundering and bootlegging or arms smuggling. The hell with Medicare and gasoline tax fraud, and all the other rackets. He would rather think about lunch. Along with the borscht, he'll order a blini with smetana; he loves how the cold sour cream mixes with the heat of the blini.

The waitress arrives; she's a pretty young woman who, after nodding respectfully at Boris, promptly takes their orders. The other two men, out of deference to their pakhan, order the same dishes as Boris does.

Before he knows it, three bowls of borscht, along with blinis smothered in smetana, are sitting in front of them.

"Eat, eat, my brothers," Boris says as he spoons the soup into his mouth.

Boris knows Nadia's recipes are the best—truly a pleasure to the palate. "Wait until you taste the blinis," Boris says and then slurps another spoonful of borscht.

Grigory continues in English. "Please, Boris, we must have answer for those evil bastards. They are thinking they can take over our business."

"Ah, Grigory, for now let's just enjoy our lunch."

*   *   *

Vladimir Abramovich, a line cook at Nadia's, is taking his noon-time break.

As he walks along the boardwalk, he notices three hard-looking men strolling toward Nadia's outdoor veranda. Having worked at the restaurant for years, he's easily able to pick out mobsters—it barely matters if they're Russians, Italians, Armenians, Chechens, Israelis, Turks, or Ukrainians. These three are very likely soldiers of the Odessa mafia; they are men of death.

*   *   *

In his peripheral vision, Boris Levenko notices the same three men walking toward the veranda, huddled against the ocean breeze. They look like three of his soldiers coming to Nadia's to enjoy a midday meal.

He's about to take another spoonful of borscht when there's a popping noise and he sees Grigory thrust violently backwards. Boris hears Oleg shout, but his voice is muffled, and a gurgling sound comes from his mouth as blood spurts onto the table, which is now tilting and splintering, and suddenly Boris feels an impact so powerful he's hurled backwards. There's another thumping shock, and another, and he feels his heart bursting as his flesh blows apart and he's lying beside the overturned table with borscht, blinis, bowls, and silverware everywhere. He's shivering while peering up at the sky as seagulls soar overhead and the light dims in one last shimmering moment of awareness.

Then comes darkness.

*   *   *

Vladimir Abramovich, the line cook, hears what sounds like an air hose spitting bursts of air from its nozzle. Then come more pops—one after another—and lurching to a stop, he turns back toward the café.

He sees those same three men holding pistols fitted with suppressors. They fire again and again and the men at the table go down; their bodies buck and spasm with blood spattering everywhere.

The three shooters empty their pistols, turn, and dash from the veranda toward the ramp leading down to Brighton Sixth Street. They pile into a waiting van on the street below. The vehicle speeds off, fishtails, then makes a sharp right turn onto Brightwater Court and is gone.

Moving closer, Vladimir sees the bodies of Boris Levenko and his two aides splayed in grotesque positions amid silverware and shattered dishes with wood splinters, blood, borscht, and blinis everywhere as people gasp at the horror that meets their eyes.

CHAPTER 2

Bill Madrian sits at his desk clearing up some insurance company paperwork.

Glancing at his watch, he sees it's nearly 7:00 p.m. Alex, the last patient of the evening, will soon arrive. The guy travels from the Bronx for his counseling sessions; he drives to Bill's office on 75th Street between Park and Lexington on the Upper East Side of Manhattan.

Alex—formal name, Alexander Bronzi—is thirty years old and still lives with his parents. Though he's an adult, Alex projects an almost childish quality. Despite his being five years older than Alex, Bill sometimes finds himself feeling paternal toward his patient. It's clear that Alex's dependency is a double-edged sword; while depending on his father's largesse, he also resents him. Deeply. "My father's a ball-buster," Alex said in their first session nearly a month ago.

"Working for a father can be rough," Bill said. "What kind of business is it?"

"We're in the trucking business," Alex replied in his Bronx patois. "We ship freight all over the country. No matter what I do, my father puts me down in front of everyone, so they don't respect me."

During last week's session, Alex also talked about his mother. "She wants me to move out of the house. 'Get married,' she says. She's tired of doing my laundry and cooking for me. But hey, Doc, I got it great at home. Why would I give that up?"

"But there's a cost to you, Alex. Your independence . . . your sense of self."

At the end of their last meeting, Bill handed Alex the bill for the month's three sessions.

"I got it covered," Alex said, opening the envelope and glancing at the invoice. Reaching into his pocket, he extracted a roll of hundred-dollar bills, peeled off nine, and held them out toward Bill.

"I can't accept cash," Bill said.

"Why not?"

Sensing Alex was testing him, Bill explained, "Everything's gotta be aboveboard in our sessions."

It was important to send Alex a clear message: Bill won't even allow the *appearance* of being willing to evade taxes by accepting under-the-table cash. With certain ground rules firmly established, Alex can feel—as would any patient—that his psychiatrist is a straight shooter. Alex can remain confident that Bill won't do anything shady or questionable, and that, among other things, he'll never betray a patient's confidence.

The intercom sounds: three short buzzes. Bill presses the button sending a signal to the lock on the lobby-entrance door. A moment later, Alex enters the consultation room.

Instead of his usual nylon track suit, Alex wears dark slacks, a burgundy-colored turtleneck beneath a sleek, finely tapered gray sports jacket. His charcoal-colored eyes flash in his fleshy face, and as usual, his hair is stylishly barbered. "I got a date tonight, Doc. I gotta look good."

Before sitting in the patient's chair, Alex reaches into his breast pocket, whips out a check, and hands it over. Bill catches a glimpse of it as he sets it on a side table. The check is for nine hundred dollars, covering the last three sessions, and is drawn on a bank in Belize.

"Belmont Trucking Company?" Bill says glancing at Alex.

"Yeah, Doc."

"Don't you have a personal checking account?"

"Na. The business takes care of things for me."

"You know, Alex, we've been talking about how much you depend on your parents . . ."

"Yeah, I know," he says, shrugging and canting his head. He actually appears a bit embarrassed.

"Not having your own checking account is part of that. Everything centers around your parents, especially your father. And of course, the business . . ."

A sheepish grin spreads across Alex's lips. "I know, Doc. I've been thinkin' about goin' out on my own . . . you know, leaving the business . . ."

"Becoming more independent can begin with small things, like having your own checking account or taking your laundry to the cleaners, maybe even getting a place of your own . . ."

"I hear ya, Doc. But it ain't easy just to pick up and leave."

Bill remains quiet, lets the exchange sink in. There's no point in pressing the issue further; doing so would seem like a criticism to Alex, and would be a repetition of his relationship with his father, which isn't why Alex comes for the counseling.

Finally, after what seems a long pause, Alex looks toward the consultation room door—as though checking to see it's securely closed—then fixes his gaze on Bill. "Hey, Doc, everything we talk about here is confidential, right?"

"Absolutely."

Alex's lips spread into a thin line. "You know, I'm Albanian . . ."

"I never really thought about it, Alex. I thought your family was Italian, that maybe the name was shortened from something longer."

"No way, Doc. Bronzi's a good old Albanian name. We're proud of it." Alex pauses, and then, in a voice barely above a whisper, says, "So, if I tell ya somethin' confidential, it stays in this room, right?"

"Yes, of course."

Alex's eyes narrow and he says in a steely voice, "Hey, Doc . . . ya wanna know who clipped Boris Levenko?"

Stunned, Bill's skin feels electrified, and his lungs feel like they've been emptied of air.

Holy shit! Alex Bronzi is referring to the mob rubout that happened near the boardwalk a few days ago in Brighton Beach, Brooklyn—the shooting death of Boris Levenko, a Big Boss in the Russian Brotherhood. Huge headlines in the *Daily News* and the *New York Post* shrieked about the murders. The story was on television, radio, and even the *New York Times* ran a front-page story about the killings.

Every nerve in Bill's body feels like it's firing in a neural shitstorm.

Hey, Doc . . . ya wanna know who clipped Boris Levenko?
What kind of question is that?

An offer of inside mob information.

It's an offer Bill can *definitely* refuse.

"No, I don't want to know," he hears himself croak through a throat that's Saharan dry.

This is unbelievable. A patient whom he's seen three previous times trusts him enough to talk about the biggest mob rubout since the 1985 murder of Paul Castellano in front of Sparks Steakhouse in Manhattan.

The Boris Levenko killing?

The biggest crime story in decades?

And Alex Bronzi expects Bill will say nothing?

What the hell have I just heard? Where does this go from here?

There's patient confidentiality. There are HIPAA laws.

You can't say a word to anyone about a patient's health status or utterances without the patient's explicit permission. And for sure, that includes anything said in a psychotherapy session.

Omerta. Just like in the mob.

But can there be *omerta* in the psychiatrist's office?

"I guess I shoulda been more up front with ya, Doc," Alex says. "Some of the business is a little on the shady side. Especially in the construction end of things, the garbage hauling, and restaurant supply operation. I thought maybe you wouldn't wanna see me if you knew more about the family's connections."

Bill feels his scalp dampen and a low-level humming begins in his chest.

Then, as though he's revealed nothing of consequence, Alex begins rehashing his usual complaints about his father treating him like a child.

As Alex continues talking, Bill barely hears a word of what's being said. His thoughts are roiling . . . *Hey, Doc . . . ya wanna know who clipped Boris Levenko?*

It's unbelievable. Bill has just been presented with the chance to learn about a major mob felony, one of the biggest to ever occur in New York City.

As Alex rambles on, a series of questions churns through Bill's mind:

Does Alex's mobster father—or, for that matter, anyone in his family—know Alex is seeing a psychiatrist?

That Alex is visiting *Bill*?

And if anyone *does* know, especially his father, what does he think Alex talks about in their sessions?

Does his father think his son is disclosing family secrets?

That he talks about illegal activities?

Drug deals?

Extortion?

Payoffs to politicians and judges?

Prostitution?

Truck hijackings?

And any of a number of criminal activities that are part of the family's business model?

Especially murder?

Can this shrink be trusted to say nothing to anyone?

It hits Bill like a punch to the stomach: no matter what is—or *isn't*—said in their sessions, someone in Alex's "family" might *think* Alex is spilling mob secrets to his psychiatrist.

Then what happens?

To Bill?

And to his family: his mother and sister, Laurie? To his brother-in-law, Roger, and to Bill's two little nieces? This is beyond the pale.

As Alex continues with his litany of complaints, Bill wonders why he hadn't followed up on his initial misgivings about Alex's family business. The trucking business is frequently infiltrated by mobs; Bill knows it's true from years of reading newspapers and from movies like *Hoffa* with Jack Nicholson and *The Irishman* with Robert De Niro.

On top of that, Alex didn't come to Bill through a referral by a colleague. Instead, he'd gone online, and out of scores of Manhattan psychiatrists, he'd randomly picked up the telephone and called Bill.

It's almost as though Alex Bronzi dropped out of the sky.

And here Bill is: sitting only a few feet away from a mobster's son, a guy who's casually mentioned knowing who committed three grisly mob murders a few days ago.

Suddenly, Bill's thoughts turn to the fictional Dr. Melfi of *The Sopranos*.

Jesus, I'm in the same boat as she was.

But unlike Tony Soprano, who said nothing about his crime family's activities, Alex Bronzi wanted to talk about the biggest mob rubout in years.

What's Bill supposed to do? His profession demands that he never betray a patient's communications.

And what about members of Alex's family? They have to know how immature and unthinking their son is. Even without the recent murders in Brooklyn, it's likely Alex would be divulging far too much about the business to his shrink.

Bill glances at the Belmont Trucking check lying on his desk.

He knows the kid had to have asked someone at the company to write that draft.

Of course, that means they know he's seeing a psychiatrist.

Hey, Doc . . . ya wanna know who clipped Boris Levenko?

That question is so loaded, it weighs on the entire treatment.

When Alex leaves the office, Bill's thoughts are consumed by what he heard.

Is Bill a potential witness to murder?

Is he now in danger?

Should he call a lawyer?

The police?

Or say nothing, just keep Alex's revelation confidential?

What are his responsibilities to his patient, his own family, to himself, and to the law.

With his heart pulsing erratically, he picks up the telephone.

CHAPTER 3

Dr. Alfred Wallace's office has a lobby entrance in a white-glove co-op building on Park Avenue just off 84th Street

Wallace's consultation room reminds Bill of pictures he's seen of Freud's Vienna office at 19 Berggasse. The room has framed sepia-toned photographs, prints, and black-and-white sketches on the mahogany paneled walls. Glass-encased bookshelves hold rows of gilt-edged, leather-bound volumes relating to medicine, psychiatry, and law. Ornate Kashan rugs cover the floor.

Wallace, a sixty-something man, is a legend in both medical and legal circles. Not only is he a physician and psychiatrist, but he has a law degree from Columbia University. As a forensic psychiatrist, he specializes in cases where psychiatry and the law intersect. He provides expert testimony at both criminal and civil trials, appears at inquests, hearings, and depositions, and does psychiatric evaluations for both prosecution and defense attorneys.

He was one of Bill's supervisors during his residency, and they've maintained a cordial relationship over the years since Bill completed his training.

Wallace, a distinguished-looking man with a full head of white hair and a closely cropped beard, is dressed in old-fashioned tweeds, and smokes a Meerschaum pipe. The room is redolent of Cavendish pipe smoke.

Sitting in his leather chair across from Bill, Wallace says, "I couldn't help but notice, Bill, there was urgency in your voice last night. You said this case is troubling . . . so tell me about it."

Bill explains the situation with Alex Bronzi. Sticking to the rules of confidentiality, he doesn't mention the patient's name or provide any identifying details, but describes Alex's lifestyle and what he revealed during the last session.

Wallace listens carefully while nodding his head.

"Tell me, Bill . . . you said this young man is somewhat boastful. Is there a chance he was merely trying to impress you in his own immature way?"

"That's a possibility, but I had the gut feeling he actually knows plenty about the murders."

"Always trust your gut," Wallace says, relighting his pipe. "This young man wasn't completely honest with you, was he? Of course, that's a rhetorical question. He didn't mention what clearly is a mob connection until the fourth session, correct?"

"Yes. That was when he asked if I want to know who clipped Boris Levenko."

Nodding, Wallace says, "You did the right thing, telling him you didn't want to know about it."

Bill knows his instincts had been right. "But I have a question . . ." he says . . . "knowing what I do, am I obligated to inform the police?"

"No, you're not," Wallace says. "The law places enormous weight on the issue of confidentiality—whether it's the doctor-patient relationship or the priest-penitent situation. That being said, if a patient tells you he *intends* to commit a crime, you're obligated to inform the authorities or at least warn the potential victim. If you don't do that, you could be considered an accessory *before* the fact and could face criminal charges.

"In fact, Bill, if you *suspect* a patient will harm someone, you're obligated to inform the intended victim *and* the authorities. The Tarasoff decision made that clear. The California Supreme Court decided that a mental health professional has a duty not only to a patient, but also to warn anyone who might be threatened by that patient. And that decision's been adopted by most states. It's now accepted that confidential patient communications must take second place to avoid imminent danger to others."

Sucking on his pipe, Wallace's head is shrouded by a corona of smoke.

"But your situation's different than the one in the Tarasoff case," he continues, raising a finger. "Here, you're not dealing with a crime *about* to be committed. Your patient claims to have knowledge of a crime that's *already* been committed. The confidentiality exception remains intact. What he said was told to you in strictest confidence. And no crime is *about* to be committed. So, the Tarasoff ruling doesn't apply here. Therefore, you're not obligated to say a word to anyone."

"Understood. But I don't know if I can go on treating him."

"That's completely understandable. This young man may brag again and talk about a crime that's *about* to be committed, which will put you in a *very* difficult situation. And if you *do* go to the police, these criminals may want to silence you. Or, if they suspect you *already* know too much, they may want to shut you down, which of course, is a source of considerable worry."

"I gotta confess . . . that's what's *really* bothering me."

"And that leads us to the *next* important question. What's your ethical responsibility to this patient? Are you concerned that if you end the treatment you could be accused of abandoning him?"

"Yes, that also worries me."

"Abandoning a patient is a tort—a civil wrong—and a physician can be sued for malpractice if that occurs. But let's look at your obligation to this man, or really, to any patient. What is it?"

"To do the best I can to help him."

"Yes. It's a duty to care about his well-being, to maintain confidentiality, and not abandon him."

"And if I terminate his treatment after what he said . . . ?"

Wallace sets his pipe in an ashtray. "Let me put it to you this way: discontinuing the treatment *won't* be an abandonment. Your obligation to *this* patient doesn't include *endangering your own life*, which is obviously your major concern, yes?"

"Absolutely. I'm worried about what his family *thinks* I might know."

"That's completely understandable. Then you're under no obligation to continue treating him. Because of worries about your own safety and that of your family, you're well within your rights to terminate the treatment."

"I'm scared shitless." The words slip from Bill's mouth. "The people in his family have no idea what he says to me in the sessions. They could assume he's told me something that would expose them to prosecution. My treatment of this guy could be like me signing my own death warrant."

"Yes," Wallace says, nodding. "That's a rational kind of worry. And furthermore, if you *did* go to the police, all you could offer is hearsay . . . a statement provided by an unreliable third party—an immature young man who may have been simply trying to impress you. My advice is to terminate the treatment. But do it kindly and in a way he can understand. So he won't feel you kicked him out. At least you have to hope he understands your reasoning."

"That's what I'll do."

"Does his father or anyone in this organization know he's been in treatment with you?"

"I don't know, but he paid me with a check drawn from the family business."

Shaking his head, Wallace says, "I'd be scared shitless too."

CHAPTER 4

Kostandin Bronzi—known to his associates as Kosta—makes his way down the staircase of his Tudor-style house on Shore Road in the wealthiest enclave of Rye, New York.

The house is a private retreat only twenty-five minutes from the Bronx, where he got his start at the lowest level of the Malotta clan. And now, he's *Kyre*, the head of the Albanian clan's Bronzi faction.

It's a beautiful spring morning as he steps onto a terrace with a view of Van Amringe pond and their swimming pool with its cedar-shingled cabana. Holding his mug of Skenderbeu Albanian coffee, he gazes out at their stretch of private beach.

The morning breeze is a refreshing reminder of how far he's come from his impoverished beginnings in the filth-ridden port city of Durres in Albania. It was one of the main cogs in the country's corrupt system under the godforsaken communists. It was a dog's life there and he was lucky to have escaped alive.

Yes, life here in America has been good. As a highly respected—and feared—boss of the most notorious faction of the Malotta clan, he has everything a man could want. Had he stayed in Albania, he'd have suffered a cruel death years ago.

Boss of Bosses, Kazim Malotta, personally told Kosta that his group is the most profitable of the entire clan, including those in Europe. That's because he's been cagey and resourceful, has never let an opportunity pass without a thorough vetting of its chances for success. And he's then taken advantage of that prospect.

His many operations have gone smoothly and will continue to do so for as long as politicians, corporations, and banks are willing to do business. All this has enhanced Kosta's power base. There's even the chance that someday he could replace the Boss of Bosses, Kazim Malotta.

And now, Kosta's moving in on part of the Odessa mafia's business. The Odessa mafia—Boris Levenko's organization—had a profitable bootlegging operation running out of the Newark port in New Jersey. Until Levenko's death, they shipped tanker loads of 100-proof alcohol distilled from cereal grains. And to ensure there would be no complications, the vodka was dyed blue and poured into plastic bottles labeled as windshield washer fluid.

When the contraband reached Russia, the dye was extracted and the contents repackaged into one-liter bottles labeled as vodka, then distributed as genuine Russian-made vodka. Until Boris Levenko died an unfortunate death, the distilleries were under his control. But now, Kosta's people are in the process of taking over the operation.

Yet, despite these successes, Kosta feels an undertow of worry. It's because his son, Alex, is a braggart and loves the soft life. Like so many in this younger generation, he's frivolous and knows nothing of the dread-filled times back in Albania where Kosta, now sixty, grew up. Alex: thirty years old and acting like a man-child. Still living at home. Still suckling on mother's milk.

Kosta's encrypted cell phone trills. It's safe to talk. The readout says it's Besim, his most trusted captain. "Yes, Besim . . . ?"

"Hello, *Kyre* Kosta," Besim says in Albanian. "The Uzis and the Heckler & Kochs have arrived and the buyers are waiting for delivery."

"What about that matter in Brighton Beach?"

"It's taken care of. Sulfuric acid leaves nothing behind. Such snakes those Serbs are. They have loyalty to no one."

Kosta nearly recoils at the mention of the Serbs. Even though they're speaking on safe phones, you can never be too careful. "Remember, Besim, say nothing to anyone. War is bad for business and we don't want trouble with the Odessa mafia."

"It's all taken care of."

"Good. Once everything is in place, we can begin shipping out of Newark. And soon, from Greenpoint, Brooklyn. We'll do it gradually so we don't arouse suspicion."

"It will begin in two weeks."

"Well done, Besim. Well done." Kosta Bronzi clicks the OFF button.

Glancing up, he sees Alex coming down the stairs. He must learn what nonsense his son has been up to. "Alex," he calls. "Come here. I want to talk to you."

Alex walks out onto the terrace. His eyebrows arch as a querying look spreads over his face.

Kosta can sense his son's wariness. Yes, something is going on with the boy. And whatever it is, it isn't good.

"Sit down, Alex," Kosta says in English, gesturing toward a chair.

Alex heaves an exaggerated sigh and says, "What's up, Dad?"

Reaching into his bathrobe pocket, Kosta says, "I want you to tell me what this is . . ."

He sets a folded piece of paper on the table.

Regarding it with a furrowed brow, Alex unfolds it.

Peering at the paper, his face goes pale.

"Who is Dr. William Madrian?"

Kosta notices the skin over his son's chin begins quivering.

Alex shakes his head and clears his throat.

Kosta knows his son is about to lie, but the boy isn't even good at that.

"What's this about?" Kosta says, grabbing the photocopy of the bill and shaking it.

"It's only nine hundred bucks."

"I don't care about the money. And that's not my question."

"How . . . how'd you get this?" Alex stammers.

"Your mother found it in a pocket before taking your pants to the dry cleaners. Now answer my question. What is this bill for, and who is this Doctor Madrian?"

"He's a doctor I saw . . ."

"A doctor? Of course, he is. There is 'M.D.' after his name." Kosta's voice seethes with annoyance. And he feels acid bubble up his gullet. "This bill says you saw him three times in April, once a week. What kind of health problem do you have?"

His son blinks rapidly as though he's frantically trying to think of an answer.

"He's a . . ." Alex pauses. His lips twist into a pale knot and he averts his gaze. "I was feeling a little . . . a little upset, so I went to see him."

"Upset? About what? What's wrong . . . tell me."

"It was something emotional," Alex says in a warbling voice.

"*Emotional*? So, he's a psychiatrist? A headshrinker?"

"Yes."

"Tell me, what was upsetting you?"

Kosta can hardly believe his son is upset about anything because he has such an easy and good life. And besides, a real man would never visit a headshrinker to solve his problems. He'd take care of whatever it is by himself, or maybe with the help of his compatriots. He'd never go outside the family for help.

"It's about . . . my social life."

"Your *social* life? Are you unhappy with the whores you visit?"

Alex's eyes remain averted. He remains silent.

The boy is an embarrassment to me and to the clan. It's clear that he's trying to think up an answer.

"Do *not* lie to me, Alex."

Alex looks down, as he always does when Kosta confronts him. *The boy has no spine.*

"So you've been seeing a headshrinker. Without telling me or Besim. And what do you tell this Dr. Madrian?"

"I already told you . . . I talk about my social life."

"Alex, I'll ask you one more time. *What do you talk about?*"

Alex's face is chalk white. "It's personal."

"There's nothing personal when it comes to the family's business."

"We don't talk about the business."

"I know better. You're a braggart, Alex. Besim and the others tell me you bray like a donkey. You talk too much to everyone. And you cannot keep a secret. Now tell me what you told this doctor."

"Nothing important."

"Tell me what you told him that's not *important*."

"Just that I've been unhappy."

"Did you mention anything about the business?"

"No."

"You said *nothing* about the business? Adnan told me you asked him to authorize a company check to pay this doctor's bill. Yes?"

"Yeah."

A film of sweat glistens on Alex's cheeks. And he's blinking like a broken traffic light, a surefire sign of nervousness. And for sure, he's not telling the truth.

"So this doctor, this headshrinker knows something about the business, yes?"

"Just that we're in the trucking business. And sanitation."

"Alex, I'll ask you one more time. No, I won't ask, I'm *demanding* to know what you said to him."

Alex fidgets, then says, "I just joked with him . . ."

"You *joked*? About what?"

"He mentioned something about the Brighton Beach murders, and I made a joke, that's all."

"Why would *he* mention those murders?"

"I have no idea. Maybe it's because he knows I'm Albanian."

"You made a joke? What was this joke?"

"I don't remember."

"Of course you do." Kosta Bronzi's hand slams heavily on the tabletop. "Tell me what you said to this headshrinker."

"He asked if I knew what happened in Brighton Beach, and I joked by asking him if he thinks I might know who clipped Boris Levenko. I was only joking."

It feels to Kosta like his blood has caught fire, as though he'll combust at this very moment. "He asked if you knew anything about those *murders*?"

"Yeah, he brought it up. So I joked with him."

"*He* brought it up?" Kosta rockets up from his seat. His hand sweeps through the air and lands a heavy slap across Alex's cheek.

Alex cringes as tears well in his eyes.

"*Ridiculous.* I don't believe you."

"We were joking, Dad."

"You mentioned *Boris Levenko.* You joked about knowing who killed *Boris Levenko?*"

"Listen, Dad, I—"

"You fool. Now you have put our entire clan in danger."

"I didn't—"

"Not only is there danger from the Odessa mafia, but if Kazim Malotta finds out, our family will be put out of business."

Rubbing his cheek, Alex shrinks back in his chair.

"Now, you've done it," Kosta snarls. "Your bragging will be the end of our family. I cannot believe our own flesh and blood is such an idiot."

Kosta's thoughts whirl as he considers the dangerous complications that could come about from Alex's revelation to this psychiatrist. This headshrinker. This could be the end of everything.

Turning to Alex, he says, "You cannot be trusted. You shouldn't even be an errand boy."

"But, Dad, I was joking and—"

"Shut up and listen to me. This is what you'll do. You'll no longer see this headshrinker. Never again will you see him. And you are never to go to Adnan and ask him to write a check for *anything. Ever.* Is that clear?"

Still rubbing his cheek, Alex nods.

"Does anyone else know you visited this doctor?"

"No."

"You're telling me the truth?"

"Yes."

"You had better tell the truth now because you've put us *all* in danger . . . including this headshrinker."

"But, Dad—"

"Not another word from you."

Kosta Bronzi knows his blood pressure has shot skyward. In fact, he now has a throbbing headache—the pulsing shifts from his forehead to a spot behind his eyes—and if this goes on, he'll end up in the hospital. Dr. Kelmendi warned him about his blood pressure as high as it is. And right now, it feels like his head will explode. On top of that, he feels stomach acid that's climbed up his gullet and now scorches the back of his throat.

Calm? How can I remain calm with such a dolt for a son.

"You boastful fool," Kosta says with a sneer. "Now I'm forced to have this taken care of."

CHAPTER 5

Bill has always felt that walking at a brisk pace clears the mind. When his heart pumps harder and faster, his brain is perfused with more oxygen-rich blood and his thoughts stream more quickly, more efficiently. It almost feels like he's walking in a trance. In its way, it's a form of therapy-in-motion.

At seven thirty in the evening the sun has set, but the street is well-lit. The last patient of the day left a while ago and Bill walks uptown on the west side of Third Avenue. Striding quickly, he hits a steady rhythm, passes scores of restaurants and retail shops with people streaming in and out of them. The route on Third from East 75th to East 84th is slightly uphill; the gradual climb gets his heart pulsing. He's barely aware of the wail of sirens, the honking horns and the pounding of 18-wheelers barreling north on Third Avenue toward Hunts Point and the Bronx Terminal markets.

He tries to obliterate the gnawing sense of dread boring through him after Alex Bronzi's words two evenings earlier.

You wanna know who clipped Boris Levenko?

Some helluva question.

Wallace's admission that *he'd* be "scared shitless too" compounds the feeling, leaving Bill with a raw sense of danger. For the first time in his thirty-five years, he realizes not only his own mortality but contemplates his imminent death.

How fragile and perilous our existence is. You can be gone in an instant.

Like what happened two years ago to his fiancée, Olivia. Thoughts of her intrude as he passes the SoulCycle outlet on the corner of 82nd and Third. He hasn't changed his walking route, realizing he almost nurtures the crushing ache washing through him when he passes the place. Each time he walks past the storefront, his thoughts flash to the terrible day he got a phone call from Joyce, Olivia's closest friend.

Bill . . . Olivia's in the hospital. She passed out at our SoulCycle class. We're here at Lenox Hill. They're doing a scan of her brain. The doctor said it could be a stroke.

He'd dropped everything, sprinted over to Lenox Hill Hospital where he learned that while sweating rivulets from cycling at jackrabbit speed, Olivia had dropped off her bicycle to the blood-pumping music of "Holy Grail" by Jay-Z.

An MRI revealed a brain aneurysm that burst open because of her strenuous cycling. Olivia had bled into her brain. An hour later, his fiancée was dead. The shock was so enormous he nearly fainted. It was as though her death smashed in the walls of his life and everything good ended at that moment.

God, I miss you, Olivia. I miss you so much I sometimes don't know how I manage to go on.

He occasionally wonders if there's a way to heal the wound to his soul her absence left behind. He realizes he missed out on her whole beautiful life, and when she was lowered into the ground, he felt as though part of him went with her.

He still hasn't recovered from the loss. Without having been aware of it, grief has taken on a different dimension; it's morphed from a searing pain to a smoldering ache he feels each day. He sometimes wonders if he's merely pretending to be living a normal life, and each year, as the anniversary of Olivia's death approaches, Bill feels gut sick with loneliness. It feels as though something has broken inside him, that he no longer has the capacity to love. Not the way he loved Olivia.

Grief changed everything.

He quit his part-time job at Lenox Hill Hospital; he could no longer tolerate being in the building where Olivia died. He's kept up his private practice, despite it being a solitary day-to-day existence in which he has contact only with his cadre of regular patients. There would be no banter with colleagues and staff, and he's no longer in the hospital hallways or wards. Remaining in his office to help people with their problems relegates grief to a back corner of his mind.

Or does it?

He knows he should put the co-op on the market. The one-bedroom apartment he and Olivia shared is suffused with too many memories.

I'm clinging to what could have been. I know that's what I'm doing, but how do I get past it?

Less than a block from his apartment on 84th Street, he enters Angelo's, a restaurant on East 84th Street. Though he's twenty minutes early, he expects Frank Olivieri, a friend since their college days, to show up soon. The guy's usually early whenever they arrange to get together.

The restaurant is clubby-looking with a bar on the right as you enter. It's one of the few establishments that doesn't have a flat-screen TV mounted over the bar; it's just an old-fashioned place where you can go for a drink.

"The usual?" asks the barkeep, a thirty-something guy with a Van Dyke beard. The guy's been there for years and knows Bill by sight.

Smiling, Bill nods.

The bartender sets a wineglass on the bar and pours a glass of Pinot Grigio.

Warming his belly, the alcohol begins infiltrating his brain. After a few sips of wine, Alex Bronzi's revelation doesn't seem so filled with portent; Bill wonders if he's making a mountain out of the proverbial molehill.

Or is he now trying to minimize the danger of what Alex said in that session? When Bill is halfway through the glass of wine, the tension in his neck and shoulders begins subsiding.

Moments later, a tall, thirty-something woman enters the place. She makes her way to the far end of the bar and perches on a stool.

The other guys at the bar eye her. Bill's certain she attracts men like a magnet sucks in metal filings. Sitting demurely, she orders a glass of red wine.

She has honey-colored hair and a certain Slavic beauty. She wears a blouse and skirt and sits with one long leg crossed over the other. She doesn't wear much makeup, and there's no polish on her finely sculpted fingernails. And there's no wedding ring on her left fourth finger. She has more than simple sex appeal; she's got sexual charisma.

Bill is pleased he noticed her. It's a small step . . . a bit of progress toward rejoining life.

He drains the glass of wine, then orders another.

While waiting for Frank, he's exquisitely aware of the woman; he can *feel* her glancing at him. Or is he imagining it? There's no way to know and he won't take a chance on looking her way. He sometimes wonders if he's too shy, unwilling to make a move. He's confident with friends and patients, but those situations are different than what's going on at this moment.

And the few times he's approached a woman in the last two years, the memory of Olivia brought on a tidal wave of guilt.

Right now, there's enough on his plate to keep him occupied. Mainly, Alex Bronzi and the murder of Boris Levenko. And what might happen since Alex's question. Besides, Frank's gonna show up soon, so any overture to this woman would be a waste of time.

Trying not to look in her direction—why start something he can't finish?—he stares at the battalions of bottles stacked behind the bar. Halfway through the second glass of wine, he feels a gentle tap on his shoulder.

It's Frank Olivieri.

"Hey, buddy, sorry I'm late," Frank says, sitting on the next stool. He orders a Dewar's on the rocks.

"How're you doing?" Frank asks.

"I'm good," Bill lies.

But it *is* good to see Frank. The guy's an administrator at Lenox Hill Hospital and has a Ph.D. in bureaucratic bullshit. He navigates hospital politics with an ease few can ever hope to attain. He'd have been a success in the corporate world, but hey, medicine has become increasingly corporate, so he's in the right milieu for his skill set. And he's a really good guy; they've been friends since their undergraduate days at the University of Michigan.

"I have some good news if you're interested," Frank says, sipping his scotch.

"I'm always interested in good news."

"The hospital's gonna expand the psychiatry department. They'll be looking for a shrink to head up a new eighteen-bed ward. If I drop your name in the hat, you'll be first in line for the job."

"No thanks, Frank. I'm happy with how things are right now."

"*Happy?* C'mon, guy. Happy's the wrong word. Let's face it, Bill, a full-time private practice has gotta be lonely. You've got no contact with anyone except your sad-sack patients. I don't understand how you can spend all your time listening to people whine about their first-world problems." Frank sighs and shakes his head.

Bill always tolerates Frank's friendly jibes with humor. "I'm not that lonely, Frank. I have contact with you, right? And my family and friends. I don't need to socialize at work."

"C'mon, man. A solo practice is a downer. You sit there all day and listen to your patients bellyache about their shitty little lives. It's gotta be a drain. Something on the ward will give you more contact with people and you'll still have time for your private practice."

Bill laughs and guzzles the rest of his wine.

"Listen, Bill, if that doesn't work for you, I can squeeze a few balls and get you a teaching position at the hospital. And there's another development I just heard about; New York Presbyterian's setting up a new ward at the 70th Street facility. I know an administrator there and a good word can go a long way. It'd be regular hours and the money's damned good. And you wouldn't be working at Lenox Hill."

"Thanks, but not right now."

"That's really a 'No,' isn't it?"

"I guess so." Bill shrugs.

Frank waits a beat before he says, "You know, Bill, life goes on . . ."

"It's just . . . the hospital atmosphere I can't stand . . ."

"Look, I know it's where Olivia . . . it's where she died, but you gotta move on and get past it."

"I'm working on it."

"I hope you'll forgive me if I say you're being self-indulgent."

Knowing Frank is the only guy in the world who can criticize his misery, Bill says, "I get it, but it's not the sadness that keeps me away. I hate the rules and regulations. You know, assholes like you telling me I gotta have a quicker turnover, fill out the right forms and all that bullshit. It drives me crazy."

"Okay, okay. So I have a black belt in bullshit," Frank says. "But that's not why you're turning down the job offers."

He wraps an arm around Bill's shoulders, lifts his drink, and says, "Here's to overcoming bullshit and sadness."

"As long as we're talking about work," Bill says, "I had a strange thing happen at the office."

Without mentioning the patient's name, he tells Frank what Alex Bronzi said.

"Wow," says Frank. "That's some kinda weird shit. And you don't want to go to the police?"

Bill describes the consultation with Alfred Wallace.

"I guess it's best to wait and see what happens," Frank says. "I doubt this guy would tell anyone he was seeing you. I'm sure he'd be embarrassed to let people know he's visiting a shrink."

"That's what I'm hoping."

"People's minds are a mystery to me, always have been." Frank lowers his voice to a near whisper. "At least what I do doesn't involve people telling me about mob rubouts."

They laugh but Bill is aware of a sense of unease slithering through him.

Frank nudges Bill and says, "Hey, guy, there's a good-looking woman down the end of the bar. She's been eyeballing you. Why not go over and introduce yourself?"

"I'm here with you tonight, Frank."

"How long's it been since you've been laid?"

"Cut the shit, Frank. Let's grab a table and have dinner."

As they walk toward a table at the rear of the restaurant, Bill feels the woman's eyes riveted on his back.

CHAPTER 6

Later that evening, Bill strides down the hallway toward his apartment.

His neighbor across the hall, a fifty-something woman, is locking her apartment door, and before leaving, shoots him a smile as he heads toward his place.

He nods and smiles in return, mouths "hello," and keeps walking.

She's a good-looking divorcée who wears too much makeup and looks like Cochise about to go on the warpath. Whenever they pass each other in the hallway, Bill gives her the obligatory smile but holds his breath so he doesn't gag from the cloying scent of perfume in which she seemingly bathes.

Entering his apartment, he's consumed by the emptiness of the place—the utter stillness always unnerves him. It's a stark reminder of Olivia's absence. Sometimes, he catches himself half-expecting to hear her voice as he traverses the foyer.

Honey . . . how was your evening with Frank? What'd you have for dinner?

But there's nothing, and he'll never hear her voice again.

I've gotta sell this place and move on. Frank's right. Enough of this self-indulgent bullshit. It's eating me alive.

In the bedroom, he changes into jeans and a t-shirt. Memories of Olivia are imprinted on the bed, the chair, in her closet where her clothes still hang. Sometimes, he thinks he can smell her presence, on the pillow, on the bedsheets, anywhere in the apartment.

There isn't a day that goes by when you're not in my thoughts.

He then wonders: *Why can't I let go of you? Why am I torturing myself?*

In the living room, he plops down on the sofa they purchased at Bloomingdale's.

How many times did we sit here and watch television? He's surrounded by her, enveloped in memories, and yet, some part of him knows the mourning must eventually come to an end.

Tomorrow he'll call a broker and make arrangements to sell the place. He'll either rent something or buy another apartment in the Seventies, somewhere close to the office.

Frank's right. I've gotta get on with my life.

He picks up the remote and clicks on the television.

MSNBC, FOX News, CNN, C-Span, one after another: All politics, all the time. It's sickening. He flips through the channels; catches the ten o'clock news—the Fed's raising interest rates; there's a coup d'état in some African country; there's been a minor earthquake in California, not to mention wildfires, and more tornados scouring the Midwest.

Jesus, the world's gone off its tracks.

There's nothing about the Levenko murder. It's surprising because it's still a big story in the local rags and on the radio.

Trying to distract himself, he grabs the remote, flicks up and down the channels, comes to a *Seinfeld* rerun. He doesn't recall this one. After five or six minutes, he realizes he's not getting the humor or perhaps it's a slice of city life he just doesn't appreciate anymore. Maybe laughter feels frivolous while he's gotta contend with more serious stuff.

Like the question Alex Bronzi put to him two evenings ago.

Could it be the question doesn't really matter?

No, that's what he *wishes*.

Those words matter. They definitely do.

He has to wait it out and see if anything develops.

Like what?

Some guy steps out of a crowd and *clips* him?

Meanwhile, there's the tension of not knowing if other thugs in the Bronzi mob—whatever the hell it's called—even know Alex has been seeing a shrink. Bill wonders how best to tell Alex he can no longer continue seeing him. His next session is scheduled for Tuesday evening. He'd better come up with something plausible to tell the guy because it isn't every day that a patient's psychiatrist quits on him.

He clicks the remote's OFF button and the picture fades to black. Feeling lethargic from a heavy meal, along with too much wine, he closes his eyes. It feels good to let drowsiness take over.

When he opens his eyes, he realizes he's dozed off and it's now eleven thirty.

Time for his pre-bedtime routine: check the office voicemail for messages and call it a night.

There's one message.

"Hey, Doc, it's Alex. I . . . I won't be coming in anymore. You shoulda taken the cash. I hope I didn't say anything that'll cause you any trouble. So just be careful and stay safe."

Dropping the receiver into its cradle, Bill feels something electric jolt his chest. He's nearly paralyzed as dread rises from the pit of his stomach and it now feels like that motor is humming somewhere inside his chest. His mouth goes dry and his scalp dampens.

So just be careful and stay safe.

Alex was definitely warning him.

It would be naiveté of galactic proportions to think Alex stopped treatment because he no longer needs counseling. No, someone in the mob pressured him and forced him to end the sessions.

So just be careful and stay safe.

Every nerve ending in Bill's body is firing. A film of sweat forms on his forehead and cheeks.

This is unreal.

Maybe the Albanians suspect he told Bill more than he actually revealed.

A flutter of fear radiates down Bill's arms, reaches his hands, which are now ice cold.

For a moment, he tries to sugarcoat the message, but that's impossible. Bill wonders if his life is about to spin out of control.

He trudges to the refrigerator, grabs an open bottle of Chardonnay, and with a shaky hand, takes a swig. It burns going down, singes his gullet; his gag reflex kicks in and he feels like he's choking, then coughs. Alex sets the bottle onto the counter, does his best not to puke.

Brighton Beach. Brooklyn. Russians and Ukrainians. Boris Levenko. The Albanian mob.

He's a potential witness.

Whether by hearsay or not, the Albanians don't deal with legal distinctions.

It's very clear: the Albanians know Bill has heard something about Levenko's death and that makes him a liability, someone who can put them in jeopardy.

He'll be shot.

Whacked.

Clipped the way Boris Levenko was killed.

With dread crawling though him, Bill wonders how it came to this.

It happened after a call from Alex Bronzi who found Bill's name online and came for four lousy sessions. Alex talked about his life and problems, mostly trivial stuff. That's what you're supposed to do in psychotherapy—say whatever comes to mind, no matter how inconsequential it may seem.

And then came that question, thrown at him in the most casual way: *Hey, Doc, ya wanna know who clipped Boris Levenko?*

But a mob rubout is anything but trivial.

The Albanians have drawn their conclusions.

He heard something that could put people in prison.

Something he should never have heard.

And now, he's in their crosshairs.

CHAPTER 7

Sitting in the back seat of a taxi, Bill feels a concave depression where thousands of asses had been before his.

The driver talks nonstop about the Mets and Yankees, but Bill barely hears a word the guy's saying; he's lost in thought about Alex Bronzi, the Albanians, and his own future. For all he knows, he's on their radar screens at this moment. What the hell can he do other than go to Roger, his brother-in-law and an attorney?

You should have taken the cash. So just be careful and stay safe.

Those words sends a chill through the marrow of Bill's bones.

The deposited check from the trucking company forms a paper trail leading directly to Bill. The Albanians must know Alex has been visiting him.

The taxi exits Central Park at 86th Street and Central Park West. At 86th Street and Columbus Avenue, they stop at a red light. Bill feels exposed. Vulnerable. What if the cab is being followed? Will a bullet come crashing through the window and sink into his skull while the driver waits for the light to change? Bill recalls photos in the *New York Post* and *Daily News* of mob murders: mangled bodies strewn in grotesque positions with blood everywhere.

At the corner of West End Avenue and 86th Street, Bill gets out of the taxi, looks around to see if he's being followed, and hustles toward the building where his sister, Laurie, her husband, Roger, and their two daughters live in an eighteen-story pre-war co-op building.

After the doorman announces him, Bill takes the elevator to the eighth floor where he arrives at a semi-private vestibule. Laurie, petite, blonde, and smiling, stands at the apartment doorway. "You're definitely staying for dinner," she announces, momentarily lessening his fear.

* * *

After dinner, Bill and Roger retire to the den while the kids do their homework and Laurie, an elementary school teacher, works on her next day's lesson plan.

Roger's a wiry guy with a buzz cut who still looks like the tennis player he was as an undergraduate at Columbia. After college, he attended Cornell Law School, then began working as a criminal defense attorney for a large Midtown law firm. A few years later, he was made partner and was bumped up to corporate crime. He once said, "*Corporate crime and mob crime are just two sides of the same coin. Either way, it's all about greed and money.*"

The bottom line is clear: Roger knows people in both high and low places. If there's anyone who can advise him, it's his brother-in-law.

"Bill, you sounded upset on the phone," Roger says, closing the door and sitting in an Eames chair facing Bill. "So tell me . . . what's up?"

"'Upset' is putting it mildly. I'm freaked out."

Without revealing Alex Bronzi's name, Bill tells Roger what his former patient had said. He then describes the meeting with Alfred Wallace, followed by Alex's voicemail message.

"You're probably right to conclude this guy's mob-connected," Roger says. "The Albanian mob is in competition with the Russians and Ukrainians, so it's certainly possible the Albanians put a hit on Levenko. But just to be clear: this patient actually asked that, 'You wanna know who clipped Boris Levenko?'"

"Yes. Those were his exact words. And of course, I told him no . . . I don't want to know."

"That was the smart thing to say. And Dr. Wallace gave you good advice. You don't want anything to do with this guy. He's poison."

Bill repeats Alex's telephone message, using his exact words.

Roger shakes his head. "Yes, I would take his message as a clear warning. What's this guy's name?"

"If I tell you, I'd be violating his confidentiality and opening myself up to legal liability."

"Fuck legal liability," Roger says. "That's a civil matter and, right now, you're worried your life's in danger, right?"

"Yes, but I don't wanna pile more shit on this."

Bill hears the kids playing a computer game and laughing in the next room.

"I have to admit something, Roger . . ."

Roger nods, has a knowing look on his face. "What's that?" He tilts his head.

Bill hesitates, remains silent. Why insult Roger by telling him what he thinks of lawyers?

"Lemme tell *you* something, Bill. You can say anything to me. In fact, right now I want you to reach into your wallet and hand me a dollar bill, or if you feel magnanimous, you can make it a fiver."

"Why?"

"Because you'll be paying me for my services . . . for a legal consultation, which means you're my client. So attorney-client confidentiality exists, just as it does in your doctor-patient situation. Nothing we say here can ever leave this room. Our conversation is privileged. Got it?"

Bill reaches for his wallet, fishes out a five-spot, and hands it to Roger.

"Now, what is it you want to admit?"

"I'm a little embarrassed to say it, but I've always thought being a defense attorney is dirty business . . . whether it's corporate or criminal. You know, the tobacco industry in its own bullshitting way is just as criminal as the mob. I mean . . . you try getting people off the hook for crimes they've committed, whether it's street crime or the white-collar stuff. Everyone knows that." Bill pauses and takes a deep breath. "Shit, I hope you're not offended."

Roger smiles indulgently. "I'm not offended, Bill. Most people think that way. The simple truth is, I do what I can to keep the prosecution honest. The Constitution guarantees each of us a fair trial if we're accused of a crime. I can't tell you how many times the prosecution has tried to bury exculpatory evidence about my clients. It's part of the game they play.

"And the cops . . . forget about it. Outright lying is part of a police officer's job," Roger adds. "The term *testilying* is common vernacular for cops lying their assess off on the witness stand. My job is to keep the prosecution honest. Even the guilty deserve a fair trial."

"I never heard it put quite that way," Bill says. "It makes sense."

"You still haven't told me the patient's name."

"It's Bronzi . . . Alex Bronzi."

"That's good to know. The more information, the better."

After what feels like a long pause, Roger continues, "Okay, Bill, after what was said in that session and Alex Bronzi's voicemail message, I think there's plenty to worry about. And here's what I'm suggesting—I know a guy who's connected and who may be able to help you."

"What do you mean *connected?* Isn't that a mob term?"

"I don't mean it *that* way. He's in touch with people who can make things happen when push comes to shove. I think you should see him. That's the way to go right now."

"What can you tell me about him?"

"Not much. He's a fixer who floats around, not only here, but in other countries, too. You know what a fixer is?"

"Yeah, a guy who takes care of problems, who *fixes* them."

"You got it. And I think he can help you."

"Have you used him to *fix* things?"

"Twice before, I used his services to help a former client. And he's very good at what he does."

"What's his name?"

"He goes by the name of Rami, but I'm pretty sure that's an alias."

"Is that his first or his last name?"

"I don't know. It's the only name I know him by."

"Why would he go by one name . . . and why use an alias?"

"I can't say for sure, but I know he's had experiences with Interpol and some other agencies. And he has a background in intelligence."

"Intelligence for us . . . the U.S.?"

"I'm not sure. But he's very savvy."

"How do you know him?"

"That's not important. But what *does* matter is he's in town right now."

"What did he do for your clients?"

"I can't go into details, but suffice it to say he has resources that aren't generally available to an attorney or, for that matter, to anyone else." Roger pauses. "I want you to meet with him and tell him everything you've told me. Let's see what he can do. I'll tell you this . . . he owes me a favor."

"What did you do for him?"

"I'm not at liberty to discuss that."

"Okay. So you'll speak to him, and then what?"

"Call me at the office at eight o'clock tomorrow morning, and I'll let you know what he says."

"Got it."

"If Rami's willing to help, there's one thing you have to do . . ."

"What's that?"

"Do exactly what he tells you to do."

CHAPTER 8

Leaving his apartment building at eight forty-five the next morning, Bill heads west on East 84th Street and heads toward Lexington Avenue.

He'll take the subway downtown to the Midtown area and meet this guy, Rami. On the telephone, Roger stressed the importance of being on time. "Get there at ten," he said. "Don't be late."

At 86th Street and Lexington, he joins a slow-moving crowd plodding down the stairway to the subway station. He's allotted more than an hour for a trip that should take no more than fifteen or twenty minutes.

Though it's a few minutes before nine a.m.—the tail-end of rush hour—a mass of people is jammed on the express train platform.

Standing amid the throng, Bill notices a movement in his peripheral vision. Glancing to his left, he sees a guy whose face is covered with stubble. The man averts his eyes the moment Bill looks at him.

Another glance: the guy has edged closer.

From his position on the platform, it's clear the man came down the subway steps after Bill did. There's something off-kilter about him: he's wearing a tan raincoat on a mild, sunny day when there's no forecast of rain.

Another quick glance: the guy is even closer now. Only four or five people separate them. For a moment, Bill's uncertain if the man has actually moved toward him. It could be no more than people shifting positions, so he appears to have angled closer.

Bill fixes his eyes on the guy who stares at the tile wall on the other side of the tracks. He has prominent cheekbones, a dark complexion, and thin lips. His posture is casual. But Bill feels a twinge of wariness. He looks away, waits a moment, then again glances in the man's direction.

Yes, he's moved closer.

In a surge of primal awareness, Bill's heart begins hammering so violently, he feels his wrists throbbing.

There's a slight vibration on the platform. The Number 4 express is nearing the station. The air in the tunnel now smells of ozone. The train's racket grows louder. People crane their necks, look toward the light as it makes its approach from the tunnel. The crowd is restless; people jockey for position to enter the cars when the train stops.

Another glance: now the guy is separated from Bill by only two people.

A simple push could send Bill onto the tracks in front of the oncoming train.

Bill wheels around and barrels his way through the people behind him. Heading back toward the stairway, he slams into a man who's thrown backward. "Hey," the guy shouts, as Bill keeps bulling his way toward the staircase.

"Hey, watch it," yells another man.

"How rude!" a woman calls.

The mass of humanity seems impenetrable, but Bill shoves and slides his way toward the exit gate. He pinballs off a few people, rushes ahead, pushes the gate open, gets to the bottom of the stairs, and pounds his way up against the tide of people streaming downward.

A quick half-turn and he's at the upper level still moving against the flood of people pouring down the stairs.

Scrambling up the remaining stairway, he's on the sidewalk at 86th and Lexington.

A city bus lets out a hiss as the driver applies the brakes on Lexington, just south of 86th. It's only fifty feet away. People stand at the open front door and board the vehicle one by one. A flow of passengers exits the bus from the rear door.

Bill races to the back door, rams his way through the crowd exiting the bus, and climbs the steps to the vehicle's interior. He threads through the horde in the aisle, gets to the middle of the bus, and looks through a curbside window.

There's no sign of the guy in the raincoat.

Is Bill losing it?

Is he imagining danger?

The guy could have been maneuvering for a better position to board the train.

This is a matter of survival. Don't take any chances.

The doors slap closed and the bus lurches ahead. It moves slowly in heavy traffic.

At 85th Street, the traffic light turns red.

The bus lurches to a stop.

After what seems like a long wait, the light turns green.

Swaying gently, the bus begins moving slowly.

Grasping a vertical pole, Bill glances out a right-side window.

Jesus! There he is!

The guy's trotting on the sidewalk, abreast of the bus.

There's no doubt now.

He's coming for him.

He'll board at the next stop.

Amid the mass of people jammed in the aisle, Bill breaks into a drenching sweat.

The bus trundles from side to side in the traffic sludge.

Suddenly, a siren keens, then lets out a series of burps. An ambulance is making a run to nearby Lenox Hill Hospital.

The bus pulls over to the curb, stops, and waits with its doors closed.

The ambulance passes. When it's a block ahead, the bus resumes its crawl.

Where's the guy?

Another glance out the window.

There he is. He's keeping pace with the bus and he's gonna board at the next stop, 83rd Street.

Trapped amid the throng in the aisle, Bill's a stationary target.

Once on the bus, the guy will weave his way through the crowd and plunge a knife into him. Or use a pistol. Panic will follow as people shout and fight to get off the bus.

There's nowhere to go.

The bus picks up speed, passing 84th Street.

The guy sprints ahead, keeping up with the bus.

Hugging the right side of Lexington, the bus approaches East 83rd, its next stop.

I've gotta make a move. Otherwise, I'm dead. But which door do I use? Front or back?

Both doors will open. Passengers will discharge from the rear while people will board from the front.

The rear door is nearest the guy. He'll probably board that way, then wend his way through the crowded aisle, just as Bill did. When he plunges a knife into Bill or shoots him, the crowd will go berserk. Terrified, the passengers will shout for the driver to open the doors. There'll be an insane rush to the street as people push in every direction, frantically trying to escape the violence.

The guy will disappear amid the turmoil.

And Bill will be dead.

The bus sways and stops at 83rd Street.

Bill maneuvers toward the front door, sliding past people, angling toward the front door.

"Excuse me, excuse me. Sorry, getting off."

"Use the back door."

"Hey, don't push."

"Sorry."

"Watch it."

"Getting off. Sorry," Bill mutters breathlessly. His heart is pounding an insane tattoo in his chest.

He gets to the step-well at the front door.

The bus stops.

Both doors open.

A cluster of people is about to board.

Bill scrambles down the steps, rams his way through the throng, and gets to the sidewalk.

People stream out from the rear door.

There's no sign of the guy.

On the sidewalk, Bill looks up and sees the guy inside the bus: he boarded through the rear door.

The thug looks out a curbside window, sees Bill, and starts shoving his way back toward the rear door.

Bill sprints past a pharmacy, turns onto East 83rd Street, and races west on the long city block that intersects Park Avenue.

Traffic is heavy on Park and it's moving slowly.

Bill crosses to the far side of the street, and begins trotting downtown.

At 81st and Park, he spots an empty taxi, steps into the roadway, and hails it.

"Forty-Sixth and Park," Bill shouts as he hops inside.

As the taxi pulls away, Bill peers out the rear window; there's no sign of the guy.

The driver negotiates southbound traffic quite capably, changes lanes when necessary, and soon, Bill's at his destination. His heart is throbbing at jackhammer speed and he's sweat-drenched.

"I'll get out here," he says to the driver, tossing a twenty onto the front seat. There's no time to wait for change.

At 46th and Park, he hustles through the East Helmsley Walk to 45th Street, rushes across the street, and pushes through the revolving doors of the MetLife Building. Inside, he trots past Café Centro, then Cucina & Co., and reaches a gleaming bank of escalators.

He takes the one sliding downward, easing himself past people peering at cell phones as the escalator descends to the main concourse of Grand Central Terminal.

The space is filled with a maelstrom of people crisscrossing in all directions. Humanity vomits out of every tunnel and rampway, streaming toward their destinations with rolling suit-cases, briefcases, knapsacks, duffel bags, and travel gear.

Bill passes the information booth, zigs and zags, avoids tourists using their cell phones to photograph the vaulted turquoise ceiling with its zodiac constellation. At the far side of the rotunda, he rushes through the echoing Vanderbilt Passageway, leaves the terminal, and exits onto 42nd Street.

He walks quickly amid the squeals of brakes, the shriek of sirens, and the blare of car horns. At the intersection of Vanderbilt and 42nd Street, he dodges a swarm of slow-moving taxis and crosses to the south side of the street.

He pushes through a revolving door into One Grand Central Plaza. Bill once visited a dentist in the building and knows the lobby runs the length of the block, from 42nd to 41st Street. He makes his way toward the 41st Street exit.

Racing up a stairwell, he emerges at the rear of the building. Now what? Go where?

*   *   *

At the corner of 41st Street and Madison, he enters the Madison and Vine Bistro, grabs a chair at a table by a window. Gulping lungsful of air, his heart feels like it's quivering in his chest. He waits for his adrenalized heart to slow it frenetic pace.

Peering out the window to 41st Street, he sees nothing suspicious. No one's following. Not yet. He's probably lost the guy.

A willowy waitress with blond hair approaches, shoots him a querying look.

Between gasps he says, "A cup of espresso, please. And a scone."

Sitting alone, he ignores the other patrons fingering laptops, cell phones, and iPads. He's pumped, galvanized, completely wired, knowing he just escaped certain death.

Still breathing heavily, Bill watches the passersby on the street, now fairly certain he's eluded the guy. Meanwhile, his entire body is clenched in readiness.

If there was ever any doubt the Albanians are coming for him, it's been erased.

Goddamn Alex Bronzi and the fucking Albanians.

Glancing at his watch, Bill realizes he has time to kill before the appointment. And just who the hell is this Rami, a guy who's *connected*?

Connected to what?

How?

To whom?

Mobs?

Gangsters?

The FBI?

Interpol?

For sure, this is trouble.

This shit doesn't happen in real life. It's right out of the movies.

His breathing slows and his heart resumes a normal rate as he waits for the coffee and scone. He doesn't know if he'll be able to eat, but one thing is certain: he's chin deep in some really bad shit.

For the love of God . . . I fell asleep in one world and woke up in another.

CHAPTER 9

Fifteen minutes have passed and there's been no sign of the guy. Bill feels reasonably confident he's lost him.

He hasn't touched his espresso or the scone. No need to be caffeinated; he's way too jumpy as it is.

Glancing at his watch, he has a few minutes to kill before heading out to Rami's office.

Leaving a tip for the waitress, he gets up and exits the coffee shop.

On shaky legs, he walks along East 41st Street toward the rear of One Grand Central Plaza, only a half-block away. His eyes dart left and right as he moves along the street. It's a Stone Age kind of awareness, an animal-like sense of what he can see, hear, even the smell on the street.

Entering One Grand Central Plaza through the building's rear entrance, he clambers down the steps to the main lobby area. As with most large Manhattan office towers, ever since 9/11, it's mandatory to show identification to guards at the front desk before being admitted to the elevator banks.

He walks to the building directory. It's a huge glassed-enclosed board made of black felt with press-in white letters denoting the various tenants. Arranged alphabetically, there must be at least two hundred lawyers and consulting firms of various kinds occupying the building, along with dentists, accountants, and a wide array of small companies.

But there's no posting for Rami Associates.

That strikes Bill as odd, and for a moment, he wonders if he's in the right building.

A uniformed guard sits behind the reception counter. A computer monitor sits on his desk.

"Who are you here to see?" asks the guard.

"Rami Associates," Bill replies, repeating what Roger instructed him to say.

The guard's fingers dance over a keyboard as he scans the monitor. "That's room 4602 on the forty-sixth floor." He then requests identification.

Bill fishes in his wallet, hands over his driver's license, which the guard eyes carefully, then peers at Bill, comparing his face to the license photo. He then types away on his keyboard, copying his driver's license number.

A small camera mounted on a gooseneck handle snaps a picture of Bill's face. The guard presses a button and a building pass slips from a compact desktop printer. Along with Bill's name, the date, and office destination, the sticky-backed pass shows a black-and-white headshot of him. Top flight security. There's no doubt Bill's presence in the building has been entered into a database.

Affixing the pass to his jacket lapel, Bill walks to the elevator bank and passes through one of three turnstiles. Two guards stand nearby, making sure visitors have passes displayed on their outer clothing.

He takes an elevator to the forty-sixth floor. Looking for Suite 4602, he comes to a door with the appropriate number. There's no sign showing the name of a company or person. Only the number is etched on a plastic sign affixed to the door.

*   *   *

At precisely 10:00 a.m., he turns the doorknob of Suite 4602.

It's locked. He presses a button on the right side of the door.

After a brief pause, a soft buzz sounds from within the door's lock mechanism.

When the door clicks open, Bill enters a small reception area, not more than twelve feet wide and ten feet in length. Sparsely furnished with a Naugahyde-covered tuxedo-style couch and two chairs, the office looks transient, as though it could be vacated quickly.

A dark-haired woman wearing a Bluetooth phone headset sits behind a granite-topped counter. Her green poplin blouse and black cargo pants remind Bill of clothing worn by EMT personnel.

"Welcome, Dr. Madrian," she says. "Rami will be with you shortly."

Bill sinks into a seat, realizing it's only ten in the morning and he already feels depleted. But at least he's not on the street running for his life, and for sure, no one will come barging through the door to plunge a knife into him.

While waiting, he's aware of a trembling sensation coursing through his body. There's no getting away from the sense of danger he feels.

Gazing about the waiting room, he wonders what kind of place this is. Most reception areas are decorated, but this place is as stark as the Antarctic. There's no coffee table with magazines, no pictures on the walls; there are none of the accoutrements most office waiting rooms have.

Answering the phone, the receptionist speaks softly. Bill thinks she could be speaking Russian, or some other Eastern European language, maybe Polish or Ukrainian. A short time later, on another call, he hears her murmuring something that sounds like French, but her voice is muted and he's not certain. Yes, as Roger mentioned, Rami could be connected to Interpol. The entire setup feels eerie, as though Bill's entering a strange new phase of his life.

He can't help but feel intimidated. The starkness of the office, coupled with the multilingual receptionist, reinforce the shroud of mystery surrounding this guy Rami.

Moments later, a rugged-looking man wearing jeans and a blue work shirt open at the collar enters the waiting area. "Dr. Madrian, I'm Rami."

Bill thinks he detects a barely discernible accent, but isn't certain. They shake hands. Rami's grip is firm but not bone-crushing. The guy has nothing to prove.

"Please call me Bill."

"Sure, Bill. Come into my office and we'll talk."

CHAPTER 10

As a psychiatrist, Bill has honed the skill of making solid observations of people.

Rami appears to be about forty years old, is about six feet tall, has prominent cheekbones and flinty, blue-green, penetrating eyes. Slope shouldered and muscular, the man walked back into the office with athletic ease, the kind of preternatural fluidity Bill's seen in many athletes. His dark hair is closely cropped.

The overall look makes Bill conclude the guy is either military or ex-military. There's something inherently menacing about the man, especially in those eyes, which fix on Bill who now sits in a chair facing the desk. Bill's mouth feels parched, and a vibrating sensation radiates through his chest.

The office looks to be about the size of Bill's consultation room—ten by twelve feet, give or take. As was the waiting area, the room is sparsely furnished. There are no decorations: no book-filled shelves, no plants, no photos on the desk or pictures hanging on a wall. An open laptop sits on Rami's desk. Nothing else.

"Roger and I spoke late last night, but I want you to tell me everything."

Working backward, Bill begins by describing his harrowing experience of earlier this morning.

Listening attentively, Rami rarely blinks, doesn't nod his head or interrupt with questions. Even as he's talking, Bill feels the skin over his chin quivering. This man sitting across the desk from him is palpably unnerving.

"You had good situational awareness on the subway platform," Rami says. "It means there's a chance you'll survive."

Situational awareness? Survival? Holy shit. What have I gotten into?

"The guy must've followed me from my building, but I don't understand how they know where I live."

"Roger said you own an apartment in a condo, right?"

"Yes."

"If you own property in the city, details of the purchase are part of a public record. That's how they know where you live. Those records can be accessed from the municipal database. Either directly at the city clerk's office or by hacking into the database. Most likely they learned where you live by hacking into the database."

Bill sits in stunned silence. This is terrifying.

I'm completely trackable.

"Based on everything you've told me, it sounds like some faction of the Albanian mafia wants to silence you."

"But I don't know anything," Bill says as blood pounds past his ears and into his skull.

"They don't know *what* you know."

"They must think I know more than I do."

"I understand from Roger that you're reluctant to divulge this patient's name, but I need that information if I'm going to help you."

"Didn't Roger tell you . . . ?"

"He said you would do it."

It takes no more than a millisecond to realize that under these circumstances, doctor-patient confidentiality is bullshit. "It's Bronzi. Alex Bronzi," Bill says. "He's involved with an outfit called Belmont Trucking, out of the Bronx. But he lives with his parents in Rye."

"The fact that he lives in Rye and works in the Bronx tells me he's a relative of a high-level Albanian mafia boss named Kostandin Bronzi," Rami replies. "The Albanians have edged out the Italians in the Bronx. They have their eyes on some Russian assets in Brooklyn and a few other places."

"How do you know this?"

Ignoring the question, Rami continues, "The only difficulty is we don't know for certain if it's the Bronzi faction or another group in the Malotta clan, or even a different clan entirely which is after you. It all depends on how far word has spread through the *Shqiptare.*"

"*Shqiptare . . . ?*"

"The Albanian mafia."

"The Albanian mafia? I never heard of them."

"It's a group of organizations with branches in the U.S., Europe, South America, and the Middle East. They traffic in drugs, guns, people, and human organs, along with bootlegging and other operations. They're involved in money laundering throughout Europe and the Middle East. And they're violent."

That trembling in Bill's insides intensifies. "You're scaring the shit outta me."

"You've got to know who you're dealing with. Here in the city, the Albanians have been based primarily in the Belmont section of the Bronx but they're spreading into Queens and Westchester.

Now, they have a presence in Connecticut, mostly in restaurants and the companies that service them. They're today's version of what the Italian mafia was years ago."

"Alex Bronzi said his family's involved in trucking and a few other businesses," Bill says. "I think sanitation and construction, if I remember correctly."

"They call them *clans*, not families," Rami explains. "And the Bronzi faction, to which this fellow Alex no doubt belongs, is part of a larger group known as the Malotta clan. Each faction in a clan is led by a *Kyre* or Boss. The boss has underbosses, the way the Cosa Nostra operated in its day.

"Members have a term . . . *besa*, which means *trust*," Rami continues. "It's their version of a code of silence. What the Italians called *omerta*, meaning not only silence, but loyalty. Your former patient may have violated that code by bringing up the Levenko murder with you."

"All he said was 'You wanna know who clipped Boris Levenko?'"

"A loaded question. And it's a violation. Even mentioning the dead man's name is a breach of *besa*. It's rumored that Boris Levenko was killed by either Serbs, Chechens, or Turks, but there's been no mention of the Albanians. They could've outsourced the job . . . contracted it to another group to maintain plausible deniability. One thing is certain: if the Odessa mafia learns the Bronzi faction was responsible for Levenko's death, blood will run in the Bronx."

"The *Odessa* mafia?"

"You probably know of them as the Russian mob, the Bratva."

"Bratva?"

"The Brotherhood, which is mostly made up of Russians and Ukrainians," Rami continues. "They're international. Here in

New York, the most powerful group is the Odessa mafia out of Brighton Beach, in Brooklyn. The Russians and Ukrainians first came here when the Soviet Union began relaxing its immigration policies before it fell apart in the late eighties. Brighton Beach became known as 'Little Odessa by the Sea.' With the breakup of the Soviet Union, their brigades have spread to New York, Miami, Los Angeles, Tel Aviv, Antwerp, and Budapest."

"Brigades? It sounds military."

Rami nods. "After the Levenko hit, another war may be brewing. If a faction of the Albanian mafia is responsible for his death, there's little doubt the Bronx will be littered with bodies."

"How do you know all this?"

"It's my business to know these things."

"What business is that?"

"Part of my business is being a skip tracer."

"A skip tracer?"

"Yes, I help find people who've disappeared. People who've gone off the grid, who've skipped town for one reason or another."

"How's that gonna help me?"

"Let me put it this way . . . in addition to fugitive recovery, there's a healthy market in helping people fly under the radar."

"You mean you help people disappear, right?"

"Yes, I help people go off the grid, either temporarily or permanently."

"Permanently?"

"Yes."

"You mean something like the Witness Protection Program?"

"Yes and no. WITSEC's a federal program used by the government to protect witnesses scheduled to testify against organized crime figures. Or to protect people who've already testified in federal trials and need to disappear to stay alive. The Feds get them a new identity so they can disappear forever."

"That doesn't apply to me."

"Actually, you're not really a witness to anything. You'd never qualify for WITSEC. But the Albanians are probably worried that you'll talk to people, which you've already done, and that could open up an inquiry into their activities."

"So you run a private disappearing business?"

"You could describe part of it that way."

"You said *part* of your business is being a skip tracer. What's the *other* part?"

"It serves no purpose for you to know."

Jesus, I'm in even bigger trouble than I could have imagined.

"Are you saying I have to disappear?"

"Yes, at least for a while."

That thrumming sensation intensifies. Bill's body feels like it's vibrating.

Off the grid. Out of sight. No longer alive as the same person.

"How long is a while?"

"Right now, there's no way to know. It could be for a week or two."

"But I have family, friends . . . my practice. Jesus, I have a *life*."

"Well, you're here because you want to *keep* living. And to do that you'll have to disappear for a while. Right now, I can't predict how long you'll have to be gone."

As a swell of disbelief washes over him, Bill asks, "But how do I leave my *life* behind?"

"We'll get to that. But first, let's go over some things."

CHAPTER 11

Rami regards Bill with a penetrating look.

"They know where you live and where your office is, but that's far from all they'll learn about you."

"What else can they learn?" asks Bill, afraid to hear Rami's answer.

"Who your relatives are and where they live. And rest assured, they'll uncover these things."

Bill nearly shudders at Rami's response. The last thing he'd ever want is to put Mom, Laurie, Roger, and the kids in danger.

"My sister uses her husband's last name, Price. And my mother began using her maiden name soon after my father died."

"Why did she do that?"

"I don't really know. I was only ten when he died. Maybe it was her way of trying to move on."

"It's good your immediate relatives have different surnames. It'll give them some protection, at least for a while. But eventually, there's a good chance they'll get to them."

Bill's stomach clenches. "How'll they do that?"

"When your father died, was a death notice put in a newspaper?"

"Yes, in the *Times*."

"If they're using a skip tracer, they'll find the death notice. And they'll learn the names of his surviving relatives. It may take time, but eventually, they'll get to your family. That'll give them leverage over you. And once they have the chance to use it, they will."

"Jesus, what can be done . . . for my family and for me?"

Rami shakes his head. He doesn't answer Bill's question, but continues on. "If the Albanians have good IT people working for them, they can hack into nearly every government database. Nothing in your life is private. Everything is potentially open for them to see."

"This is . . . it's hard to believe."

"You subscribe to Amazon or Netflix?"

"Yes . . ."

"They'll hack into any streaming service and learn your credit card number. And that will lead them to other sources of information. It can be done by anyone with decent hacking skills. You drive a car?"

"I lease one. A Chevy."

Does it have OnStar?"

"Yes."

"They can track it. Where's it parked?"

"In the basement garage of my building."

"Leave it there. Don't go near the car. They can access the Motor Vehicle Department and learn the make, model, and license plate number of your car. The next thing you know, you're driving on an avenue and a motorcycle comes abreast of you and a guy sets a magnetic bomb onto the side of your car, then speeds away. It blows you and the car to bits."

"Unbelievable."

"Of course you use a credit card?"

"Yes, Chase Visa."

"Every time you swipe or tap that card at any outlet—a restaurant, a clothing store, a supermarket, a bar—you can be tracked. They'll know where you've used plastic. All your shopping habits and preferences can be traced. They can stake out those places and wait for you. In other words, your whole life becomes an open book."

"This is hard to believe."

"When you go online to any site or when you send an email, the record of your activities and messages is preserved on a server. On top of that, the city's brimming with surveillance cameras at retail stores, street corners, convenience stores, lobby entrances . . . just about anywhere you go."

"I never even thought about these things."

"When your cell phone is turned on it's a veritable GPS system for anyone who wants to track you down, so you'll have to get rid of it. We'll get into that in a while. The fact is with today's technology, we live our lives in public."

Bill's chest feels tight, as though his coronary arteries are constricting, that they'll close off completely and he'll have a heart attack.

"The bottom line is simple: if the Albanian mob has a good IT specialist, they'll track you down."

Bill shakes his head again.

What the hell can I do?

"So, let me ask you some more questions before I tell you what you have to do."

Bill waits, dreading whatever will be asked of him.

CHAPTER 12

Rami leans forward with his forearms on the desktop.

"Do you belong to any medical societies?"

"The American Psychiatric Association and the New York County Medical Society."

"Beginning today, you'll have nothing to do with them. No meetings, no calls. No emails or texts. Nothing."

Bill nods.

"Are you on staff at a hospital?"

"No. I gave that up two years ago."

"Do you work at a clinic?"

"No."

"Good. So you don't need to account for your absence to an employer. I assume you have a private practice?"

"Yes."

"As a solo practitioner or with a group?"

"As a solo practitioner."

"Good. No partners will be pressing you for explanations about your being gone for a while. For the time being, your practice is suspended. Don't go near your office until you hear from me."

"But I have patients who—"

"No *buts*. The fastest way to get yourself killed is by going there. The second fastest way is to go back to your apartment."

Dread slithers through Bill.

"Do you post entries on Facebook, Instagram, or Twitter?"

"Hardly anything . . . once in a while on Twitter."

"Anything personal . . . pictures of friends or relatives?"

"No, nothing like that. I hardly use any social media."

"Good, because they can learn about you if you post personal information on those sites. Now . . . as for money, you'll have to tap whatever savings you have or borrow from someone you trust."

"This is insane."

"But it's necessary. Are you able to get your hands on a few thousand dollars in cash?"

"If I have to."

"Then do it."

Bill suddenly realizes life as he's known it, is over.

Rami leans back in his chair. "Are you married?"

"No. My fiancée died a couple of years ago." Bill's throat constricts at the thought of Olivia.

"Is there a woman in your life?"

"No. Not right now."

"Good. Do you have a pet? A dog or a cat?"

"No."

"Good. Pets make disappearing more difficult. People never want to leave them behind."

"*Disappearing*. I have to *disappear*?"

"Yes, you do. At least for a while. I know it's hard to imagine and tough to do, but it's necessary."

"Where do I go? What do I do?"

Bill's stomach lurches.

"When you leave here, you'll get someone you trust to go to your apartment. Have that person take whatever you'll need to live for a few weeks and bring it to you at a predetermined location. Leave your laptop in the apartment and make sure it's turned off. If you have a landline, tell this person to take the phone off the hook and leave it that way. You don't want any incoming calls that can be traced. As for buying things, it has to be done with cash."

"It's like I'm being canceled . . ."

"Yes, in a way. You have to cancel your current lifestyle, at least for a while."

"For how long?"

Probably a week, maybe two, but there's no way to know for sure right now."

"I don't know if I can do this."

"You must, if you want to live."

Bill's stomach clenches. "What else do I have to do?"

"As far as finding a place to stay, you can't go to a hotel or any-place where you'll have to show identification. It's best to find a friend who'll let you stay with him . . . someone who won't be immediately associated with you if these people do an online search of social media for your family and associates. It can't be someone who's posted comments on your Facebook page if you have one. And not someone you've sent direct messages to on Twitter. It has to be someone you haven't emailed, texted, or tele-phoned frequently so there's little chance of there being a digital trail leading back to you. It has to be someone at the periphery of your social life."

Bill's thoughts streak through a roster of friends. He can't hole up with anyone he knows well and there aren't many other people in his life.

"Do you have children?"

"No."

"Good. Most people are tracked down because they can't stay away from their kids or pets. Tell me about your relatives."

"My mother lives in an apartment in the Twenties. She goes by her maiden name, Broderick."

"You can't visit her under any circumstances. Doing that could put you and *her* in danger. I'll tell you how to communicate with her in a few minutes. Your sister's married to Roger Price, right?"

"Yes."

"Does she go by her maiden name or is her last name Price?"

"It's Price."

"Good. She's safe, for the time being. You can't visit her either at home or anywhere else."

"Understood."

"It bears repeating: most fugitives are caught because they can't stay away from their families and pets."

"So now I'm a fugitive?"

"For lack of a better word, yes."

There's a brief pause during which Rami looks like he's sizing Bill up. "You look like a well-built young guy," Rami says. "I'm guessing you belong to a health club."

"I do. I wrestled in college and try to stay in shape."

"Don't go to that club. In fact, stop doing *anything* you do on a regular basis. Most people don't realize how routine their lives have become. They walk the same route every day, go to the same coffee shop, or try to sit on the same seat on a bus or train when they commute. There are a hundred trivial things we do the same way each and every day. Our lives are more predictable than we realize. Part of situational awareness is giving up these routines— the gym, your favorite coffee shop or restaurant, a bar where you go for a beer, a walk you take or a route you jog. You can't use your social media accounts, any of them . . . Facebook, Twitter, Pinterest, Instagram. In fact, don't go near your computer."

"I can't believe this."

"Before the internet, it was easier to disappear, but not today. Everything's online and anyone with the proper resources can learn about you and eventually get to you."

Bill realizes his mouth has dropped open.

"You have to live a cash-only existence. At least for a while. If these people are seriously looking for you, they'll hire an expert in fugitive recovery."

"A guy like you."

"Yes, a guy like me. These days, a skip tracer can locate you by hacking into your bank accounts, your records at a financial insti-tution, or through your credit card purchases. Or through a phone number database, a loan application, a utility bill, a depart-ment store credit card, or your driver's license."

Bill takes a deep intake of air and lets it out as his shoulders sag.

"People don't realize the wealth of information that's available through public records—things like birth or marriage certificates, divorce filings, property transactions, probate courts, and law-suits. A good skip tracer can tap into every one of them."

"You're talking about a modern-day bounty hunter," Bill says.

"Call it what you want. But if you're careless, they'll find you."

"Anything else?"

"There can be no telephone calls, no emails, no texts. Remember, you'll have nothing to do with your cell phone, your office or home telephone line, or computer. Got it?"

"Yes."

"In fact, you have to destroy your cell phone. It's a portable GPS that will give you away. You'll buy a burner phone, and two more for your mother and sister, assuming you want to stay in touch with them. Load those phones with a few hours' worth of calling time and write down the numbers so you know how to reach them. Send each of them a phone by FedEx or UPS and use cash to buy and send the phones. Along with the phone, send a note giving them your burner phone number and tell them to call you at that phone number using those burner phones, *not* from their own cell phones or landlines."

"Jesus, this is unreal," Bill says as the room seems to darken.

"And you can't explain a *thing* to them. Make up a story and tell them to call *only* your burner phone. And if you call them, use your burner phone to do it."

"I understand."

"You'll have to think of an excuse to explain this arrangement . . . so be creative."

Bill shakes his head.

This is all so insane.

"Now for cash . . . you'll go to your bank and withdraw a few thousand dollars in hundred-dollar bills along with some smaller denominations for everyday purchases. Withdraw only a few thousand. It won't take them long to know which bank you use and they may lie in wait at that branch, hoping you'll show up again. And remember, a bank must report a cash transaction over ten thousand dollars to the IRS, so make one trip only and with-draw as much as you think you'll need for the next few weeks, but don't exceed ten grand."

"How long does this cash-only existence go on?"

"It depends on certain things."

"What things?"

"There's no need to discuss it now. Worst-case scenario, arrangements can be made for you to disappear. Even perma-nently if it comes to that."

CHAPTER 13

Feeling an electric charge in his chest, Bill says, "*Permanently?*"

Nodding, Rami says, "I don't think that'll be necessary, but you should be aware of how dangerous this can be for you."

"Please, Rami, give me the CliffsNotes version of what permanently means. I have to know the worst-case scenario."

"It doesn't apply to you, at least not for now."

"Still . . . I need to know what I might be facing."

"Okay, but it bears repeating: this isn't your situation . . . at least for the time being."

"Just tell me . . ."

"First, we delete your online presence, meaning we wipe Bill Madrian off the internet and bury him in a digital grave. That's the easy part. Next comes the more complicated part. Taking on a new identity."

"How's that done?"

"Twenty-five years ago, it was easy. You went to a cemetery, looked at gravestones, found one for someone born the same year as you were, and who died as a child. There'd be no current records. You'd contact Social Security and tell them you've lost your card and need it replaced . . . in that person's name. With that new identity, you begin a new life.

"That was *then*. Today, it's more complicated. We get you a new identity, beginning with a Social Security card that's not registered with the government. It's a fake. We get you a bogus birth certificate and a driver's license. If you're permanently disappearing, you have to make up an entire life story . . . where you're from, your education, your family, your first job . . . everything. You really want to hear more?"

Bill nods as a cold feeling seeps through him. "I've gotta know how this goes down."

"You move to a small or medium-size city like Omaha or Albuquerque, where you'd be a new face in town with a ready-made background. And you'll never work again as a physician or psychiatrist."

"I think I know why, but please tell me . . ."

"Because to get a medical license in another state, you have to show your college and medical school transcripts along with proof of your internship and residency training programs, and you have to produce a valid medical license from New York State. It's impossible to get these documents—either real or forged—without compromising your identity. I know because I've helped two doctors disappear and they never practiced medicine again. One disappeared so completely that, for all I know, he's picking cherries in Oregon."

Bill feels the air leave his lungs.

"You'd have to find a job that doesn't require a background search or extensive training—something like a short-order cook or working in construction or driving a taxi."

Bill can barely imagine these changes. Driving a taxi, working on a construction crew hauling bags of cement or lumber. He can barely fry an egg no less work as a short-order cook.

"And here's the hard part . . ." Rami says matter-of-factly. "You'll never again see your family. You can't go to a wedding or a funeral or a family occasion of any kind. In fact, you'd have to sever all ties to your family for the rest of your life. Basically, it boils down to this: Bill Madrian will be gone."

"I don't know if I could do that," Bill says in a quivering voice, realizing the enormity of these changes.

Sweat prickles on his forehead and his underarms are drenched. *My God, it's like walking out of my own life.*

Rami continues, "The one or two people who disappeared and later were discovered were found because they'd returned to see their families. That's the main reason people who're off the grid get caught by whoever's coming after them: they can't stay away from their loved ones."

Bill tries to envision never again seeing Mom or Laurie or his nieces. A melancholic ache sweeps through him.

"And there's something else: in this new life, if you meet a woman and decide to get married, you can never reveal your identity to her."

"Why not?"

"Because you can never know what'll happen in a marriage. Sometimes, people going through a divorce try to hurt each other, especially if there are children. Under those circumstances, your old identity could be used against you."

"This is unreal. I'd be living a completely false life."

"Yes, that's true. The bottom line? You'd have to live a life of lies. But you'd have a *life*."

Tears well in Bill's eyes.

Rami says, "But none of this may be necessary, depending on what we learn about who's coming for you."

"Can you determine that?"

"In this world of interconnectivity, we can learn more than you'd ever think is possible."

"So it works both ways, doesn't it?"

"Yes, it does. Data is neutral; it's all nothing more than binary numbers. But I don't want to promise anything we can't deliver. The *one* thing I can tell you is this: whether this goes on for days, weeks, or longer, for a while, you have to live your life off the grid."

Bill sighs, knowing Rami speaks a simple and harsh truth.

"Now . . ." Rami adds, "when you have your burner phone, call me at this number." He hands Bill a card with a handwritten ten-digit number on it. Nothing else. "When you call, just say, 'I'm calling on my cell phone' and leave me the number of your burner. Understood?"

"Yes."

"One other thing . . . if this goes on for more than two weeks, destroy the burner phone. To do that, you remove the SIM card and the batteries and toss them down a sewer or in a public trash basket. Then, get rid of the phone far from where you threw away the batteries. Then, buy a new burner and begin all over again. And do the same thing with the cell phone you now have. Destroy it."

Bill slips Rami's card into his wallet.

"Do you have any questions for now?"

"Do you want a retainer?"

"That's not necessary."

"Why not?"

"For one, I owe your brother-in-law a favor."

"For his having done what?"

"I can't say. Speaking of payment," Rami says, "you insisted that Alex Bronzi pay you by check, correct?"

"Yes."

"What bank was it drawn on?"

"Atlantic Bank. I noticed because it was a foreign bank and when I deposited the check, I was told it would take five days to clear because it's international."

"It's an offshore bank in Belize and it's often used by shell companies for money laundering. When the check clears, they'll know not only your bank, but the branch you use, so stay clear of that branch. Which bank and what branch do you use?"

"Chase. The branch at 79th and Third."

The room is so quiet Bill hears hissing in his ears.

"Can I ask you something, Rami?"

"Yes . . . ?"

"You keep saying 'we' and 'us.' Who're 'we' and 'us'?"

"That's no concern of yours. The important thing is to follow my instructions. Get cash, buy burner phones, destroy your cell phone, and make arrangements to stay under the radar if you want to come out of this alive."

They both stand.

"A last reminder," Rami says as they head for the door. "Avoid public transportation. Isolate yourself until we learn more. Understood?"

"Yes. How long will it take for you to learn more?"

"It's hard to say. I don't want to promise what I can't deliver. I hope you understand."

"I do."

"One other thing," Rami says. "Don't come back here under any circumstances."

CHAPTER 14

For a dazed moment, Bill stands stock-still in the lobby.

What he's just been told is a massive overload of dos and don'ts; it's too much to absorb in one sitting.

He doesn't even recall the elevator ride down from the forty-sixth floor. All he can think about is the prospect of discarding his entire life to immediately begin living another. Taking a deep breath, he shakes his head and then wends his way through the lobby to an indoor arcade.

After passing a coffee shop and a store selling Irish linens, he comes to a shoeshine parlor near the steps leading up to the Madison Avenue side of the building. Outside the store stands one of the few remaining telephone booths in Midtown Manhattan. Or, for that matter, anywhere in New York City.

After dropping a quarter in the slot, he dials the office of Dr. Nancy Ketchman, a psychiatrist he knows from Lenox Hill Hospital. He's in luck; she answers the call. He won't have to leave a voicemail message.

After exchanging a few pleasantries, Bill tells her he has a family emergency and must leave town for a week or possibly, longer. She agrees to cover his practice while he's gone.

After dropping another quarter in the machine, he dials his office number and records a new outgoing message on his voicemail.

You've reached Dr. Madrian. I'm out of town for the time being. Dr. Nancy Ketchman is covering my practice.

He recites her telephone number. The recording sounds fine; there's no discernible warbling or evidence of anxiety in his voice.

Good to go.

He then checks the office voicemail for new messages.

There's one hang-up, nothing else.

His cell phone contact list has the telephone number of every patient he treats. Recalling Rami's warning and not wanting to use his cell phone, he changes a five-dollar bill in the building's coffee shop. Using quarters, he dials each patient's home or business number. He leaves voicemail messages cancelling all sessions for the next two weeks and informing the patients that Dr. Ketchman is covering for him while he's gone.

He then calls Frank Olivieri at the hospital.

Bill's apartment is only seven blocks from Lenox Hill Hospital, so Frank can easily make the short trip.

"Frank, I need a favor."

"Shoot."

"I have to leave town for a little while and can't get back to the apartment."

"What's up?"

"It concerns a relative," he says without thinking of any details to explain why he'll be away. "When you're done with work this afternoon, will you stop off at my place and collect a few things? I'll call the doorman and he'll have the porter let you in."

"Sure, I can do that. What do you need?"

He keeps it simple, telling Frank where everything's located: underwear, running shoes, a few changes of clothing—two pairs of jeans, a few shirts and other sundry items. "You'll find a satchel inside the front closet near the door. Put my stuff in there."

"Okay . . . but what's going—"

"And Frank, pull the plug on my desktop and take the battery out of my laptop . . . it's right near the desktop. And take the telephone receiver off the hook."

"Bill, what the fuck's going on?"

"My cousin is sick, but I can't explain right now. Can you do this for me?"

"Sure, but what's—"

"Listen, you know the Starbucks at the corner of Eightieth and Lexington?"

"Yeah . . ."

"Meet me there at five thirty with the satchel. Okay?"

Frank agrees to do it.

Bill's cell has the number of the apartment building's front desk.

He pops another quarter into the pay phone and dials.

"One-sixty East 84th Street," says Luis, the daytime doorman.

He tells Luis that Frank Olivieri will be coming by at 5:15 and asks the doorman to have the porter let him into the apartment. "And Luis, I'll be out of town for a while. Can you ask the mailman to leave my mail with you and will you store it in the package room?"

"Will do, Doc."

*   *   *

With those calls made, Bill leaves the building and heads to a nearby CVS. He needs to buy some toiletries and other items he didn't want Frank to bother packing.

Leaving CVS, he heads west to Sixth Avenue, and begins walking downtown to the nearest Target store.

It suddenly hits him like a punch to the stomach.

I'm as homeless as some derelict hanging around Grand Central Terminal or riding on the subways all day and night. Jesus, this is scary.

He has nowhere to sleep tonight.

Where will he eat?

In a diner?

Buy food from some guy selling hot dogs or falafel from an outdoor food cart?

Will he have to disappear for good?

Maybe never see his family again? Unthinkable.

Where does he live the rest of his days?

How does he earn a living?

How does he create a new life?

How can I do this?

Don't jump to conclusions.

Rami said I may only have to do this for a couple of weeks.

But still, I have to think about what might happen down the road.

College, med school, his residency training program, his practice, his family and friends, everything he's built or been part of for the last thirty-four years . . . it could all be over.

He's never felt so untethered, so disconnected, so completely alone.

Walking on Sixth Avenue, he contemplates the utter wreck of his life.

Lighten up. I gotta take it one step at a time.

Don't let your imagination run wild.

He has to have confidence that Roger sent him in the right direction by hooking him up with Rami. But there's something he can't afford to forget: Roger's spent all but the last five years of his professional life defending the lowest of the low . . . thugs and mobsters.

Rami could be part of that world.

In fact, that man's office setup, his menacing looks, and his evasiveness when asked reasonable questions all point in a not-so-savory direction. And when Bill offered to pay him a retainer, the guy refused the money.

There are no free lunches. So . . . what's wrong with this picture?

On top of that, he said he owes Roger a favor. For what?

Was Roger involved in some illicit shit when he practiced criminal law?

Was Rami part of it?

The whole thing reeks of secrecy, of illegality.

And now I'm part of that picture.

Could Bill be digging an even deeper hole for himself by following Rami's directives?

But what choice does he have?

So, at least for now, he'll do as he was told even as he realizes there's this other world—not one he ordinarily inhabits—an ugly place of pain, duplicity, and violence. And if he's going to stay alive, he's gotta deal with it in whatever way possible.

And right now, dealing with it means disappearing.

At least for a while.

Walking a few blocks south, he removes the SIM card and battery from his iPhone and tosses them into a trash basket at the corner of 39th Street.

Two blocks farther south, he dumps the phone into a trash basket. All his contacts and apps are gone.

He's now disconnected from the world.

CHAPTER 15

At the Target store, he wanders between aisles brimming with everything from detergent to potato chips.

The clerk in the Electronics Department is a twenty-something guy with slicked back red hair and a soul patch beneath his lower lip.

"I'd like to buy three prepaid phones," Bill says.

"Three?"

"You got it."

The clerk shows him a Tracfone Samsung Galaxy steeply deeply discounted at $35.99. "How much airtime do you want on these?"

"Fifty minutes each."

"Do you want to register them?"

"No."

"If you don't register them, you won't be able to use any apps."

"I just wanna make some calls."

"You won't be able to load in more minutes by going online. And you can't use it at an ATM."

"Not a problem."

Giving Bill a sardonic smile, the clerk places the phones in a bag.

Bill's glad he's got a few hundred bucks in cash on him.

Leaving the store, he walks back uptown recalling he'd once seen a UPS store on East Forty-First, somewhere near Lexington.

*   *   *

At the UPS store, he writes down all four phone numbers on a Post-It, which he slips into his pocket.

He arranges for two burners to be sent by overnight delivery: one to his mother; the other to Laurie. He pens identical notes of explanation on two stick-on labels and affixes them to the bubble wrap surrounding each phone.

I'm having problems with my cellular carrier. To call me, use this phone and call this number. Don't call from your landline or your own cell phone.

He knows this note will only create a shitload of questions, especially from Mom, but that's a worry for tomorrow. He'll figure out a way to handle it when the time comes. Just like he'll figure out how much more to tell Frank when he sees him at the coffee shop.

As for Laurie, it's likely Roger will have provided some plausible explanation of what's going on with Alex Bronzi. And Bill knows Laurie can keep things to herself; she won't share the truth with their mother.

He hails a taxi on Park Avenue. "Park and 72nd," he tells the driver.

Once uptown, Bill purposely walks a circuitous route to the Chase Bank at Sixtieth and Madison. A different branch than the one he usually frequents. He's reasonably certain he hasn't been followed.

At the bank, he fills out a withdrawal slip for $5,000. For sure, since he deposited the check from Belmont Trucking, the Albanians already know his account number and have probably hacked into it. If the check hasn't yet cleared, they'll know his account number very soon. For certain, they'll see he's on the run. Why else would he be making such a large withdrawal?

I've never thought about this before, but as Rami says, my life's an open book for anyone with decent hacking skills.

"For security purposes, the last four digits of your social security number, sir?" the teller, a young woman with a pixie hairstyle, asks. "And I'll need to see your driver's license."

Bill realizes his social security number is hooked into everything that can identify him.

After he recites the number, the teller smiles indulgently, enters a few more keystrokes. She also records the number of his driver's license. It seems like she's tapping away on the keyboard forever. Finally, a machine at her side spits out a thick ream of bills. All hundred-dollar bills except for the last three hundred, in twenties, tens, and fives.

He asks for an envelope and stuffs the bills inside it.

It's the largest cash withdrawal he's ever made. How long will five grand last him? A few weeks, maybe a month. Possibly a little longer. It depends on how he lives and where he stays. He'll live simply. No extravagances. No restaurants, no bars, no public places. They're forbidden anyway.

It suddenly strikes him that all these Ben Franklins are concrete proof of the drastic changes in his life: they represent days, weeks, possibly months of living off the grid. If he's got to stay hidden away for months, the money will be gone.

But he has to stay out of reach.

And he must live a cash-only existence.

Living where?

He won't be *living*. He'll be existing on the periphery of life, never writing a check or using a credit card and not seeing family and friends. He'll be sequestered away, living a clandestine life ... somewhere.

But where?

How do you do this?

How do you live in the shadows and become a ghost of your real self?

Life is with people, those you know and those you love.

But not for me, not anymore.

How do you just give it all up and become a stranger in the world?

How do you disappear from your own life?

Back on Madison Avenue, he imagines what he's up against: some skip tracer fingers a keyboard while sitting at a computer anywhere in the world—Albania or Russia or France—infiltrating every nook and cranny of his life.

This $5,000 may be the last bit of money he'll ever be able to access as William Madrian. If he has to change his identity, he'll be impoverished. He'll never be able to tap into his savings and his pension plan will go up in flames.

One thing is certain: if the Albanians have a guy like Rami working for them, they'll track him down. In a heartbeat.

And when that happens, it'll be over.

CHAPTER 16

Now he needs to find a place to stay.

Either a Y or hotel is out of the question.

Those places will insist on having ID shown when he tries to register. And that would pinpoint exactly where he'd be staying.

There's a chance he could hole up in some roach-ridden hovel on the Bowery, if there are any left these days what with gentrification galloping ahead like it's been doing for the last few years. But even if some down-and-out places are still around, they're not realistic options. With this stash of money, he'd be mugged in a heartbeat.

He could ask Frank to bunk out at his place, but the guy lives in a fourth-floor rental apartment on East 85th Street and lives like a slob. But why put Frank at risk? There's a long digital trail between them: they've emailed, texted, and telephoned each other hundreds of times over the years. The Albanians could easily find him at Frank's place. And they'd probably want to eliminate Frank, too.

He can't stay at Laurie's apartment or with Mom; doing so will expose them to danger. And if he sets up temporarily with anyone else, he's gotta think up some bullshit explanation.

Leaving the bank, he runs through a roster of other friends and acquaintances. Pausing, he realizes he may have one feasible option. Standing on Third Avenue amid the rush of passersby and the squall of traffic, he thinks Greg Jeffries may be the guy to call.

He knows Greg from the health club, where they play four-wall squash every other week. One day last week, Greg mentioned he wouldn't be available for their usual game because he and his wife, Linda, were headed to their beach house on Aruba.

If Bill can reach Greg by phone, and if the Jeffries agree, maybe he can stay at their townhouse on Seventieth between Park and Lexington. He was there a couple of times and the place is certainly large enough to accommodate him.

It's worth a try, especially since there are no other viable options. He doesn't think he'd be putting Greg and Linda in danger. His relationship with Greg is strictly limited to the health club. They don't exchange emails, texts, or phone calls. It's impossible to imagine how the Albanians could ever track him through his relationship with Greg.

True, soon after Olivia's death, he was invited to their place for dinner, but that was nearly two years ago. And recently, Greg has hinted he knows a woman he'd like to introduce to Bill, but the squash games have really been the extent of their contact. But there's no digital trail from Bill to Greg, at least nothing that's been recent.

Bill is confident Greg and Linda would feel comfortable giving him access to their home. They're generous people and they know Bill's a responsible person. It seems there's a decent chance they would go for the setup.

He has to come up with some bullshit story about why he needs to stay at their place.

Bill's memory is what got him through medical school. Recalling Greg's cell number, he dials it on the outgoing burner.

"Who's this?" Greg says, sounding annoyed.

"Greg, it's Bill. Bill Madrian."

"Hey, Bill, how come your number didn't come up on my cell? I thought you were some fucking robocall."

"I'm calling from a new phone . . . haven't registered it yet."

Greg's voice fades out.

"I'm losing you, Greg. You sound far away."

"I *am* far away," he says as the connection improves. "Like I told you at the club, we're in Aruba for the next ten days. Good to hear from you. What's up, buddy?"

"I need a favor."

"What is it?"

"My apartment's been flooded . . ."

Where did I come up with that? I'm a better bullshitter than I thought.

"Flooded? On an upper floor? How'd that happen?"

Without hesitating, Bill hears himself say, "Last night, a pipe under the bathroom sink broke, and the place overflowed. I was asleep and never knew what was happening. When I woke up, the apartment was a mess. Water flooded everywhere, and the parquet flooring's separated from the subfloor. I have to vacate for a few days while the building makes repairs."

A brief pause.

Greg must think this is a ridiculous story.

"Can I stay at your place for a couple of days until the repairs are done?"

"Wow. That sucks. Hold on. Lemme speak with Linda."

Greg's voice is muffled as he talks to his wife.

Bill waits, marveling at his newly discovered capacity for bullshit.

Greg is back on the phone. "Yeah, it's fine with us. Like I said, we won't be home for another ten days."

"Thanks, Greg. I can't tell you how much I appreciate this."

"No sweat, buddy. Here's what you gotta do: our downstairs tenant is a woman by the name of Elena Lauria. She lives in the apartment on the ground floor, the one with the door beneath the outside staircase. She's a librarian at the branch on 79th Street and gets home most evenings at five thirty. She has the key to the house. She can give you the key and the code for the security system. I'll call her and explain the situation."

"Thanks a million, Greg."

"Hold on . . ."

Greg's voice is muffled again.

"Linda says the biggest guest room's the first one on the second floor. It's on your right when you go up the stairs. It has an en suite bathroom with clean towels, and the bed has fresh linens. Wait a minute, Bill . . ."

Greg's voice is muffled for a few moments. He gets back on the phone. "She says the freezer's fully stocked and you can defrost whatever you need."

"I'll replace whatever I use."

"No need to, Bill. The stuff's there for guests . . ." Greg's voice drops to a near-whisper. "You know Linda . . . she hardly ever cooks. We eat out for a living." He chortles. "Hey, when we get back, how 'bout a little four-wall?"

"I'll whip your ass."

"We'll see about that." Greg's laugh sounds like a distant snicker.

"Thanks again, Greg. I really appreciate this."

"No sweat. I hope things turn out all right with the apartment."

CHAPTER 17

One block away from the bank, Bill peers warily at the intersection of 80th and Lexington: there's the tide of traffic, a sanitation truck grinding up garbage, a cable company panel truck at the cross street, and plenty of pedestrians.

There's nothing out of the ordinary.

Bill is aware his nervous system's on five-alarm alert and his heart is thudding a persistent drumbeat into his skull. He has to kill a few hours before this woman, Elena Lauria, gets home from the library. He could head over to Carl Schurz Park and Finley Walk where he usually jogs along the East River, but as Rami said, it's best to avoid familiar routines.

After that encounter on the subway platform this morning, it seems risky to be even within a mile of the apartment, but he decides to spend time at the Starbucks where he'll meet Frank. It's a storefront café on the corner of 80th and Lexington, four blocks from the apartment. There's little chance the Albanians will be looking for him here. And Frank won't have a long walk from the apartment to the coffee shop after he collects a few things for Bill.

Entering the café, he's exquisitely aware of his surroundings: the aroma of coffee brewing, the hiss of the espresso machine, the grinding of coffee beans, the clinking of spoons and cups, a guy talking loudly on his cell phone, the barista calling out "Macchiato," then "Soy Milk Latte."

After ordering an Americano, he grabs a seat at a corner table where he can peer through the window and keep an eye on Lexington Avenue. He sees nothing that looks threatening or out of the ordinary.

Feeling a tensile readiness throughout his body, he glances out the window every few minutes. There's the usual flow of passersby on a weekday afternoon. And a phalanx of vehicles barreling south on Lexington.

He decides to familiarize himself with the burner. It's like his regular cell phone, except he has no internet apps. No big deal. He's now off the grid so not having internet access is no loss.

He'll be reachable by only three people: Rami, and by tomorrow, Mom and Laurie. And possibly Roger, assuming he uses Laurie's burner.

Removing Rami's card from his pocket, he memorizes it and then dials the number.

"Leave a message," Rami's voicemail says.

Bill recites the number of the burner for Rami to use if he calls.

He's certain when Mom's burner is delivered—tomorrow morning—she'll call and demand to know what's going on. He can almost hear her voice: *Why can't I call on my regular phone?* She has a finely tuned nose for bullshit. What can he say that won't sound absurd? He'll worry about it when the time comes.

Pocketing the burner, he sips his coffee. It tastes bitter—no surprise. Would anything taste good right now? It doesn't matter. He ordered something merely to justify taking up space at a table. He wishes he had something to read, but realizes he'd be unable to concentrate.

*   *   *

At five thirty, Frank enters the coffee shop.

"Hey, man, here it is," he says, handing Bill the satchel and sitting down. "What's going on with your relative?"

"She had a nervous breakdown and is at the Cleveland Psychiatric Institute. I need to go there to help out."

Jesus, I'm a better bullshitter than I thought.

"I didn't know you have relatives in Cleveland."

"Yeah, a cousin I was close to when we were kids."

"You sure it's got nothing to do with that patient?" Frank leans toward Bill and in a near-whisper says, "That mobster's son?"

"Na, nothing like that," Bill says, knowing the bullshit he's handing Frank isn't selling.

"Sounds like you're handing me some crap, buddy. Why take the phone off the hook?"

"I don't want a million robocall messages."

"Sure . . . sure," Frank says in a sarcastic tone. "But I have a dental appointment, so I gotta go." Frank glances at his watch. "You're sure everything's okay?"

"Yeah, sure. Go get your teeth fixed."

"Goddamned mouth carpenter. You know what he charges to have a hygienist clean my teeth and then he sneaks a peek in my mouth? *Three* hundred bucks. Fucking rip-off." He pushes away from the table. "Lemme know how things work out with your cousin. And watch your back."

CHAPTER 18

Glancing at his watch, Bill realizes it's nearly time to head to the townhouse and pick up the key.

About to leave Starbucks, he sees the woman through the window.

Yes, it's her, the one who'd been sitting at the bar at Angelo's. He'd recognize her anywhere.

She's standing on the sidewalk holding a cell phone to her ear, some five feet from where he's sitting. They're separated by nothing more than the coffee shop's window.

Unaware of his presence, she's staring at the other side of the avenue. He fixes his gaze in the same direction. But amid the clamor of Lexington Avenue, he sees nothing that would draw her scrutiny.

It's strange to see her again, only a few blocks from Angelo's. She must live or work nearby, somewhere in the East 80s.

He has a better view of her than was possible at the bar. She's wearing form-fitting, faded jeans, a white blouse, and a waist-length black leather jacket. Her hair is pulled back in a bun, which accentuates her features. She has high cheekbones and a sculpted-looking nose—natural looking, refined—and it flares slightly at the nostrils, sort of a Julia Roberts nose. She's kind of Spanish looking, but she could pass for Eastern European, if he had to guess. She could be named Nadia or Tatiana or Carmen or Liliana—either Slavic or Latina.

She's every bit as exotic-looking as she appeared at Angelo's. And now he can look her over without her being aware of it.

While talking on her phone amid the roar of traffic, she has her left hand over her other ear trying to blot out the street noise.

Bill guesses she's having an intimate conversation, probably with some guy she's seeing. Maybe it's sexist to think this way, but a woman with her looks always has a man in her life, or is being pursued by one. It's a law of nature.

Still holding the phone to her ear, she turns and faces the coffee shop window. She nods as though making an emphatic point. Her eyes appear unfocused—like she's listening intently to whatever's being said—and a moment later, her gaze drifts past him. She turns and again faces the avenue. For sure, she couldn't see him through the street reflections on the store's pane of glass.

She then hits the OFF button, slips the phone into her purse, and begins walking north on the avenue.

He realizes if he weren't in a life-changing bind, he'd be tempted to rush out the door, catch up with her, and start a conversation.

Weren't you sitting at the bar in Angelo's last night?

But this is no time for romantic games. His life's tipping over the edge of a cliff and he's about to go into seclusion.

Beyond the next few days at Greg and Linda's place, he hasn't the vaguest idea where he'll be holed up. Or for how long. What a nightmare this is.

How do you reinvent yourself, your childhood, your parents, your education, everything?

Become a short-order cook scrambling eggs, making sandwiches, ringing a bell like the guy at the Lenox diner does where Bill sometimes chows down at the counter for lunch?

Do construction work, like he'd done for two summers during college?

Drive a taxi, hauling people around some mid-size city in the Pacific Northwest?

Alone and unknown, starting over again. From scratch.

Fucking Alex Bronzi and the Albanians.

But that's the worst-case scenario. Don't dwell on it. Don't go down some rabbit hole of your imagination. Rami said this may go on for a week, maybe two. Just deal with it.

He has to depend on the guy to get out of this bind.

But what can Rami do?

So, he's a skip tracer with some "connections," whatever they may be: Interpol or maybe the FBI, though that seems unlikely. And who in the world goes by a single name? Cher, Madonna, Shakira, Sting, Jay-Z, entertainers, that's who. Just who the hell is this Rami?

Moments later, he's on the sidewalk watching Lexington Avenue traffic rumble its way downtown. It'll be tough to get a cab because it's rush hour.

Normally, he'd walk the short distance to 70th. Greg and Linda's townhouse is only ten blocks downtown and half a block west of where he's now standing. But being out in the open is dangerous.

Every passing taxi is occupied. He begins walking downtown on the east side of Lexington Avenue.

One short block later, at 78th and Lexington, a taxi pulls to the curb and a woman gets out in front of a hair salon. Bill sprints to the still open left rear door and jumps in.

"Lexington and 70th," he tells the driver.

It'll be a short walk to the house he'll have to view as home for the next week or so.

After that, who knows what'll happen?

CHAPTER 19

E ast 70th is a tree-lined street with attached brownstones and townhouses on both sides.

Walking the short distance to Linda and Greg's place, he tries imagining what it will be like living alone in a four-story house.

Greg once mentioned the house has 5,500 square feet of floor space and cost the couple a huge pile of dough when they bought it some years ago. Bill knows plenty about the house because he once looked it up on Zillow. And from conversations with Greg. He and Linda spent a fortune renovating the interior—all four stories and the ground-level apartment, where this woman, Elena, is a tenant.

*   *   *

Tucked beneath the stairway leading to the building's front door is the entrance to Elena Lauria's street-level apartment.

Bill opens a waist-high, wrought-iron gate, heads down one step, and gets to the apartment door. He rings the bell.

Moments later, the door is opened by a dark-haired, thirty-something woman who must be Elena Lauria. She's tall and athletic-looking. She has a heart-shaped face with luscious-looking lips, expressive brown eyes, and her black hair is pulled back in a scalp-tightening ponytail. She wears jeans and a loose-fitting sweatshirt with the logo "Tufts" on its front.

Bill experiences an instant stirring he recognizes as a frisson of attraction. Yes, beauty impresses him, but there's more than that in her looks: he senses kindness, which attracts him every bit as much as her looks.

Even as he feels drawn to this woman, he feels a pang of guilt, realizing there hasn't been a day since Olivia died when he hasn't yearned for her. The only thing that's kept him going has been his practice; listening to patients spew their troubles keeps him from dwelling on his own.

But the woman standing in the doorway touches something within him. It's completely unexpected; it's an emotional ambush, but he stifles the feeling.

This is no time for games or romance.

There's only time for staying safe. For staying alive.

"I'll bet you're Bill Madrian," Elena Lauria says as her lips curl into an inviting smile.

There's something about that smile; it's warm, even generous in a way he's never quite noticed in anyone else.

"And I'll bet you're Elena Lauria," he says, realizing the attraction is mutual.

Don't get sidetracked. Your life's at stake. Anything you feel at this moment is because you're in danger and desperate for a connection.

Nodding, she tilts her head in a way he finds captivating. Her eyes glitter in the late afternoon light.

"It's good to meet you," she says as that smile reaches her voice. "Linda told me what happened to your apartment. That's terrible. Would you care to come in for a drink?"

"I'd love to, but I can't right now," he says, realizing he's too charged up to be decent company at the moment. "I have to take care of a few things . . ." Hoping she doesn't think he's standoffish or indifferent, he adds, "But I'd like a rain check. Maybe in a day or so we can have that drink?"

"That would be lovely," she says, as her smile broadens.

Yes, there's something gracious in her voice and in that smile, and he's surprised at how he regrets putting off the invitation. But survival surpasses all else.

"How about tomorrow evening, or the next one . . . if you're free," he says.

"That'd be great," she replies with a nod, half turning back to her apartment. "Just wait and I'll get the key."

Returning a moment later, she asks, "Do you know where everything is?"

"Oh yes. I've been here before. You're a new tenant aren't you," he says, aware he's prolonging the conversation."

"I've been here for a few months."

"Yes, I recall Greg mentioning something about a new tenant. Greg and Linda are great people."

"I couldn't ask for better landlords. Here's the key," she says, handing it to him. "And on the back of my business card is the code for the house alarm." In addition to her telephone number at the library, the card also has her cell number. "Feel free to call me if you have any questions."

Or if I want to come to your place to share a drink.

"I'll definitely do that. And I hope I have a rain check for that drink," he says, trying to make amends for turning down her invitation.

"You've got it," she says as she shoots him that alluring smile.

He turns and heads back the path toward the steps leading to the townhouse's front door.

CHAPTER 20

Entering the house, Bill finds himself in a spacious gallery where modern lithographs hang on teakwood walls.

He deactivates the alarm system, then commits the code to memory.

The foyer floor is polished blond oak with inlaid, diamond-shaped medallions of a darker wood, probably mahogany. No expense was spared by Greg and Linda in renovating this old townhouse.

The dining room is decorated in an eclectic mix of modern and ornate Edwardian pieces. Colorful Persian area rugs are everywhere to soften the look of the hardwood floors. Linda's skilled hand as an interior decorator is evident throughout the house.

The kitchen overlooks an enclosed backyard with decorative plantings and an ailanthus tree. It strikes Bill as odd that the only access to such a lovely outdoor space is through Elena's garden apartment.

Though neither Linda nor Greg cook—*We eat out for a living*—the kitchen is equipped with the latest high-end appliances. There's an eight-burner La Cornue stove sporting cast iron, steel, brass, and porcelain enamel. There's the obligatory Sub-Zero refrigerator, two sinks with brushed aluminum faucets, a marble-topped middle island on which sits a contraption labeled "Krups Barista One Touch Automatic Espresso Machine." It has levers sprouting everywhere and has a built-in coffee bean grinder.

The entire house is emblematic of an uber-rich financial services guy who went to Wharton and got into private equity before managing his own hedge fund.

Bill checks out the contents of the freezer. It's stacked with a glut of frozen foods: Newman's Own uncured pepperoni pizza, Birds Eye Alfredo chicken, Stouffer's five-cheese lasagna, El Monterey chimichangas, and an assortment of Lean Cuisine entrées.

For as long as he's here, Bill won't have to do any food shopping. He can stay isolated in this place until Greg and Linda get back from Aruba.

What does he do when they return?

But this is no time to think about that. Besides, there's the possibility Rami will have come up with something in a few days, or will he?

Though feeling a pang of hunger, he decides to first check out the rest of the house. The master and guest bedrooms are on the second floor. He climbs the stairway and finds the guest bedroom exactly where Greg said it would be.

The third floor has a fully equipped gym with a Nautilus treadmill, an elliptical machine, free weights, a Peloton bike, and a Bowflex Power Rod all-purpose workout machine.

Yes, Bill can definitely stay here for a few days and live in isolated comfort.

*   *   *

By ten in the evening, after having gobbled a microwaved pizza, the day feels like it's been endless. It's hard to imagine the chase along Lexington—which flashes with sickening clarity through his mind—and his meeting with Rami, happened only this morning. It seems like they occurred a week ago. It's amazing how your sense of time can either telescope or expand depending on circumstances.

As he thinks about time, it suddenly strikes Bill that he's living moment to moment and hasn't thought of a long-range game plan to deal with this situation. Before today, he had an orderly, predictable life. Everything had its time and place. Each day was filled with an array of quotidian tasks. He never had to think about survival.

How did it come to this: that his major—really, his *only* concern—is thinking about how to stay alive for the next few days? Or weeks. Or maybe, if things turn really ugly, for the rest of his life?

Rami's words come to him, *But you'll have a life.*

From a strictly practical standpoint, if he stays sequestered for too long, he won't get his mail—at the office or at home—and bills will go unpaid. Interest will be tacked onto his credit card balance and he'll fall into arrears on his maintenance for the co-op. All the bills—office rent, telephone, electric, health club, the cable company—will gather dust in the building's package room. And he'll be cut off from all these basic services.

And a long absence from the office means his practice will dry up and disappear. There'll be nothing left to sustain himself. He won't be able to earn a living and his entire life will turn to dust.

And he now realizes these everyday little chores—from writing out checks to picking up dry cleaning or walking to the office—are done without thinking about a long-range trajectory.

These barely-thought-about routines, these bits of flotsam and jetsam of daily obligations, are the small occurrences that comprise a life. You never really give much thought to where it's going and what it all means.

But now there's one primal concern: survival.

And there's one soul-searing question when it comes to disappearing:

Does his life have any meaning beyond the few people who will miss him when he's gone?

Boiled down to basics, his life means nothing in the larger scheme of things.

Christ on a bike, it's all so demoralizing.

I can't let myself think like this. It negates me.

So to distract himself, he grabs the remote and turns on the flat-screen TV. It's the local news on Channel Five.

There's an item about a subway mugging in Manhattan; there was a hit-and-run accident in Queens and a few other local items. After a break for an ad, the newscaster returns and says,

Police are still investigating the gangland killing of mobster Boris Levenko in Brighton Beach. They're asking anyone with information to call the police tip-line.

The call-in number flashes at the bottom of the screen.

That question keeps echoing in Bill's mind: *Hey, Doc, ya wanna know who clipped Boris Levenko?*

What kind of question was that?

It was a lethal question.

My God, this is scary.

Icy tentacles spread from Bill's neck to his shoulders, and a tingling sensation forms around his lips. He closes his eyes, leans back on the sofa, and tries to slow his breathing.

In and out . . . slowly.

Don't freak out.

There's a chance you'll get beyond this.

The news report continues.

There's speculation Levenko's shooting was a result of tensions between different families in the Russian mob, though police aren't ruling out a territorial dispute involving rival ethnic groups.

There's no mention of the Albanians.

Bill tries to suffocate the memory of that guy trotting alongside the bus—but it's impossible to forget. And his body is humming like a tuning fork. He peers about the room. This place feels so strange, so alien, and he feels more alone than he's ever been in his life. Even the soundlessness of this well-built townhouse is disturbing.

There's a good chance Rami's right: the Albanians will get to Mom, Laurie, Roger, and the kids. Yes, in today's digital world, privacy is a lost luxury.

Can they track him to this house? Greg and he have occasionally called each other using their cell phones. But that was months ago. If the Albanians get their hands on his phone records from Verizon, there'll be hundreds of calls on the readout, with only a couple made to Greg's cell. They'd have to sift through reams of digital information to see a pattern pointing to Greg—not that there *is* one—so they'd never suspect he's staying here. It'd be like trying to find a contact lens on a sandy beach.

But they'd see he's made plenty of calls to Mom, Laurie, and Roger. It's only a matter of time before they get to them. Rami made one thing clear: these Albanian crime families—or clans—have resources far beyond those available to ordinary citizens.

And what kinds of resources does Rami have?

He works out of a hole-in-the-wall setup in a building on 42nd Street. He recalls the receptionist speaking on the phone in a foreign language, maybe two or three different languages, so there's a chance the guy has international connections. But so what? This isn't a matter for Interpol. And Rami's operation is a one-man pony show. How much can he possibly have in the way of resources compared to those of the Albanian mob?

Bill feels his heart punching a savage rhythm in his chest. It still feels like adrenaline is pouring through his bloodstream, reaching every organ in his body, saturating every cell. Needing to burn off some pent-up anxiety, he heads upstairs to the gym.

Getting on the treadmill, he begins a slow walk, then increases the speed and sets the machine at a moderate incline.

After ten minutes of a steady jog, a sweat sheen has formed on his body. The treadmill's readout shows his heart rate has soared to 160 beats per minute and it feels like a hummingbird is lodged in his chest. He jumps from the machine, turns it off, and sits on a workout bench to cool down before he'll hit the shower.

He heads to the guest bedroom and enters the en suite bathroom.

Looking into the mirror, he wonders if he should do something to change his appearance?

Shave his scalp, go bald?

Nah, not the way to go.

Grow a beard? A mustache?

That'll take time.

He strips off his clothes and steps into a massive shower stall with multiple jets protruding from three sides of the cream-colored stone tiles. He could probably fill his apartment with new furniture using the money Greg and Linda spent on this shower alone.

Standing beneath the cascade of hot water, Bill soaps up and lets the deluge slosh over his back and shoulders and then sluice down his sides and thighs. The needles of water feel like a heated wrap, relaxing, soothing. Just what he needs.

As often happens in the shower, his thoughts wander in a series of recollections. He recalls the trip he and Olivia took to France where they drove along the Dordogne River and stayed at a series of small country inns, eventually getting to Paris where they booked a room in a small hotel near the Luxembourg Gardens. How romantic it seemed when they drank a bottle of cheap Bordeaux in their garret of a room and made love as though they were Bohemians in a Puccini opera.

But that's all over.

It's gone and will never return.

Not in this lifetime.

As an ineffable ache overcomes him, he begins shivering, turns off the water, steps out of the shower, and towels himself dry. It's frightening to think how temporary it all can be—your memories, your thoughts and feelings, your job, the people you know, those you love, your very life. They can all disappear in an instant.

Toweling himself dry, he thinks, *Get hold of yourself. Just calm down. Give it some time. See what this Rami guy can do.*

In the guest bedroom, he dresses, knowing it's useless to even *think* about falling asleep. He'll toss and turn as his thoughts spin to a bottom-line question:

Will he have to renounce his life and live the rest of his days as a different person?

Until the end of his time on earth.

Until he's dropped in the ground.

Somewhere.

CHAPTER 21

Close to midnight, feeling lost in the expanse of the house, Bill wanders from room to room.

It feels strange being alone in this immense place with its lofty ceilings, decorative cornices, and elaborate furnishings. And of all things, there's a dumbwaiter from the kitchen to the upper floors, a vestige from the 1800s. It apparently goes downstairs to the garden apartment below. No doubt, the live-in servants or cook were quartered where Elena Lauria now lives.

Bill finds himself standing in the hallway outside the master bedroom. Feeling an urge to enter, he realizes it would be an invasion of Linda and Greg's privacy, an intimacy to which he's not entitled.

Yet, here he is, standing outside the bedroom door.

Because he has a hunch and he has to see if it plays out in a tangible way.

Greg's an aggressive guy, a real force of nature. Both in business and in his personal life. Bill knows this from the way Greg plays four-wall squash and from talking with him each time they compete. You'd think his *life* depends on winning every game. The guy didn't get to be a multimillionaire because he's a laid-back slacker. He's uber competitive in every conceivable way. Being who he is, it's probable that if an intruder got into the house, Greg would be like a honey badger protecting Linda and himself. He's got tons of money and plenty of connections, and Bill thinks he recalls Greg once mentioning something about a handgun. There just might be one in the bedroom.

He enters the master suite and stops at the foot of the bed. It's king size with a huge, quilted headboard.

He goes to one of the night tables—really, a bedside chest—and slides the top drawer open. Inside is a paperback romance novel, a few hairpins, some other assorted things but nothing like what he's looking for. The other two drawers are empty. This must be on Linda's side of the bed.

Moving around the bed, he opens the top drawer of the other nightstand.

Bingo: a pistol lies there. With its sleek lines and black matte finish, it looks lethal.

Bill's never held a gun in his life. He has no idea how the thing works. But he can tell it's not a revolver. It looks like what's called a semiautomatic. Each time you pull the trigger, a bullet is fired.

He lifts it out of the drawer. Gingerly.

It feels heavy in his hand, so weighty, it must be loaded. But it has a comfortable feel, as though it's an extension of his arm and hand. Having no idea if a bullet's in the chamber, he makes sure to keep his index finger away from the trigger.

He's gotta learn how to use the thing. He's seen enough movies to know you pull back on the top—he thinks they call it a slide, or something like that—and a bullet pops into the chamber from a magazine sitting inside the weapon's handle. But that's the extent of his knowledge. It's not enough to even *think* about using the thing.

How does he learn something about this pistol? There's no handbook and his burner phone has no internet access. Now what?

Then it comes to him.

*   *   *

In the den, a desktop computer sits on a workstation table.

He sets the gun on the desk, sits at the computer, and pushes the power button.

A whirring sound comes from the device as a green light on the unit goes on. A few movements of the mouse and the monitor's screen comes alive.

Welcome, Greg appears on the screen.

A rectangular box appears beneath the welcoming message.

Shit! The thing's password protected.

To be expected.

Trying to guess the password would be an exercise in futility.

And it's likely that after three failed attempts, the computer will lock him out and he'd never gain access.

He's gotta game it out.

If Greg is like most people, he carries a piece of paper in his wallet on which he's jotted down his usernames and passwords. But on the chance he might lose or misplace the wallet, he's probably also written the passwords on paper located somewhere in the house. For convenience, it's most likely stored somewhere near the computer. That's what Bill's done, and he knows Frank Olivieri's done the same thing. Chalk it up to human nature. Keep things close at hand and convenient.

He opens the top drawer of the workstation. Rummaging through it he sees a pair of scissors, a bunch of pens, Scotch tape, a box of paper clips, a stapler, some cassette tapes, a package of AA batteries, rubber bands, and a roll of stamps.

Inside the second drawer, there's a small cardboard box with a slip-on lid.

Bill opens the box. It's filled with a stack of 3 x 5 blank index cards. He lifts the first blank card.

He comes to the second card in the stack: there it is!

Printed neatly is a list of usernames and passwords for Greg's cell phone, his Twitter and Facebook accounts, along with the username and password to log into the computer.

After typing them into the space, Bill has access to the computer.

Clicking on the Chrome icon, he's online.

In the Google browser's address bar, he types in "YouTube," hits the ENTER key.

The YouTube web page comes up.

The pistol on the desk has a logo etched on the side of the barrel: Glock 26.

In the YouTube search box he types in "How to use a Glock 26 pistol."

He now has a choice of demonstration videos.

He watches a sixteen-minute video describing the weapon's basics.

The gun is described as relatively lightweight, easy to conceal, and smooth edged so it won't get caught on a waistband when it's drawn. The narrator says, *The Glock 26 is a subcompact semiautomatic pistol designed specifically for concealed carry use. G26 is a gun you can count on at the moment of truth.*

The video demonstrates how to load and use the Glock along with warnings and safety precautions. Examining the pistol, Bill notices the safety button is in the ON position. By pushing it so the button protrudes with a red edge showing means the safety lever's in the OFF position.

The narrator says, *Red means dead. Always remember that. When you see "red," the safety mechanism's off and the weapon is ready to fire, so be very careful.*

Red means dead. Easy to remember.

He replays the video and follows the instructions, pausing it now and then to practice each step demonstrated. He presses the lever to release the magazine. It drops into his left hand. Yes, the gun is fully loaded.

He checks: there's no cartridge sitting in the chamber. He clicks the magazine back into the frame and with the safety lever in the ON position, practices holding the pistol in the two-hand grip demonstrated on the video.

By the end of the video, he knows how to load the handgun, rack it, hold it, take aim and fire. He now feels reasonably confident that in an emergency, at least he'll have a chance to protect himself.

He'll carry the gun with him, if and when he leaves the house. Suddenly, doubt spreads its tendrils through his brain.

It's more than doubt. It's certainty that he'd have trouble aiming the gun at another human being and pulling the trigger.

Yeah, sure, like I'm gonna go Clint Eastwood on these bastards. Who am I kidding? Life isn't a movie where the good guy takes care of business in two hours. If it comes down to a shootout, I'm toast.

The reality of it hits him: he's trucking in the *illusion* of being able to protect himself.

Then again, you never know what you're capable of when the shit hits the fan.

*   *   *

By one a.m., he's so keyed up, his heart is hammering his rib cage, and he knows he won't fall asleep.

He goes downstairs to the living room and sits on a sofa. The events of the last twenty-four hours stream through his mind: from the chase at the subway platform and then the bus, to being with Rami, to meeting Elena Lauria—yeah, maybe they'll share a drink—to then finding and learning to use a Glock—all in one day. It's a dreamlike stream of events replaying again and again in his mind.

For no particular reason, he switches off the living room lamp. In the dark, he approaches a window at the front of the house.

The sycamore trees lining East 70th Street haven't yet sprouted their full canopy of foliage. A nearby sodium street lamp casts a pinkish light through the night air. He has a good view of the roadway and sidewalk on both sides of the street.

A dark-green panel truck is parked and idling across the street. Yes, the engine is running because even though the vehicle's headlights are off, he sees exhaust fumes billowing out from the tailpipe.

Feeling a jolt of dread, he wonders if he's being watched. Or is he so keyed up he's now misinterpreting everything through a lens of suspicion, as though strictly neutral events pertain to him. Is he becoming paranoid?

C'mon, man, you're a psychiatrist. You know the mind can play a million tricks, can fuck you up in the worst ways. But this is real. It's not some fantasy.

Though the interior of the van is dark, he can make out movement behind the wheel. There's at least one person inside. Bill decides he's gotta wait: will the van drive away or stay in place? If it's the latter, he's definitely being watched.

How the hell do they know I'm here in this house?

His mouth goes dry.

A moment later, the headlights flare and the van pulls out of the parking spot, then heads toward Lexington Avenue.

He's jacked; it's adrenaline overdrive. He's so on edge he's jumping at every little thing and assuming the worst. This must be what paranoia feels like. Every little sight or sound takes on threatening portent. It's an exhausting way of being in the world. How long can this go on?

Grabbing the burner phone for outgoing calls, he dials his office.

The answering machine picks up. He punches in the code.

An electronic voice says, "You have three messages."

Playing them back, he hears the distinct sound of three hang-ups—one at eleven thirty a.m., another at one p.m., and the last at four p.m. They're calling the office, checking on him.

He dials his apartment number and gets a busy signal. Yes, Frank took the telephone off the hook.

His hands grow cold. A queasy sensation forms in the pit of his stomach. This is what it feels like to know your life is in danger, that unknown men are tracking you, wanting to kill you.

Returning to the window, he peers out to the street.

Where the van had been, there's now a sedan, parallel parking into the spot. He watches as a man and woman get out of the car and walk down the street.

No danger.

He's way too amped, strung out on fear.

What am I doing? What would Olivia think if she could see me now? Enough of Olivia. I've got to depend on myself. There's no one who can help me except Rami . . . maybe Rami . . . whoever he is and whatever he may be doing.

He decides to check that the house is secure and the windows can't be breached.

Holding the Glock against his thigh, he goes downstairs and checks the front door. It's thick and securely locked. Iron grill-work covers the first-floor front windows, so there's no need to worry about entry through them. He activates the alarm system.

He checks the first-floor windows at the rear of the house. They too are covered by iron grills.

There's no way anyone can enter the house from the first floor. He's safe.

CHAPTER 22

Kosta Bronzi lights a cigarette and sucks in the smoke even though his throat is raw from the last one.

He's under so much stress these days. Maybe when things calm down, he'll quit smoking—this time for good. It's a filthy habit and why kill himself with tar and nicotine when there's so much to live for?

He sits across the table from Besim, a man he trusts with his life. They're closely bonded. In fact, Besim is married to Kosta's first cousin, which is part of the clan's practice of keeping things in the family. Kosta knows there's nothing stronger than blood ties.

"I have good news, Kosta," Besim says. "Our Turkish friends have guaranteed the goods will be shipped to Eastern Europe with no problem. And they've agreed to take only ten percent."

"Good, good, Besim. And what about our friends in Tel Aviv?"

"They said the bank is ready to receive the funds, but it can only be done in small amounts. They don't want the government to get suspicious."

"What do they mean by a small amount?" Kosta crushes the remains of his cigarette in an ashtray.

"Only two million at a time. And it can't be more than one transfer a week."

"Why so little at such intervals?"

"Because their banking system is highly regulated."

"Why not use another country's system?"

"It would look suspicious if we bank in Turkey or, for that matter, in any of the Muslim countries. And there's too much illegal activity by the other clans in France, Germany, Greece, and Italy. We have to stay away from those countries because they're flooded with laundered funds. Israel is the only choice."

"But why only two million at a time?"

"Because larger amounts could raise suspicion. The Shin Bet could get involved. Or even worse, the Mossad could start sniffing around. And we don't want to deal with them."

"May Allah forbid it."

"If we flood their banking system, they'll put operatives on the situation and it could all go up in smoke," Besim says. "One of these days we have to learn how to use cryptocurrencies. That's the way to get around all these bank regulations and money transfer issues."

Kosta nods. "And the shipments . . . ?"

"All set and ready to be sent. Twenty crates."

"As usual, Besim, you've done fine work. Everything is good with the family?"

"Yes, and Marie is expecting any day now."

"Congratulations again. We'll have a great gathering when the child is born."

"Thank you, Kosta. It will be an honor."

If only Alex could be like Besim, Kosta thinks. The man is not only loyal and trustworthy, but he doesn't brag or run his mouth off about the businesses.

The trouble with Alex is what Kosta sees in all the young ones growing up in America. Their eyes are glued to their cell phones; they're obsessed with Facebook, Instagram, and all those dating sites. There's some foolish thing called Snapchat, whatever that may be. They can't appreciate what their parents and grandparents endured back in Albania. They don't know the value of hard work and want nothing more than to lead frivolous lives.

Kosta contrasts his son's life to his own. He was born when Albania was part of the Soviet bloc. Life under the communists was chaos. Hundreds of mosques were destroyed and the churches fared no better. Crime and corruption were rampant, especially in Durres where he, his mother, and father lived. The clans took over everything, terrorized innocent citizens, and demanded protection money.

When Kosta was eleven years old, he watched as his father got shot down like a mongrel on the streets. He recalls holding his father's bloodied body in his arms and seeing him draw his last breath. To this day, Kosta's heart aches when he remembers that day.

Why did one of the clans kill him? Because he wouldn't pay protection money to keep his little vegetable store going.

In a cauldron of desperation, in order to help his mother and himself survive, Kosta became a burglar.

One night, when he was fifteen, while sneaking into a darkened house, he found himself staring into the muzzle of a pistol. Holding the gun was Velo Memia, a kingpin in the Albanian mafia. "You little snot," Memia snarled. "I'll teach you a lesson."

Kosta was dragged to a clan hideaway where in a dank basement room, he was beaten mercilessly and held prisoner.

On the second day of captivity, Memia forced him to his knees, whipped out his cock, and said, "Choke on it, you little bastard." Knowing he was going to die anyway, Kosta did the only thing he could: he clamped his teeth onto the shaft of Memia's member and yanked. He then spat the organ onto the floor. Screaming in agony, Memia dropped to his knees as blood spurted from the stump.

Kosta rocketed to his feet, grabbed Memia's pistol, squeezed the trigger, and the man's skull exploded in a cloud of red mist. When two clan members came pounding down the cellar stairs, Kosta emptied the gun into both men. He then dashed up the stairs and sprinted home.

But the house was empty.

Frantic, he barged into a neighbor's house. The husband's lips trembled as he said, "Kosta, your mother died."

"What happened?" Kosta asked, reeling with shock.

"She thought they killed you, so she drank rat poison. We could do nothing for her."

With sorrow, and fear in his heart, Kosta knew he was marked for death. He stowed away on a cargo ship berthed in the port of Durres, and sailed across the Adriatic to Bari, Italy. Joining other fugitive Albanians, he made his way north, crossing the border into Austria and eventually making his way to the port city of Hamburg in Germany. There, he boarded a ship bound for New York.

Arriving in the city, he traveled to the Bronx, where his cousin Jakov lived. Based on his relative's endorsement, the clan welcomed Kosta and became his family.

By dint of determination and guts, he's risen to become Kyre of his own faction, the most distinguished boss of the Malotta clan. Kosta knows that to survive he must have the same ruthless determination he did as a youngster.

But his dolt of a son has endangered the entire clan by mouthing off to some Manhattan headshrinker. He violated *besa* by even *mentioning* Boris Levenko. Alex's loose tongue could have deadly consequences for Alex, for Kosta, and for the entire clan.

Besim is the only other person who knows what Alex had said to that headshrinker. If the Boss of Bosses, Kazim Malotta, ever learns that Kosta ordered the hit on Levenko, for sure he and Alex would end up in a ditch. Edonia's heart would be broken to lose both her husband and son.

So, for the well-being of Edonia and Alex, and to preserve Kosta's position in the Shqiptare, this headshrinker must go. Soon. Because the longer he's alive, the greater is the chance he'll talk to someone.

Coming out of his rumination, Kosta regards Besim's bony face, his black hair, and Van Dyke beard. He's a hard-looking man who will do whatever is asked of him. For Besim, life seems simple. He does what must be done. As far as Besim is concerned, killing a man is like slaughtering a chicken.

"You know, Besim, we do what we must do in order to survive . . . in order to prosper for ourselves and our families. And we must take care of the business at hand."

"You mean that headshrinker, yes?"

"Of course. You have people who can deal with this situation?"

"Yes. They're searching the area. We're quite sure he's still in Manhattan on the Upper East Side, either in the Seventies or Eighties. It's only a matter of time until we locate him."

"The longer it takes, the more likely it is he'll contact the authorities. Tell me, Besim, they know what he looks like?"

"Yes. His picture's online . . . on sites called Healthgrades and Zocdoc. They're websites for doctor referrals." Besim pauses, then adds, "But we need to find his relatives, too. We can use them to force him to give himself up."

"Madrian . . . it's not a common name, right?" Kosta asks. "There can't be too many of them."

"We've located two other people named Madrian in the city. Neither appears to be related to him."

"We must find this headshrinker quickly. Can you access his phone records?"

"Yes, we'll get them very soon."

"Good. That might lead us to his family."

"As you know, Kosta, he was spotted at a Starbucks on Lexington Avenue. We're certain he's staying nearby."

"This is urgent. I want you to use that skip tracer, the one we've used for the last few years, that fellow McMillan, the one with an office on Wall Street. Do you still have him on tap?"

"Yes, I'll give him a call."

"How many people do you have looking for Madrian?"

"Five, all good people."

"Do they know why we want to find him?"

"No. They only know he's the target."

"Good. Make sure they never learn why we want him."

"Of course."

"And, Besim . . . this is important for all of us. So, make it happen quickly."

CHAPTER 23

After a restless night's sleep, Bill tries to use the coffee machine, but there are too many levers and buttons.

This high-tech contraption is beyond his ability to use without detailed instructions. Is this what's become of him? He's so nervous he can't figure out how to make a damned cup of coffee?

He could leave the house to get breakfast at the coffee shop on the corner of 70th and Lexington, but no way will he chance hanging around a diner, even for two minutes. He won't use DoorDash because he can't use a credit card.

At Greg's desktop computer, he uses Google Maps; types in "70th Street & Lexington Avenue, NYC," brings up the intersection, and then goes to "Street View." He sees Neil's Coffee Shop, not even a half block away. Googling it, he gets the telephone number, calls, and orders two cornbread muffins and three containers of coffee to be delivered.

A few minutes later, the front doorbell rings.

After checking through the peephole, he opens the door, pays the guy with a twenty, and says, "Keep the change."

It's wise to tip generously. After all, it's likely he'll be ordering in most of his coffee from Neil's.

Though he's been staying in the townhouse for less than a day, he's already feeling the mind-numbing effects of confinement. It's not only the isolation; it's also the realization he's being hunted. One wrong step and he could be annihilated.

After eating breakfast and needing to blow off some anxiety, he goes upstairs, gets on the treadmill, and spends half an hour walking at a leisurely pace. No need to work up a sweat. But after thirty minutes, despite slow walking slowly on a flat surface, he's sweating rivulets. And his pulse is ramped up to well over one hundred beats a minute.

Stepping off the treadmill, he's lightheaded, feels as though he'll faint. For years, he's heard patients complain about this sensation. It's stress overload—a case of raw nerves that has him feeling this way.

When his burner lets out a high-pitched trill breaking the tomb-like silence, it startles him. Letting out a gasp, he feels his chest tighten.

It's Mom.

"William, I just got a UPS delivery . . . a telephone with the strangest note from you. What on earth's going on?"

"Nothing, Mom."

"What do you mean *nothing*? Why this phone . . . and why can't I call you from *my* phone?"

"I've been having trouble with my cell phone. You'll have to use that one until I get a new one."

"I understand you have some sort of temporary phone, but why do I have to use *this* one to call you?"

"It's a different phone company and they're not the same carrier. It's too complicated to explain," he says, knowing she has zero tech savvy and will most likely accept this bogus explanation.

Like many older people, she loathes even using her cell phone. "It'll be taken care of in a few days. I don't want you to—"

"William, is everything all right? You sound . . . I don't know . . . upset."

"Sure. Everything's fine."

"Are you in the office?"

"No, I've taken a few days off."

Sighing, she says, "You know, even when you were a child, I always knew when you weren't telling the truth. You're lying to me. I can tell by your voice. Please tell me what's going on."

"Nothing, Mom. This is just a temporary thing that—"

"I tried calling you at your apartment and there's a constant busy signal."

"I know. The line's out of order. It's the same carrier I use for the cell phone."

She sighs again.

Bill's thoughts race. No way is she buying this story. He needs to think up something more convincing, something she won't question.

"William, dear . . . what's wrong?" Her voice is soft, plaintive.

"Nothing, Mom. Believe me, I'm fine."

"Listen, dear, I know that ever since Olivia's . . . ever since then it's been hard for you . . ."

"It's not that."

"Then what is it?"

"Mom . . . I don't . . . I can't . . ."

"It's coming on two years now," she says, "and I know June's a difficult month for you. Believe me, I understand. After your father died, for the first two years I had a very hard time each September. That terrible night seemed to come back in my mind, again and again. So, I understand that . . . well, for lack of a better word . . . that the anniversary's coming soon. I know what you're going through, but you're still a young man and as trite as it may sound, life goes on. The world doesn't stop because of your loss."

"I know, Mom. I know. It's a lot easier than it was this time last year."

"I just want you to be happy."

"I know. Believe me, I'm—"

"Please, William, just reassure me that things are okay?"

He can't fool himself, so how can he fool his mother?

"Everything's fine, Mom. You have to believe me."

Surprisingly, his voice is steady, even, calm.

"William, why don't you come downtown and have lunch at my place?"

"I can't. I have some things I have to do."

"What do you have to do that's so important you can't see your mother?"

"I had to take the day off because of a leak in the apartment. They're coming to fix the floor."

"A leak? What happened?"

He tells her the story about the apartment flooding. "They're coming today to assess the damage to the parquet flooring, so I have to let them in."

"Can't you have your superintendent do that? Please, come downtown. I haven't seen you in weeks. I can whip something together and we'll have a lovely lunch."

She's been a widow for so many years now. Even though she has friends, it's a lonely life. No matter what's going on, I can't push her away.

"I have a better idea, Mom. How about I meet you at that restaurant you like, the one on 26th Street?"

"Uncle Joe's?"

"Yes, like we always do, we can have small Caesar salads and pizza."

"That would be lovely. Why don't you come up to the apartment first and we'll go there together."

He can't even *think* about exposing her to danger.

"Like I said, Mom, I wanna be around when they come to repair the leak and look at the floor. They're coming in the early afternoon. How 'bout we meet at the restaurant, and let's make it one thirty, okay?"

"It's a bit late because I have a hairdresser's appointment at two thirty, but I'll make it work. I'm looking forward to it."

They hang up.

Is leaving the house too great a chance to take?

Maybe. But if he runs to the corner, grabs a taxi, and heads downtown, he'll be on the street for no more than a minute, maybe two. It'll be in the middle of the day when taxis are more available than in the morning or evening rush hour.

Under the circumstances, it's too bad he can't use an Uber. But the burner has no apps. Besides, Rami said not to use a credit card for any reason.

A quick trip down to 26th Street won't expose him to danger.

CHAPTER 24

t's 1:05 in the afternoon.

Before leaving the house, Bill tucks the Glock into the waistband at his back.

Rummaging through the hallway closet, he grabs one of Greg's windbreakers and slips into it. It hangs down low enough to hide the pistol's bulge.

Though it may not be wise to do, he'll risk a few minutes on the street trying to grab a taxi.

He sets the house alarm, steps outside, locks the door, and makes his way down the steps to the street.

Traffic rushes by on Lexington. Every passing taxi is occupied. It's typical midday congestion on the Upper East Side. It was a fool's notion to think catching a cab would be easy.

He walks south on Lexington to 68th Street, keeping an eye out for an unoccupied taxi. He comes to the 68th Street subway station. He could hustle down the steps and take the local to 28th Street, only a few blocks from the restaurant. But Rami warned him about public transportation. He was lucky to have noticed that hit man yesterday on that crowded platform.

So, he bypasses the subway entrance, crosses 68th Street, and stands in front of the Hunter College Building. People stream in and out of the place so it could be a good spot to snag a taxi. Sure enough, a cab pulls up and a woman gets out.

She's out of the taxi for no more than a half-second when Bill jumps in.

"Second Avenue and 26th Street," he tells the driver.

"Ah . . . the Kips Bay area," the guy says.

"Yup." Bill says nothing more. He's in no mood to make idle conversation. He just wants to get downtown, meet his mother, and spend some time reassuring her that everything's okay. Then it'll be back to the house.

It's slow-going on Second because of bus and truck traffic. Suddenly, at 58th Street, traffic comes to a standstill. It's bumper-to-bumper gridlock with no end in sight. Horns blare and sirens wail amid a pall of ash-gray smoke drifting across the avenue. Looking ahead, Bill sees fire trucks blocking traffic. Cop cars, uniformed police, emergency vehicles, and firemen are everywhere.

Bill recalls Rami's warning about a guy on a motorcycle pulling up and attaching a bomb to the side of a car, then speeding off. That could happen now, even in a traffic tie-up, because there's enough space between the lines of cars for a motorcycle to speed away.

Craning his neck, Bill looks back. Traffic is at a standstill. They're boxed in mid-block and there's no way to get to an alternate route downtown.

Moment later, the clattering roar of a motorcycle comes from behind and to the right. A guy on a Kawasaki is speeding between the lines of vehicles.

It's coming; a guy on a bike with a magnetic bomb.

A shiver winnows down Bill's spine as he prepares to pop open the left rear door and jump from the cab. But the guy keeps going;

there's no clunk of something being attached to the taxi. A moment later, the motorcycle is far ahead of the taxi, still zipping between two lines of cars and trucks.

Bill feels a droplet of sweat slither down his torso. He takes a few deep breaths, inhales deeply, leans back in the seat, and waits for his racing heart to slow.

The backup has been caused by a small fire at a storefront one block ahead.

Bill and the cabbie sit, waiting in silence.

Knowing he'll be late, Bill whips out his burner and dials Mom's burner. No answer. She's probably at the restaurant and left her burner at home.

Maybe he should dial her cell, but he recalls Rami's words. He can't call either her landline or cell. But it's probably better to dial her cell using a different phone. He won't take a chance calling her even using his burner.

"Do you have a cell phone?" he asks the driver. "Mine can't get a signal here."

"Yeah, man." The cabbie turns and hands him his phone.

He dials Mom's regular cell number.

She picks up. "Yes . . . ?"

"Mom, it's me. I'm in a taxi. There's a fire in a store on Second Avenue and we're stuck in traffic. Nothing's moving. I don't want you to worry, but I'm gonna be late. It could be a while before traffic begins moving."

"I'm glad you called, William. I'm already at the restaurant and I'll wait as long as I can, but I do have that hairdresser's appointment. If I have to leave before you get here, I know you'll understand. Then, we can talk later . . . this evening. Promise you'll call me then."

"I promise."

After a few more words, they hang up.

The cabbie apologizes for the delay. "I'll turn the meter off," he says and he does precisely that.

Thanking him, Bill knows he'll give the guy a generous tip. After all, he's losing time and money with this delay.

Sitting there, Bill's thoughts drift to Mom's having mentioned the anniversary of Olivia's death. He thinks back to the night they met. It was the beginning of the Memorial Day weekend two years ago at Rory's on Second Avenue in the East 90s. The noise level was ear-bleeding, so bad he wanted to walk out, but he couldn't because he was with Frank Olivieri and Don Landon, guys who loved the noise, the frivolity, the ambience.

He remembers the moment he saw her—that image is etched in his brain.

Sitting at the bar with Frank and Don, he noticed her walking into the place. Alone, she took a stool at the bar, off to his right, maybe twenty feet away. He even recalls what the lighting was like: soft, subtle, a buttery glow that highlighted her blond hair.

There was something alluring about her; it was more than her looks. It was her poise, her confidence, yet there was no appearance of arrogance. How he managed to perceive those qualities in those few moments is still a mystery, but that was the impression she made. And it turned out to be a truth he came to know over time.

While Frank and Don talked about the Mets and Yankees, they suddenly realized Bill wasn't listening to a word of their conversation.

"Hey, Bill, where's your head at?" Frank asked.

"Huh? Nowhere."

"Bullshit," said Don. "He's been staring at that woman down the end of the bar."

Frank craned his neck, turned back to Bill, and said, "She's good-looking. Why not go over and say 'Hello'?"

"Not my style, Frank."

"C'mon, Bill. Get off your ass and walk over."

Knowing they'd razz him, Bill decided to approach her.

Getting off his barstool, he ambled in her direction.

Patrons were bellied up to the bar three-deep. The mass of people seemed to heave back and forth amid the hubbub of conversation and music piped in through ceiling speakers.

As Bill neared her, a guy wearing a double-breasted suit—looking like a Wall Street type—slithered through the bar crowd and began spinning his version of charm. Bill felt a juvenile kind of jealousy.

At that moment, the randomness of the universe brought Bill what he came to realize was the luckiest moment of his life. The crowd's movement shoved him into her. When their bodies collided, the drink she was holding spilled onto the bar.

"I'm so sorry," he said.

Feeling idiotic, he compounded the misstep by gently grabbing her wrist.

"Oh, that's all right," she replied, swiveling on her stool to face him.

At that moment, he actually found himself wondering if he was experiencing what was meant by the expression *love at first sight* or was it a *coupe de foudre*, the French expression meaning *lightning strike*? It was a favorite saying of his Montreal-born father, who frequently peppered his English with heavy doses of his native tongue.

"It's not your fault," she said, laughing gently, as the warmest smile Bill had ever seen spread across her face. "This place is so crowded," she continued as she took his hand in hers.

"Can I buy you another?" he asked.

"I'd like that."

Wall Street Guy melted into the mass of humanity.

A moment later, the woman sitting to Olivia's left vacated her stool.

"Why not sit here," Olivia said, patting the seat. Turning to the bartender, she said, "I'd like another vodka gimlet, please." Facing Bill she said, "And my friend here is drinking . . . what?"

"I'll have the same."

"I'm Olivia."

"I'm Bill."

"Well, Bill, this is a strange way to meet . . . just bumping into each other. Why do you think that happened?"

"I'm at a loss for words." Smiling, he hoped he didn't look sheepish.

"Well, maybe if we talk for a while, the words will come to you."

That was how it began.

*   *   *

The taxi arrives at the restaurant nearly forty-five minutes after the appointed time.

Getting out of the cab, Bill looks both ways.

I have to develop an awareness of what's around me. As Rami would say . . . situational awareness.

There's nothing unusual, just the bedlam of Second Avenue: cars honking their way south, trucks rumbling downtown, hordes of people on the sidewalks walking amid the pandemonium.

He's so late, he's certain Mom's already left the restaurant.

Trying to appear casual, he walks toward Uncle Joe's.

CHAPTER 25

Uncle Joe's is a family-style Italian trattoria.

Serving Neapolitan-inspired food, the place is a warm, comfortable room with tables napped in white cloth. The restaurant appeals to an older crowd, isn't *au courant* like so many of the watering holes on the Upper East Side.

Mom and Bill have had lunch here quite a few times. They usually order personal pizzas—thin crust, well done—and small Caesar salads. She ends up taking half of hers home each time.

He enters the place and is greeted by Antonio, the maître d', who recognizes him. "Your momma waited as long as she could and then left," he says. "She asked you to call her later."

Sitting at a table near the window, Bill thinks about his mother. She's made a better adjustment to losing Dad than Bill's made after only two years of living with Olivia. She's gone on with her life—yes, it's a different one now, but she has friends, a few other widows and one late-in-life divorcée—goes to movies, the theater, and plays bridge with a group of women.

Bill sometimes wonders if there'll ever be another man in her life. If that happens and makes her happy, he'd be fine with it. That's what his father would have wanted for her. Yes, Bill would welcome that, at least in the abstract, though he wonders how he'd *really* feel if another man appeared on the scene and "replaced" his father.

Bill orders a personal pizza and a small Caesar salad. He scans the room. The restaurant is moderately filled with a lunchtime crowd, but there's nothing that arouses suspicion or tickles his radar. Yes, as Rami would say, he's developing situational awareness.

After a brief interlude, the waiter approaches. "Your pizza will be out in just a few minutes. Would you like your salad now?"

"Sure, that's fine."

The waiter returns to the kitchen.

Peering out the window to his right, Bill sees a black Lincoln Navigator pulling up to the curb on Second Avenue, only twenty feet from where he's sitting. The curbside back door opens.

Two hard-looking men emerge. They have stubbled faces, wear dark blue jeans and black leather car coats. One guy has the coldest-looking eyes Bill's ever seen.

With their hands buried in their coat pockets, both men glance up and down the avenue, then walk toward the front door of the restaurant. The Navigator waits at the curb with its engine running.

Holy shit! They've gotta be Albanians. It's a mild day and they're wearing leather coats with their hands thrust in their pockets, no doubt locked onto pistols.

Bill shoots up from the chair and heads for the kitchen.

He blasts through the swinging doors, knocks a waiter against the wall, rushes past a grill, scrambles past a deep fryer, then a dishwasher, and bounces off a table holding a huge kettle, keeps going amid the clutter of pots and clanging pans, glances left, then right, sees a back door, opens it to a narrow alley with a pile of black plastic garbage bags, clambers over a low fence, and on legs feeling like jelly, he dashes along a narrow passageway to East 26th Street.

It's a residential side street, quiet, not much traffic and only a few pedestrians.

He races toward First Avenue, then runs south, turns onto 23rd Street, and gets back to Second Avenue. Now three blocks south of the restaurant, he jumps onto the roadway and hails a taxi.

It pulls over.

He rips open the door, leaps in, and says, "Head downtown."

"Where downtown?"

"Just downtown."

"You got it."

Maybe I should go to the FBI at Foley Square or the NYPD at One Police Plaza. We're heading in that direction anyway. I can tell them what Alex Bronzi said and describe how I've been targeted. But what can I tell them other than what some immature thirty-year-old said in a counseling session? On top of that, I can't prove anyone's coming after me. The cops will think I'm nuts. Maybe I should ask Rami first, if he thinks it would be best to go to the cops. Right now, it's best to just lie low.

The ride down Second Avenue seems agonizingly long. Bill keeps glancing back and notices the driver peering at him through the rearview mirror.

It then hits him like a mallet to the chest: how did the Albanians know he'd be at Uncle Joe's? After leaving the townhouse, he was on the street for no more than three minutes. It was only another few seconds before that woman got out of the cab in front of Hunter College and he jumped in. But he could have been spotted on the street.

After hearing what Rami said about locating people via the internet, it's conceivable they can find him in a hundred different ways.

Maybe they followed him when he went to the bank, or at Target or the UPS store. Or somewhere else.

Or maybe they were monitoring Greg's computer.

How would they be able to do that?

Or Bill's burner.

Do they have that kind of capability?

Rami said, or implied, that a burner couldn't be tracked. Or did he? For sure, he advised Bill to use only burners. Who knows what kind of spyware is available these days?

Jesus, they'll find me anywhere. Maybe I should leave town.

It's absolutely unreal; Bill's minute-to-minute existence is filled with doubt and desperation.

Right now, fear is the landscape of his life.

Why's he heading downtown? Does it matter where this taxi goes?

He has to leave as much distance as possible between himself and his family.

Bill's hands tremble and a weak sensation courses through his body. His legs feel rubbery. And weak. He didn't have to go to medical school to know it's the feeling you get after an adrenaline surge. His body was flooded with hormones the instant he saw those guys; he was so jacked that when the adrenaline dump subsided, every muscle in his body began feeling like spaghetti. And there's this gut-sick feeling in his stomach, as though he'll puke.

He's being driven by fear and suspicion.

Is he becoming paranoid?

No, it's just that he wants to live.

Bill suddenly realizes something: when he spotted those guys—hit men or not—in that moment of panic, not for a nano-second did he think of pulling out the pistol and getting ready to fire. There was no way he could hold a gun, point it at a person, and shoot to kill. Killing isn't in his DNA.

Why did he even *think* of meeting Mom for lunch?

A dumb mistake.

One he won't make again.

Should he call Rami?

Leave a message?

Tell him what happened?

And say *what*, exactly?

Rami, you gotta do something. I'm being tracked by the Albanians. They followed me downtown.

Downtown? Where were you going? I told you not to go anywhere.

And what about Rami? And why did he keep saying "we" and "us"? Does he belong to some criminal organization? Or maybe it's Interpol?

The only familiarity Bill's had with any of this stuff has been the movies. Or what's in newspapers about the Italian mafia. He'd never even heard of the Albanian mob.

Maybe Roger knows more than he's letting on. Exactly what's his connection to Rami? Is Roger hooked into some criminal organization? Don't they usually have their claws embedded in politicians, the police, judges, and lawyers? Crime and corruption are everywhere.

Is Roger *connected*?

One thing is clear: if you look under the hood of anyone's life, there's a good chance you'll come up with some dirt.

And Roger's no different. He could be tied into some criminal enterprise.

But enough about Roger and Interpol and mafias. If I don't do something soon, I'm a dead man. But do what? Go where?

He can't go back to the townhouse, at least not during daylight hours.

Can he stay with Don Landon for a while?

No, that won't fly. The guy has a live-in girlfriend. He'd never go for that setup. And besides, he and Don have had too many phone conversations over the years, both cellular and landline calls. If the Albanians can access his phone records, there's an easily detectable pattern leading directly to Don. Staying there's a big zero.

It's as though Bill's now poison and anyone he touches will be contaminated.

He realizes the more people he contacts, the more likely it is he'll be tracked down. And he'll be putting other people in danger. He might as well have leprosy. He's gotta get back to that townhouse and his own private lockdown.

It was stupid to leave the townhouse. Just plain stupid.

Maybe he should let Rami get him a new identity so he'll be able to live in some small to medium-sized city. Alone, disconnected, uprooted, knowing no one. Completely alone.

Face it, the life you've known could very well be over.

CHAPTER 26

Second Avenue ends at the intersection of East Houston Street on the Lower East Side.

There's no need to go farther downtown. Forget the FBI or the police. He can't offer them anything useful. It'll go nowhere, and it'll just stir up the pot of poison in which he's already drowning.

He can't go back to the townhouse during daylight.

Where to go?

East Houston Street's as good as anyplace else.

To do what?

He hasn't got a clue.

Just hang out.

Somewhere.

Anywhere.

He tells the driver to turn left onto Houston. They proceed one block east and Bill asks the cabbie to stop at the intersection of Forsythe and East Houston. He pays up and gets out of the taxi.

Standing on the street, he looks around and sees rows of old tenements. He hasn't been to this area of Manhattan in years.

He spots The Gatsby Hotel, a six-story brick building.

Forget staying at a hotel; he can't use a credit card.

Jesus, I never even thought of these things. Escape, evasion, going incognito. This is all so unreal.

There's no place where he can feel safe. He's homeless, just floating aimlessly through the streets, uprooted, unattached, a complete stranger. To everyone.

Forget about a flophouse near the Bowery. Take a room there and a bunch of down-and-out guys would beat the shit out of him, then scrounge through his pockets for a lousy nickel.

In a staggering moment of awareness, he realizes he's a vagrant, no different from the homeless guys sleeping on subway gratings or using the trains as shelters. As for eating, he's never even seen a soup kitchen. He's never had to wonder where his next meal would come from or where he'd be sleeping at night.

We take so much for granted in our little lives.

Walking along Houston, he suddenly realizes in the middle of the fucking *afternoon*, he *needs* a drink—there's gotta be something that'll tamp down what feels like a motor vibrating in his chest. God, he's amped, absolutely electrified. That gut-sick feeling rises from his stomach and weakness is still leaching through his muscles. It's pure fear, the terror of knowing your life could be over today or tomorrow or maybe the day afterwards. And there's nothing you can do about it.

He comes to the Z-Rock Bar & Grill at the corner of Attorney Street and East Houston. It looks like a dump, but it's out-of-the-way and probably safe. It'll be just to kill some time until it's dark and he can get back to Greg and Linda's house.

The tavern's interior is dimly lit. Three grungy-looking guys are sitting at the bar, sucking down juice in the middle of the afternoon. With his thick stubble, faded jeans, and wearing an ill-fitting windbreaker, he looks like he belongs here.

The resinous scent of marijuana hangs in the air, blending with the odor of piss and malt. The Glock in his waistband feels reassuring, though it would take extraordinary circumstances for him to pull the thing out.

Bill spies a small stage in the rear room. The place must have live music at night. It's a good bet when the band is playing, the bar area is jammed amid deafening rock played by up-and-coming heavy metal groups like Megadeath, the kind of shit Frank Olivieri loves.

A weather-beaten bar's on the right side of the front room. Brigades of bottles are stacked behind it. There are no top-shelf brands in this place. Just beer and lowlife hard stuff—Old Crow or Four Roses. Maybe some rotgut jug wine is available if that's your preferred poison.

Three tables are arranged haphazardly in the front room, maybe ten feet from the bar. They're surrounded by bentwood chairs.

Bill grabs a seat on a vinyl-topped barstool.

An unkempt-looking guy sitting to his left slurps a glass of amber-colored stuff. Bill can smell it from five feet away. The shit smells like turpentine.

The bartender's a tough-looking woman who's somewhere north of thirty, has purple hair, a nose ring, and raptor-like features. A fuck you attitude oozes like lava from her pores. Snapping her chewing gum and peering at him with a world-weary look, she says, "There's no music 'till eight."

"I'm good with that. How 'bout a bottle of Bud?"

She nods, sighs, goes to the end of the bar, bends over a cooler, grabs a bottle, snaps off the cap, returns to where Bill is sitting, and plops the opened bottle down in front of him.

"Fifteen bucks," she says, snapping gum furiously as she stares him down with that fuck you look.

"*Fifteen* bucks? For a bottle of beer?"

"You don't like it, go somewhere else."

The chewing gum crackles between her molars.

With heat rising to his face, he takes out his wallet, then slips a ten and a five onto the bar.

She snatches it and walks away, bypassing the cash register.

He regards her out of the corner of his eye.

She pockets the money.

What a place. But the last thing I need right now is to make a scene. Just drink the beer, keep your mouth shut, and stay calm.

A foamy crown forms at the top of the bottle; he takes a sip, then a few quick gulps. Seconds later, the alcohol feels like it's seeping into his brain. The speed of the effect is a solid indicator of how much he needs this drink. When he's feeling down or distressed, alcohol leaches quickly through his brain circuits. A nearly calm feeling begins washing through him.

The Glock in his waistband feels like it's eating into his lower back. But right now, it's his best friend.

Thinking of the pistol, he momentarily imagines the door of this dive bursting open and two hit men spraying bullets throughout the room. But that's unlikely, even absurd, because there's no way he was followed from Uncle Joe's. At least he's developing some level of situational awareness, to use Rami's terminology. So maybe there's hope that he'll get out of this horror show alive.

Thinking of Uncle Joe's, he again realizes that when he saw those two guys about to enter the restaurant, he never gave a moment's thought to pulling out the piece. His first and only impulse was to run. It takes something more than he has in him to shoot a man—a certain coldness or maybe an overwhelming threat to your life—a situation of self-preservation. Even then, could he really point and shoot a man to death?

When he's partway through his second beer—and out thirty bucks—the knot of anxiety in the pit of his stomach begins lessening. How good it would feel to just go numb, maybe fall asleep at the bar like some wino who's got nothing to do and nowhere to go. But that's not gonna happen because he's gotta stay alert, but calm. It's crucial to stay focused because he may have to respond to a *real* threat, not to some bullshit fantasy like the panic-inducing demons that plague so many of his patients.

It's life or death now, in real time, not something from childhood, like when he imagined a monster sitting in the chair in his darkened bedroom—it was nothing more than a pile of clothing—while he lay in bed quaking with fear and peering at the shape.

Bill knows he can face the specter of the death of a loved one, having lived through his father's sudden passing and that of his fiancée, who's lovely thirty-year-old face he last saw as she lay in repose on the satin pillow inside a brass casket.

Death is familiar, and he'd seen so much of it during medical school and even more as an intern rotating through medicine and surgery before becoming a psychiatric resident.

Yes, death is part of life. But I've never had to deal with my own death . . . one that could be brought on by thugs and goons. A violent death.

He glances at his watch—it's only three thirty; there's still plenty more time to kill before darkness falls. He'll nurse this beer slowly.

He wonders how his patients are reacting to his sudden departure?

Really, his disappearance.

Yeah, I've disappeared. I might as well be a ghost.

If he's gone for too long, his patients will find other psychiatrists.

Then what'll he do for a living?

A living? He's gotta do whatever he can to keep on living.

For the hundredth time, he wonders what this guy Rami can possibly do to get him out of this hole.

It's all so surreal, it feel like a fever dream.

But it's no dream; it's a waking nightmare.

And it's disorienting. When did he meet with Rami? Was it yesterday? Or was it two days ago? He's losing track of time.

His burner lets out a trill.

He feels his heart beginning to race.

He'll take a chance and answer the phone. "Yes . . . ?"

"Bill, it's Laurie." Her voice sounds strained. "What the fuck's going on?"

"You mean the phone and the note?"

"Yes. Give it to me straight."

"Hold on, I gotta get some privacy," he says, moving away from the bar and sitting at a corner table. "Nothing's going on, Laurie . . ." he says softly with his hand cupping the phone.

"Come off it, Bill. Roger and I don't keep secrets from each other. He said that because of a patient you're in trouble with some Albanians. A mob connection of some kind."

"It's just . . . I was seeing a guy in treatment . . ." he says, trying to sound casual, yet knows his quivering voice is a giveaway. "But not anymore. He quit."

"Yeah, yeah, and this patient knows who's behind the murder of that mobster in the news, right?"

Laurie knows what's going on. There's no sense in playing it down.

But he remains silent.

"Bill. I know you're in trouble," she continues.

"It's all under control."

"Bullshit," she cuts in. "Give me the full story."

"I can't talk about it."

"You can't *talk* about it? Listen, Bill, this could involve the family . . . Mom, me, Roger, and the *kids*. What're we going to tell Mom?"

"We don't have to tell her anything."

"Yes, we do. We have to be on the same page."

"I told her I'm having trouble with the phone company. And that there's a leak in my apartment . . . the sink."

Or did I tell her the toilet overflowed . . . I'm so nervous my memory's getting jumbled.

"And they're coming to fix the flooring. So I can't go back there for the time being."

"That doesn't cut it, Bill. What did you tell her about these burners?"

"Just that I'm having trouble with the phone company."

"That's absurd, Bill. It doesn't explain a thing. For everyone's sake, you have to get out of the city. Remember I told you about our place at Crystal Lake upstate, near Middleburgh? Roger says you can head up there and stay until this gets sorted out."

"I have to wait and see what this guy Rami can do. Has Roger talked with him?"

"Not since he referred you to him. And he doesn't know much about this Rami guy. He's doesn't even think that's his real name."

"Laurie, he's my only option. And I found a safe place to stay."

"Listen to me, Bill, they can get to you through your family . . . which puts all of us in danger. How do we deal with that?"

"No they can't. You guys have a different name from mine. I have to depend on this guy, Rami."

"This is off-the-charts weird, Bill. You should call the police," she says in a hushed voice.

Her near-whisper makes Bill wonder if maybe Roger is home, not at the office. Is she trying to advise him *sotto voce* because she doesn't want Roger to hear her?

"I can't do that," he says.

"Why not?"

"What can I tell the cops?"

"That this patient confessed to three murders," she says in a voice far louder than before.

No, Roger isn't home now.

"No, he didn't confess to a thing," Bill says. "He just said he knows something about them and he might've just been bragging to impress me."

"If *you* don't call the police, *I* will."

"No, *don't* do that. It'll just make things worse."

"*Worse*? How could they *possibly* be worse?"

"Laurie, it'd be a big mistake."

She sighs. "I can't have the kids exposed to this kind of thing. Or Mom . . . or Roger and me."

"I have to speak with Roger."

"About what?"

"I'll call him."

"Bill, just listen to me. I don't—"

"Laurie, I gotta go."

He presses the END CALL button.

*   *   *

After going through the receptionist and Roger's secretary, he gets his brother-in-law on the phone.

"Roger, what else do you know about this guy, Rami?"

"All I know is that he's connected to some people . . . probably in law enforcement."

"*Probably?*"

"Yes, but I don't know for sure."

"Which law enforcement people?"

"I don't know. And he has some other connections."

"What kind?"

"I don't really know and, besides, it doesn't matter. Just pick yourself up and get out of town."

Roger sounds cagey, evasive. What's he hiding? And who the fuck is Rami?

"Is he with Interpol?"

"I don't know."

"So, he's a skip tracer, but what else does he do?"

"I don't know, Bill. That's the God's honest truth."

Is anything true? Does everyone lie? What kind of web am I caught up in?

"Is he reliable?"

"Yes, he's good people."

"Whaddaya mean, *good people*?"

"C'mon, Bill, that's just an expression."

"How'd you meet him?"

"I don't remember. Listen, Bill, you need to disappear for a while. Laurie and I have a place—"

"I know, I know . . . at Crystal Lake. But I'm safe now."

A woman's voice comes through Roger's intercom. It's his secretary.

"Bill, I gotta go. I have an appointment," Roger says. "We'll talk in a day or two, okay? Just get out of the city—right now—it's your best move."

The line goes dead.

CHAPTER 27

One more beer and a few hours later, Bill is still at the bar, thinking about the exchanges with Laurie and Roger.

The cabin they own is more than a hundred miles away.

On face value, it sounds like it might be a good place to lie low.

It's near Middleburgh, in the middle of farm country, deep in the heart of the rust belt, somewhere between the Catskills and the Adirondacks.

Would the Albanians even think of looking for him there?

Maybe they would if they checked online for any second homes Roger and Laurie own. But that seems an unlikely thing for them to even think of doing.

But he'd be so isolated, especially at this time of year, when all the other summer homes around the lake are still shuttered.

God, he hopes Laurie doesn't follow through with her threat to call the police. And what's gonna happen when Mom and Laurie talk, as they inevitably will later today?

They're both strong-willed women.

It's likely they'll decide to take matters into their own hands and call the police or the FBI.

This thing is mushrooming way out of control.

Glancing at his watch, he sees it's nearly five thirty. It's still too light to head uptown.

A few more people have come into the place and are sitting at the bar. The barmaid's shot him a few sullen looks: she wants him to either order another beer or take a hike. So, he'll ask for another Bud and pretend to nurse it. He can't afford even a slight buzz.

Stay focused and stay sharp.

Remember that guy on the subway platform. If Bill hadn't been fully alert, he'd have ended up beneath the wheels of an onrushing train.

He knows he can't afford to let his guard down. And now, he's gotta wait until dark before venturing outside.

*   *   *

A few hours later, after leaving the pub, he walks into a Dick's Sporting Goods outlet on 14th Street.

He selects a lightweight blue silk jacket with the orange Mets logo, and a matching baseball cap.

After making the purchase, he asks the clerk to cut off the plastic tabs so he can wear both items outside.

The salesman obliges and gives him a bag in which to place the windbreaker he's been wearing. Bill walks over to a quiet corner of the store near the exit, where he strips off Greg's jacket, making sure no one can see the pistol stuffed into his waistband. He dons the Mets windbreaker and puts the cap on his head.

His reflection in a nearby mirror confirms he now looks considerably different from when he left the townhouse.

At 23rd Street, he hails a taxi and tells the driver to take him to 70th and Third.

Remembering the idling van parked outside the townhouse last night, when the taxi reaches 70th Street, Bill decides to walk the short distance back to the building. This way, he can look into every car parked along this quiet side street.

All are empty.

From a slight distance, he sees the only light coming from the townhouse is a soft glow from the front window of Elena's apartment. The rest of the building appears to be shrouded in an almost tomb-like grayness .

As he'd anticipated, there are only a few people walking along East 70th. Most are couples, strolling home from having had dinner at one of the many restaurants along Lexington or Third Avenue.

A few solo pedestrians pass by.

None of them arouse the slightest suspicion.

He approaches the townhouse. The climb to the front door is out in the open so he rushes up the stairway, unlocks the door, enters the house, and deactivates the alarm.

He was visible on the stairs for maybe ten seconds.

He resets the alarm, removes the pistol from his waistband, and slips it into the satchel; he hangs the Mets jacket in the hallway closet and sets Greg's jacket on another hanger.

Despite its size, the house feels like a crypt.

Can he tolerate another night alone and confined, feeling hunted and on edge?

How long will he have to wait to hear something from Rami?

And what will the guy say?

That he can get me to a place where I'll live a life in exile. Is that preferable to this?

That feeling of dread envelops him once again, bringing on a tightening in his chest. His heart throbs mercilessly and he realizes he's too cranked to read or watch television. His thoughts orbit around a simple fact: his entire life's headed down the drain.

He's gotta divert his mind, anything to get him off this carousel of fear and uncertainty.

Opening his wallet, he takes out Elena Lauria's card.

There's no danger in using Linda and Greg's landline.

Jesus, I have to think before I do something as simple as making a phone call.

He dials her number.

She picks up on the second ring.

"Elena, this is Bill Madrian."

"Oh, hi. How're you?"

"I'm fine. And you?"

"Everything's good. How's it working out at the house?" she asks.

"It's good. I was thinking about taking you up on that offer of a drink."

Surprisingly, his voice isn't quivering. He feels calmer just by being on the phone with her. Maybe the prospect of doing something normal makes him feel less antsy.

"Oh, that would be lovely. Where are you?"

"Upstairs. If it's convenient, I could drop by now."

"That's fine. Let me tell you how to get down here so you don't have to bother with the front door."

"Sure."

"In the kitchen, just behind the pantry area, you'll see a door. It's usually locked from your side. Just unlock it on your end and it opens to a stairway that leads down to my kitchen. Back in the old days, the cook used to live in what's now my apartment. I'll unlock the downstairs door on my side. But don't set the alarm for the upstairs house. If you do, when the door to my kitchen opens, the alarm will go off and the alarm company will send the police."

It's a lucky break. He'll deactivate the alarm but won't have to go out onto the street to get downstairs to her place.

CHAPTER 28

Smiling, she opens the door leading into her kitchen.

"Wow, you've grown the mandatory stubble. It looks good on you."

He manages to share her laugh.

After a few casual words, she shows him around the cozy garden apartment.

There's a book-lined living room with a gaslit fireplace surrounded by pink- and bluish-colored stones. The furnishings are traditional, comfortable-looking, homey. Colorful Kashan rugs cover the parquet floor. Knickknacks and framed photos—no doubt, of her family—give the place a personal touch. A few pothos plants sit in ceramic pots on a windowsill facing the street. An eat-in kitchen is located behind the living room. To the rear is a bedroom with a door leading outside to a small brick patio and a garden behind the house.

"What're you drinking?" she asks.

"Whatever you're having."

"Is a Chardonnay good?"

"Absolutely."

He settles into a tuxedo couch set perpendicular to the fireplace. It's the first time today he feels relaxed.

She returns from the kitchen with two glasses of white wine. Bill notices she moves with an athleticism he finds alluring. The way she moves and places her feet reminds him of a ballet dancer.

And she's even prettier than he remembered. As she hands him a glass of wine, he notices her eyes seem to change color—from hazel to a light shade of green—depending on the shimmering flames inside the fireplace. There's a floral scent to her, not a perfume or body wash; it's her skin, dewy in texture. And he now realizes her features are perfectly proportioned. It's strange, he didn't really notice how lovely looking she is when they first met.

Yes, when he saw her for the first time and she gave him the key, he was too amped to have appreciated the beauty now staring him in the face.

Jesus, was it only yesterday when they met? It seems like a week ago. It's strange how time is malleable, can collapse or expand, can get distorted into a fear-filled continuum.

Yes, stress and fear can warp anything.

She sits in the other tuxedo sofa facing him.

The wine feels soothing going down; the tension begins draining from his muscles and his thoughts coalesce in a coherent stream. It's a different feeling from while he was nursing beers at the Z-Rock bar.

"How long have you been living here?" he asks.

"About four months. It's such a cozy place and it's so near work—I have a short walk to the library on 79th Street. And Greg and Linda are good people."

"Yes, they are."

Good people. The same phrase Roger used about Rami.

She asks how he knows Greg and Laurie, and soon, they fall into conversation.

Despite the harrowing events of the last two days, he realizes he wants to learn about her.

She's originally from the Boston area, Charlestown. "We lived in a triple-decker on Concord Street, not far from Bunker Hill," she says. "My mother and father still live there. Dad runs a stone masonry company. He's still very involved with the business and works seven days a week. And my mother's a homemaker, but now that my brothers and I are out of the house, she works part-time at a local garden center." She describes her two brothers who are partners in a landscaping business.

She's always adored books and loves reading. "I ended up as an English major at Tufts, got a Bachelor's in American literature, then a Master's in library science."

Talking about her life, she's refreshingly open. At twenty-five, she met a man. "Six months later, we got married. But Eric was lousy at monogamy. We were divorced within a year," she says and shoots Bill a quick smile. "I never took his name. So here I am in New York City, beginning a new life."

"A new life . . ." he murmurs.

How do you find a new life?

Elena's offhand comment hits so close to home.

"What do you do for entertainment?" he asks, trying to shake off the dread her words reactivate.

"Oh, I see friends, go to movies, and sometimes we go to galleries and museums. I belong to a health club and take a mixed martial arts class. It keeps me in shape. It's good discipline, keeps me focused. I'm still finding my way around the city. How about you?"

He tells her about growing up in Queens, about college at the University of Michigan, followed by medical school at the State University in Albany, then psychiatry.

"So you listen to people's problems all day?"

"Yes," he says, thinking he's never encountered a patient with the kind of problem he's facing.

"What about your family?"

"My mother's a widow, lives in Manhattan. My father was French-Canadian and became an American citizen when he was twenty-nine. He was an accountant. He died of a heart attack when I was ten."

She nods while a subtle grimace appears on her face; she doesn't hand him the obligatory "I'm sorry for your loss."

He doesn't tell her how, when he was ten years old and at a cousin's wedding reception, his father's head suddenly dropped onto his plate while the guests were eating their entrées; how the table tilted and dishes and silverware clattered to the floor; how people gasped in horror; how an uncle frantically did CPR; how the EMS technicians arrived and used a defibrillator but couldn't revive him as his heart quivered uselessly in his chest until he died minutes later.

He says nothing about how his father's sudden death still feels like a splinter embedded in his soul; how in moments of shocking clarity, he believes we live with ticking time bombs buried within us, that disaster is always lurking in the wings, waiting to grab us and upend everything. That it can all go down the tubes in a flash, like what happened to his father or the fate that befell Olivia while she was at SoulCycle or the nightmare that began when Alex Bronzi asked a question that changed his life in an instant.

And he says nothing about how losing a loved one early in life can leave you with an empty space that feels like it can never be filled.

And he decides not to mention Olivia's death, at least not tonight.

Instead, he describes his private practice and how he enjoys seeing patients, "though sometimes it seems isolating, even a bit lonely."

"Lonely? You mean without hospital connections and colleagues you see every day?"

"Yes, it can feel that way, but I still have friends from the hospital, guys I've known for a long time. We enjoy grabbing a few drinks and the occasional dinner."

"Do you have family in the city?" she asks.

He mentions Mom, Laurie, Roger, and the kids; how he adores his nieces, and for a moment, thinks of his last visit to them—it seems like a hundred years ago when Roger referred him to Rami.

A twinge of apprehension overtakes him as he recalls the conversation with Laurie only a few hours earlier. This nightmare has to end soon. But how? How do you put an end to something when you don't even know where it's coming from or what's going to happen next?

But the worry subsides as she leans toward him.

"Is there anyone special in your life?"

He simply shakes his head.

Silence fills the room. Then, Elena says, "I know what happened to your fiancée. Linda told me about it and also told me quite a bit about you." The corners of her mouth turn down.

Nodding, he's thankful he won't have to talk about Olivia.

After a momentary pause, he says, "You think Linda and Greg wanted us to meet?"

"Of course," she says as a grin begins forming on her lips.

He nods again, then out of nowhere, hears himself say, "I have to get past it . . . I can't let it be who I am."

Her eyes look wet.

Or is it just the flickering lighting coming from the fireplace?

"Life's partly about getting beyond what's happened to us," she says. "And moving on, even though it can be tough to do."

"Yes, it is," he says, surprised at how calm he feels, realizing sadness hasn't overtaken him with the mention of Olivia's death.

A quiet interlude settles over them. The only sound in the room is the rhythmic ticking of a clock sitting on the mantel. It's a comfortable silence. It strikes Bill that they both seem content to be together.

"The past is always part of us," Elena says, breaking the stillness, "but we have to move on and get beyond it the best way we can."

"Yes, we do."

"Isn't that what you do as a therapist?" she asks. "Helping people get beyond what haunts them from years earlier?"

"Sometimes I think that's the essence of psychiatry," Bill says, "helping people move beyond what happened to them years ago."

She pauses, sets her wineglass on a small table.

"You're very much in touch with your feelings, Bill, aren't you?"

He nods. "I guess so, but sometimes, they can be overwhelming."

More silence, but sitting quietly with her is comforting. There's no need to fill the conversational vacuum with words.

Elena gets up and refills their wineglasses. "Do you think that right now we're on a date?" she asks, as she hands him a cocktail napkin.

Her candor surprises him. He's somewhat upended by her openness, but decides he likes this kind of frankness. "I guess so.

I mean, we said we'd get together for a drink. That's a date, right?"

"And . . . ?"

"And I'm glad I dropped by."

"I am, too."

They drink a bit more and continue talking.

And now it seems the wine's going to his head and his toes are tingling, then begin going numb. Her place is so cozy, has such a welcoming warmth, he knows he could stay here for hours and hours. Yes, he's decompressing and it feels so damned good. Soon, his eyelids feel heavy and he could fall asleep on the sofa in this book-lined living room with its flickering fireplace.

He could swear she's leaning closer to him. Those magical eyes are changing color, or he again wonders if it's the shimmering light coming from the fireplace. Her dark hair falls softly across her face as she inches toward him.

"Why don't you come by for dinner tomorrow?"

Her voice, as soft as it is, startles him back from his reverie.

Instantly, the ugliness of his nightmarish situation engulfs him.

"I don't know if . . ."

How can I ever explain . . . ?

"You don't know what?"

There's the back stairway down to her place. If I use that, I don't have to go outside and expose either of us to danger.

"I'd really like that."

CHAPTER 29

Nikolai Golovkin, strides into the conference room.

As he enters, the eight other pakhans stand in unison. It's a sign that this newly appointed pakhan in the Odessa mafia is regarded with the respect due him.

After Boris Levenko's murder, it's important that this replacement boss be extended every sign of acceptance. The nine men gathered are all brigade pakhans, and collectively wield global power stretching from New York through the Middle East to Moscow.

They cannot allow the Levenko assassination to do more damage than it's already done.

Men wired with transmitters and earbuds are stationed along Brighton Beach Avenue. Another two stand on the platform of the elevated train trestle running past the building. Two men armed with Para Micro Uzis are standing guard at the bottom of the stairway leading to the second-story conference room. Security has been doubled since Boris Levenko's assassination.

Golovkin is encouraged by the turnout. His call for a council meeting of commanders was heeded quickly with no reluctance by the other pakhans. They're all present: from Miami, Los

Angeles, Atlanta, San Francisco, Brussels, Moscow, London, and Tel Aviv.

And of course, he represents the Odessa brigade of Brooklyn, the most powerful of them all. There's a male muskiness to the room, now redolent of cigar smoke and aftershave lotion.

Golovkin makes his way to the head of an oval-shaped table.

"Ah, Nikolai Golovkin," says Anton Sakharov, commander of the Los Angeles brigade. "It's good to see you," he says in Russian, "but it's a shame we're meeting under such terrible circumstances."

"Sit, brothers, sit," Golovkin replies in English as he takes a seat in the chair nearest the window. "We have important things to discuss and, of course, we must speak English so we can all take part in the discussion."

As each man sits, the room falls quiet.

"The council mourns the loss of Brother Levenko," says Sergei Dubov, a thin, wiry-looking man and commander of the Miami contingent. "And . . . Nikolai, we're glad you're now a pakhan," Dubov adds. "No one is more qualified than a man whose great grandfather was Chief of Staff of the Russian Imperial Army."

Sheer flattery, thinks Golovkin. *Dubov's voice reeks of cynicism. He's the only man here I don't trust. His words about Boris Levenko are tripe. He had only bad things to say about the man when Boris was alive.*

"It doesn't matter who's in charge," Golovkin says. "It's crucial that we maintain cordial relations with each other, and with other organizations, be they Italian, Chechen, Albanian, Dominican, or any others."

Golovkin is heartened as words of agreement resound around the table.

"Boris Levenko grew complacent," Dubov says as his lips curl into a sneer. "He lost his taste for the *zhizn*, for the *life*, which requires, above all, vigilance. But from what I heard, Boris wanted only to feast on his blinis and slurp his borscht. And when weather permitted, he'd sit at his restaurant near the Brighton Beach boardwalk, which made him an open target for anyone passing by. No wonder he was shot down. I suspect he grew tired of the Brotherhood and what it demands of us."

Dubov glances about the table, looking for confirmation of his words. But no heads nod in agreement. And no one speaks.

The silence in the room seems to throb in Golovkin's ears. It's broken by the passing of the Q train rumbling by on elevated tracks not far from the window.

When the train has passed, Dubov continues in a raspy voice. "We must find out who killed Brother Boris and exact revenge."

"We've put out feelers," Golovkin says.

"And what have you learned so far?" Dubov asks.

"We have some people working on it, but so far, nothing definite has come up."

"Which people?"

"I can't say right now."

"Why not?" asks Dubov.

Just like Dubov to press for no other reason than to be obstreperous.

"Because we don't want to blow their cover," says Golovkin. "The less known for the time being, the easier their task will be."

"So you don't trust the people in this room," Dubov counters as his lips twist into a semi-smirk.

Dmitry Federov of the Atlanta brigade rolls his eyes and shakes his head. He has little patience for Dubov's contrarian tendencies.

Golovkin is aware the brigade commanders know Dubov has trouble accepting authority. They also know he craves being in the limelight—that he often argues for the sake of argument alone—and resents Nikolai Golovkin's position as titular head of all the brigades.

When Boris Levenko was Boss, Dubov always peppered him with sand trap questions, and now, it's Golovkin's turn to face the gauntlet of Dubov's probing. Boris had confided in Nikolai many times about Dubov, saying, "He's a thorn in my side. The man has ambition—he wants to be in charge of everything."

Nikolai Golovkin is certain Dubov is testing his patience. This meeting could end in discord with the specter of rivalry threatening to erupt between Dubov's Miami people and Golovkin's Brooklyn brigade. But this is no time for animosity since they face a common threat, most likely, the *Shqiptare*, although that has yet to be proven.

Avi Golan of the Israeli brigade narrows his eyes and his jaw looks like it's tightening. He's known to have a hair-trigger temper and could explode in a barrage of curses aimed at Dubov if the Miami pakhan keeps up his argumentative tone.

"I most certainly *do* trust our brothers," Golovkin says, "each and every one of you." He hopes his voice sounds reassuring. The last thing he needs is a cloud of suspicion hanging over this meeting. "We are all brothers," he goes on. "I trust you all, but you know the old proverb . . . 'A secret is like a dove. When it leaves your hand, it takes wing.'"

Chortles sound around the table. The others nod in agreement.

But not Dubov. He stares icily at Golovkin. "It certainly sounds like you don't trust us with *this* secret," he says, casting an eye around the room.

Once again, silence prevails. Golovkin notices some of the men peering down at the table. The stillness in the room is reassuring or it could be ominous because you never know what men like these are thinking, or even planning. But for the moment, Golovkin feels certain they're with him, not siding with Dubov.

"It's best left a secret and that includes each of us without exception, " says Avi Golan, the Israeli commander, with an edge creeping into his voice. Nikolai Golovkin knows this could be the prelude to an outburst. "And I trust Brother Golovkin completely," Golan adds.

Dubov's fist pounds the table. "We must act without delay," he shouts. "There's evidence the Albanians were the ones who put Boris Levenko in the ground."

"How do you know this?" Golovkin asks.

"I have my sources."

"Tell us who they are."

"I don't want to blow their cover," Dubov says as that smirk threatens to break out on his face. Then his lips twist into a smile, one that doesn't reach his eyes. "And besides," he adds, "as you said, 'A secret is like a dove. If it leaves my hand, it will take wing.' We should contact our people in Europe, have them send a few dozen men, and we can wipe out the Albanians, every one of them."

Golovkin's chest tightens. "We don't even know which *faction* of which clan was involved . . ." he says. "We don't even know for sure if it *was* the Albanians. My sources tell me it was Serbs who did the actual shooting. Of course, whoever set it up could have outsourced the killing to them, but we don't know that yet. And the last thing we need is an all-out war. With the Albanians or any other group." Golovkin knows a cold tone is infiltrating his voice.

"Maybe you don't have what it takes to be a *pakhan*," Dubov says as the smirk achieves full expression.

Dubov's voice and demeaner reek of contempt, thinks Golovkin. *Something may have to be done about him.*

"That's uncalled for," mutters Sakharov at the far end of the table.

Ushakov from Moscow looks coiled, as though he'll rocket up from his chair and slam a fist into Dubov's face.

Golovkin glances at Ushakov; his eyes tell the Russian to remain calm even as Golovkin's stomach clenches at Dubov's insult. He can't let this sit-down blow up into a pissing match. Or worse: violence. And one thing is certain: War makes little sense whether it's between ethnic mobs or Bratva brigades. And he long ago learned to stay cool even when he feels he's running hot. A show of temper will only guarantee more animosity with Dubov. He recalls the last war between two Brotherhood brigades. The streets of Brooklyn and Miami were littered with bodies.

Trying for a soothing tone, Golovkin says, "We won't make a move until we're one hundred percent certain who was behind Brother Levenko's demise."

Avi Golan says, "War is bad for business. The only result is blood and no one profits from it."

Dubov's face curdles into a scowl. "You must know more about who was responsible for Brother Levenko's murder by now, and you choose not to tell us," he says, staring at Golovkin.

"Our contacts will know very soon."

"I ask you, Nikolai, who do you have working on it?"

"And I'll tell you once again . . . I can't say at this time."

Such hubris from Dubov. It's intolerable.

"Have you contacted our KGB friends?" asks Dubov.

"We don't have KGB on the payroll," Golovkin replies. "They're *ex*-KGB. You know full well we never work with governments or any agency of a government. Not now and not ever. We have contacts with former KGB operatives, ex-MI6 spies, ex-Mossad agents, and retired German BND personnel. We don't even *try* to recruit active government personnel."

"Yes, I know and apologize for that mistake," says Dubov, sounding less antagonistic.

"We have some of the best people working on this," Golovkin says. "It's only a matter of time before we learn who's responsible for Brother Levenko's death. That's all I can say right now."

Golovkin pauses and again, silence prevails.

"Now . . ." Golovkin says, "let's get down to the business of investigating this thing they call cryptocurrency."

CHAPTER 30

It's nine o'clock on another beautiful spring morning in early May, but Kosta Bronzi isn't sitting on his patio gazing at the waters of Long Island Sound.

And he's not smoking. He decided last night to quit that vile habit. For good. He owes it to Edonia and his children to live a long and healthy life.

He's sitting in the back seat of his Denali SUV. His driver, Skender, cruises along the Hutchinson River Parkway, then exits at the Bronx River Parkway and heads toward the Belmont section of the Bronx. Kosta has an important meeting to attend because he knows certain things must be taken care of. Expeditiously.

This headshrinker, William Madrian, must die before the problem spirals out of control. The longer he lives, the greater the danger he'll talk to someone. For all Kosta knows, the man is speaking to an FBI agent at this very moment. Or to some other person—a lawyer, the Brooklyn D.A., someone in authority, maybe a New York City detective at Central Command—and if that happens, the word will spread like an out-of-control wildfire.

And if the Bratva gets wind of who's behind the Levenko hit—even if it's nothing more than a rumor—they'll dig deeper and find out more. And then they'll look for revenge. And as certain as the sun rises in the east, they'll come after Kosta's faction.

Or even worse, they might start a war against the entire *Shqiptare*. The Odessa brigade is bad news because it's powerful. Their new Boss, Nikolai Golovkin, is a calm and decisive man, not one to be fooled with. And there's no doubt he'd call on the other Bratva brigades both in the U.S. and Europe, and for sure, blood will spill in both camps, the Odessa mafia and the Malotta clan. And everything will go to the dogs.

So Madrian must go. And it must happen quickly, before he has a chance to open his mouth. Too much time has elapsed as it is. It barely matters that he's a civilian. He's a danger to everything Kosta has worked for over the years, and certain things must be done no matter which lines are crossed. Survival dictates it. And Kosta has survived by being ruthless.

The brutality of life was pressed into Kosta's being by the time he was fifteen years old. Not only by the gruesome deaths of his parents and his torture at the hands of the Memia clan, but by everything that happened since he came to America.

At seventeen, living in the Bronx with his extended family, he was a junior member of the Malotta clan. One day, his older cousin Jakov Bronzi, a powerful underboss who owned the restaurant Kamez on Arthur Avenue, gave Kosta and two other young men an assignment.

Jakov said, "That new Albanian restaurant, Sophia's . . . the owner stole our chef, Enver, asked him to leave Kamez and work at his place." Jakov paused, looked straight into Kosta's eyes, and said, "You will go into that restaurant and slash faces—all the customers and waiters. Their scars will remind them of the price of disloyalty. Then you will tell Enver to return to work for me."

"But why not just burn the place down one night . . . why hurt innocent people?"

"Because we must send a message that no one can challenge the Bronzi faction," Jakov replied. "If you don't have the guts to do what's necessary, you can leave the clan right now."

Though it made Kosta sick to his stomach, he and three other men entered the restaurant and slashed faces, overturned tables, threw the patrons out, and set the place on fire. They then ordered Enver to return to Kamez. Any remnant of doubt Kosta had about the harshness of life ended that night.

He knows that his early life caused something inside him to wither; then it died. He sometimes wonders if he has any humanity left in him. But in the deepest part of his being, he knows he still is able to love, and can feel compassion. When he doubts it, he consoles himself by thinking of his lovely wife, Edonia, their son, Alex, and their daughter, Adriana, a medical student at Cornell. Only when he's challenged or crossed does he become like the Balkan gray wolf that roams the northern Albanian Alps. Even the wolf, as deadly as it is, kills to survive.

Pressing the button on the armrest, he lowers the glass panel separating him from the driver.

"Skender, after you drop me off, double park and walk to that bakery, Egidios's. Pick up a *trilece*, that three-milk cake my wife loves. Then wait for me in the car. I'll be back in a half hour."

"Yes, Boss. But, if I double park, I'll get a ticket."

"The cops know my car. Just double park in front of Kosova Deli and we'll be fine."

*   *   *

Once they're on Arthur Avenue, Kosta gets out of the Denali in front of Kosova Deli with its red awning showing the black, double-headed eagle. It's the enduring symbol of Albania and goes back to when the Albanians defeated the Turks in the Middle Ages. Ethnic pride should never be forgotten. *You must always be aware of your origins.*

Skender leaves the Denali double parked and walks toward the bakery.

Entering Kosova Deli, Kosta is greeted by the owners, Urtan Jashari and his wife, Lendina, to whom he leases the store for a tenth of the fair market price. He feels great sympathy for the couple. They're hard working Albanian immigrants whose son was murdered in a drive-by shooting two years ago. It was a senseless killing of a bright young man who had nothing to do with the *Shqiptare.* Urtan's and Lendina's lives now orbit around their store; and their plight tugs at Kosta's heart.

Their sad situation reminds him of his own losses so early in life. He sometimes wishes Alex were the kind of boy Urtan and Lendina's son had been: smart, studious, and serious-minded. Such a shame their son died in the turf wars because of mistaken identity.

Kosta is reminded that despite the horror of his early years, there's still a soft patch in his otherwise hardened heart. So, no matter what happens, he'll never raise Urtan's and Lendina's rent. The couple is so grateful, they virtually bow and scrape each time he walks into the place.

He acknowledges their greeting, and peers into the glass case behind which prepared food is displayed.

"Will you have tea and *shendetlie* this morning, Mr. Bronzi?" Lendina asks.

"Not this morning," Kosta replies. "I'll only be here for a short time." He then walks to the rear of the store, opens a door, and climbs a flight of stairs to the second floor. Opening a thick wooden door that is already unlocked, he's in a small anteroom. Another sturdily reinforced door leads to the conference room.

The room upstairs from the deli is a perfect front for conducting business. Kosova Delicatessen is an ordinary Mom and Pop store selling Albanian sausages, meatballs, vegetable preparations, and homemade baked goods. No one would ever suspect Mr. and Mrs. Jashari's store is the entranceway to the Bronx office of Kosta's faction of the Malotta clan.

Each week, Kosta has the upstairs swept for surveillance bugs. When telephone calls are necessary, they're made with encrypted satellite phones. No ordinary phones are allowed upstairs, not even burners. That's an ironclad rule Kosta has enforced ruthlessly. And only a few select people are allowed to use the back stairway.

The setup is nothing like the social clubs the Italians have, and Kosta avoids sit-downs in restaurants or nightclubs, lest Boris Levenko's fate befall him. In fact, Kosta's a homebody—he dines at home every night in the company of his wife, and never frequents social clubs or restaurants.

Opening the second door, he enters a room that looks out over Arthur Avenue. This is where he meets with people like Besim and a few other trusted henchmen, to take care of matters involving the Bronx and other areas of operation.

Closing the door, he greets Besim and another man seated at the table.

They both jump to their feet when he enters.

"Sit, sit," he says, waving at them with the back of his hand.

They all take seats at the table.

"So, Besim, who is this competent-looking fellow sitting across from me?" He glances at the man sitting next to his underboss.

"This is Bruno Rudaj, the most skilled tactician we know," Besim says. "He's at our service."

Kosta turns to Bruno, a thin man with closely set eyes, dark, slicked-back hair, a thin face, and a Van Dyke beard. His look reminds Kosta of the nose-horned vipers—deadly, venomous bastards—he used to see in the woods near Durres. As is this man reputed to be: a fellow with a penchant for killing remorselessly.

Kosta extends his arm and they shake hands. "Let's speak in our mother tongue, Besim," Kosta says. It's another precaution he takes, even though Kosta is certain the room isn't bugged. Albanian is spoken almost exclusively since the NYPD and the Feds have very few Albanian-speaking personnel. "Tell me what happened with the headshrinker."

"He can be elusive," Besim says in Albanian. "Our people tracked him from the corner of East 68th Street and Lexington Avenue to a restaurant on Second Avenue in the Twenties. When our men finally got there, he was gone. They rushed back on the street and searched everywhere, but there was no sign of him."

"You said he was seen at Lexington and East 68th Street?"

"Yes. We think he's staying nearby, probably somewhere in the Seventies. He's been spotted a few times, but we haven't seen him enter or leave any house . . . yet. The people looking for him have explicit instructions to call me the moment he's seen."

"Good. Don't let up. He must be found quickly. And put a few more people on it."

"It'll be done," says Besim. "And when we're sure of his location, Bruno will take care of him."

"Bruno," Kosta says, turning to the assassin, "they say you're an excellent tactician."

"I do what I do," Bruno replies in perfect English. There's not a trace of an accent.

"Where did you learn to speak English so well?" Kosta replies in English.

"I took lessons to lose my accent so no one would know I'm from Albania. And I can mimic other accents."

"Tell me, Bruno, do you know why we're after this man?" Kosta says, reverting to Albanian.

"It's none of my business," Bruno replies, also in Albanian.

"Very true," Kosta says, nodding his head. "Perhaps, if you do this job neatly, we can use your services in the future."

"It would be my pleasure."

"Where are you from in Albania?"

"Originally, Tirana."

"Ah, only thirty kilometers from Durres, where I came from."

"Yes, they're near each other."

"Things are better there now, yes?"

"But not as good as they are here."

"Very true." Kosta nods, then says, "I'm glad to have met you. I must stress this situation is very important to us."

"I understand completely."

"When we locate this man, you'll hear from Besim, and then you'll take care of it."

Bruno nods. "It will get done."

Peering at the assassin, Kosta likes what he sees: a hard-looking man and one of few words. Yes, they could give him a great deal of work in the future.

"And now, Bruno, I must ask you to leave because Besim and I have other things to discuss."

*   *   *

When Bruno Rudaj leaves the room, Kosta waits until he hears both doors close.

Regarding Besim, Kosta then says in a soft voice, "Can this Bruno be trusted?"

"Yes, I believe so."

"Then it won't be necessary to take care of him once it's done. Correct?"

"Yes, that's correct. He just does what he's paid to do. As you can see, he asks no questions. He's quite skilled and we may be able to use him for other assignments."

"Good, but make sure he knows nothing about why we want this headshrinker."

"Absolutely."

Kosta pauses. "Now tell me, why haven't we found him?"

"Our IT man is out sick, and we haven't been able to access Madrian's phone records yet."

"Let's use our skip tracer, the one located on Wall Street? That fellow McMillan."

"He's out of town on a job for the Alameti clan. He'll be away for another week. But no matter who we use, it'll be hard to trace this Madrian fellow by the usual methods. If we don't get lucky

and find him on the street, we'll have to see if he leaves an electronic trail . . . if he uses a credit card or an unencrypted cell
phone. Or if he goes back to his apartment or office."

"I see."

"But based on what we've seen so far," Besim continues, "he's
unlikely to do any of those things. We already know he made a
large withdrawal from his Chase account. It appears he's travel-
ing beneath the radar for the time being. For all we know he's
contacted his own evasion expert. If he's done that, we may end
up following false leads because a good expert can create a phan-
tom trail which will lead us on a wild goose chase, as the
Americans say."

Kosta Bronzi sighs. "Yes, I know . . . and since McMillan is
unavailable, I want you to find another skip tracer. And make sure
it's someone who's never been used by any other organization, if
you know what I mean."

"I'll put out feelers, Kosta."

"And, Besim, whichever skip tracer you find, don't say a word
about why we want Madrian tracked."

"Of course not."

"We don't have much time. I've been contacted by one of the
highest-ranking members of the Malotta clan. They're proposing
that the heads of all factions meet to discuss the Brighton Beach
matter and what we can do about it. After all, we want to stay out
of trouble with the Odessa mafia. We can't have this problem lin-
ger because if it becomes known who was behind the Levenko
thing, *we'll* become targets of our own people.

"The clans don't want to go to war with the Russians and
Ukrainians," Kosta continues. "The Odessa mafia has too many
soldiers. And besides, right now, we're moving into the distillery

end of things, and it looks like we're only filling a vacuum left by Levenko's departure."

"I understand. I'll take all necessary precautions."

"As for this headshrinker, we must locate him quickly before he goes to the police."

"If he does, it would only be an accusation by a man who couldn't pin a thing on us."

"True, but it would bring *attention* to us," Kosta says. "We can't afford even a *hint* of suspicion about Levenko. So, Madrian has to disappear. Soon."

"It will be done."

CHAPTER 31

Stirring, Bill looks up at the ceiling in a gossamer moment of semi-consciousness, then rolls onto his side.

At first, there's no coherence to his thinking, but a moment later, he's alert and realizes he's covered in sweat; yet, shivering.

How crazy is this? Shivering and sweating at the same time?

His body is reacting as bizarrely as his life has become.

A clock ticks on the side table near the bed. It's discordant, disorienting, and he wonders for a moment if he's fully awake. Then in a spasm of panic, the nightmarish reality of his life floods him: the Albanians want him dead.

He's wide awake, and his heart is pounding a sickening drumbeat as he tries to calm himself. *My God, how long will this go on? It feels like I've been hiding forever.*

Sitting up, he swings his feet to the floor. Bleary-eyed and glancing at his wristwatch, he notices his hand shaking.

Gotta settle down and let this feeling pass.

It's nearly ten thirty. He hasn't slept this late in years. But it makes sense: he's exhausted because of what he's been through in the last two days. It's a feeling of depletion.

First things first: he'll shower, get rid of this film of sweat covering his body.

Never before has a morning shower felt so refreshing, so calming. Once out of the stall, he looks into the mirror and sees a bristly growth of beard and dark circles crouched beneath his eyes. He tells himself that despite the insanity of what's happening, things will somehow work out. But a slithering sense of unease snakes its way back into his awareness. He can't will himself to be optimistic. But at least that inner trembling has subsided.

When he's dried off and dressed, he heads for the kitchen.

Elena let him borrow a Melitta coffee maker, a few filters, and a can of Folgers. She also gave him four English muffins.

The time spent with her was a lovely respite from the horror his life has become. But right now, he can't think of anything beyond the next few hours.

Cleaning the dishes, he decides to call the office for voicemail messages, but won't use the house landline. The Albanians are probably monitoring his office telephone. Maybe they have a way of tracing a caller's number, getting the address from a reverse directory, and then . . . showing up here. Not only would that threaten his life, but it could put Linda and Greg in danger. A shiver crawls up his spine at the thought.

Using the burner, he calls the office and retrieves three more hang-ups. They're still checking the office telephone.

He wonders how long it will be before Laurie, Roger, and the kids are targets. Or Mom.

There's one no-brainer in this situation: if they become the price he must pay, he'd give himself up in a heartbeat.

He can't remember the last time he hung around doing nothing on a weekday morning. Even on holidays, he had things to do: go for a three-mile jog, make or return phone calls, or run errands.

Or call a friend and arrange to meet for dinner. Before this, his days had structure and a comfortable predictability.

But now, he has no idea of what awaits him. He's not even certain how he'll spend the next minute, much less the hours until this evening.

Being sequestered in this empty house and waiting—for what?—has his nerves on edge.

Will he hear from Rami today?

Will today be the day his hiding place is discovered?

And if it is, what can he do?

He forces himself to think about his patients. How strange they must find his recent behavior: suddenly taking time away from the office and their sessions. If this isn't over in a week, two at most, he'll have no practice left.

But he reminds himself that's the least of his worries.

*   *   *

Just sitting around and waiting for something to happen makes Bill feel even more on edge, so at one p.m., he decides to go online and see what he can learn about the Albanian mafia.

Knowledge is power, and as trite as it may sound, it's probably true.

Sitting in front of Greg's computer, he enters the password.

He types "Albanian mafia" in Google's URL box.

With his heart thudding, he reads about the Albanian mob's structure and its international reach. There are dozens of links to articles about them with titles like "The Piranhas from Tirana" to "Kings of Cocaine: How the Albanian Mafia Seized Control of the Drug Trade." And there's one called, "The Brutal Rise of the Albanian Mafia and the Secret *Besa* Code They Live By."

Besa . . . the code Alex Bronzi violated in that session.

Hey, Doc, ya wanna know who clipped Boris Levenko?

The question that changed my life.

Bill clicks on one hyperlink after another and learns they traffic in drugs, weapons, and human beings, especially migrants from Africa and Eastern Europe. Sex trafficking's a big source of income. They enslave young girls, shipping them to brothels all over the United States, Europe, and the Middle East. They even sell human organs: mostly livers and kidneys, which they take from their sex slaves once they've grown older, and can no longer be marketed sexually. After extracting their organs for sale, they kill the women and dispose of their bodies in crematoria or landfills.

Yes, there's that term Rami used: *Shqiptare*, signifying the Albanian mob. Their families—known as clans—can have hundreds of members in various countries—with tentacles spreading along the Balkan route from Turkey to Western Europe and North America. Sometimes, bloody turf wars erupt between clans. There can even be conflicts between different factions of a single clan.

Bill's heartbeat ramps up as he reads about clan activity in the New York metropolitan area.

An article says, *By the 1990s, they were battling the Lucchese and Gambino families for territory in Queens, the Bronx, and Westchester County. They managed to overtake the Italians. The only mafia organization that outguns them is the Russian Brotherhood, also a worldwide operation.*

He's heard of the Russian mafia, but not the Albanian mob. Why not?

Has he been living with his head up his ass?

But then again, why would he know a damned thing about Albanian gangsters? They've never been romanticized in movies like *The Godfather* or *Goodfellas* or *Casino*. Or on television with programs like *The Sopranos*. And there's never been an Albanian mafia boss to compare with the likes of John Gotti or the mythic Al Capone. The Albanians have managed to stay under the radar.

But they're now at the forefront of Bill's life.

Maybe Laurie was right: he should take off, go upstate. It wouldn't be smart to go to their cabin at Crystal Lake; maybe it would be better to find a small town in the Adirondacks, a spit of a place where he could hole up for a few weeks without being noticed.

But how would he get there? He can't rent a car since he'd have to use a credit card and show a driver's license, and that's a surefire way to create a digital trail. He could take a train upstate, but he knows you have to show ID to get on Amtrack.

Could he take a bus?

Maybe, but he doesn't know if Greyhound requires passengers to show ID; and anyway, it would be foolish to go to the Port Authority Terminal, a place likely being surveilled by the Albanians.

He thinks about friends he knows who live in the city.

None of them own a car, so borrowing one isn't an option.

There's gotta be a way to feel less endangered, but how do you downsize fear?

A vortex of helplessness fills him as he thinks about his lack of options.

It all came about because of a random phone call from Alex Bronzi.

A random event—like what happened last year when a twenty-two-year-old woman stepped off the curb at Third Avenue and 79th Street as a taxicab hurtled around the corner and she was killed instantly. Had she stopped for a moment to look in a boutique window, it never would have happened.

Or like what happened on 9/11.

Bill had a patient who's still alive because on the morning of the terrorist attack, he stopped at a Starbucks before heading to his office on the eighty-ninth floor of the south tower.

Random occurrences were the difference between life and death for them.

Starting with Alex Bronzi's going online and randomly picking out Bill's name and number when that kid wanted to see a psychiatrist; that's how this horror show began. And it's funneled down to this lousy predicament in which Bill now finds himself trapped.

All random.

How and when will this end?

CHAPTER 32

Twenty minutes later, his burner lets out a shrill tone.

It's his mother. She's not using the burner; she's using her own cell phone.

"Mom, why're you calling me from your cell? I told you to use the one I sent. What's—"

"William dear, I don't want to talk about some stupid phone. I'm standing here in your lobby with the doorman and Mr. Gomez, the super. You never called me after we missed our lunch appointment, and I tried you this morning at the office and the apartment. The office voicemail says you're away and someone is covering your practice. And I get nothing but a busy signal on your home phone. What on earth is happening?"

"Mom, I—"

"Your super knows nothing about a leak in your apartment, and the doorman said you're away. What's going on?"

His thoughts whirl in a cauldron of confusion, but nothing comes to him. "Listen, Mom, I can't tell you because . . . I'm . . . I'm in trouble . . ."

Jesus, that just slipped out.

"Trouble? What kind of trouble?"

"I . . . I can't say."

"You can't *say*? This is absurd. What's going on?"

"I can't give you any details. That could put you in danger . . . Laurie, Roger, and the kids, too."

"*What*? *Danger*? What kind of danger?" Her voice, now shrill, sounds disbelieving.

"Mom, I'll explain in a few days."

"Where *are* you?"

"I can't tell you."

"This is insane, William. I'm calling the police."

"*Don't* do that, Mom. I have to get off now. If we stay on the phone any longer, it could be dangerous."

"William, I—"

"Sorry, Mom."

He presses END CALL.

This is a disaster. It's all falling apart. Mom, Laurie, Roger, and the kids will soon be targets.

And he'll have to come out of hiding.

CHAPTER 33

He decides to call Laurie's burner.

"Laurie, I just got a call from Mom," he says. "She sounds hysterical. I'm sure she's headed your way. She went to my building and made a scene in the lobby. She wants to know what's going on and I can't tell her. I just hope she's not being followed."

"She just called me and she *is* coming over here," Laurie replies. "I think there's no choice but to go to the police. Or the FBI."

"Listen, Laurie. I just spoke with Rami. He'll have something by tomorrow," he lies, aware it's a wish, not a fact.

"What's going to happen tomorrow?"

"I don't know. Let's just hope for the best."

"Something better happen soon, Bill. If not, we're going to the police."

*   *   *

Roger is home early from the office.

Laurie's been doing her best to calm her mother down. Mom's face is pale and her hands are shaking. "I had to come right over," she says. "I'm so upset."

She recounts for Roger the revelations gleaned while talking with the superintendent of Bill's building. With every detail, her voice grows reedier, tears begin cascading down her cheeks, and she gulps for air, growing more short of breath with each utterance.

"Try to relax, Mom," Laurie says, trying to placate her mother.

This is spinning out of control. We have to do something, Laurie thinks.

"When I got William on the phone, he said he's in some kind of trouble," her mother continues. "And what's going on with these phones?" With her lips trembling, she looks from Laurie to Roger.

Laurie glances at each of them. "Mom," she says, trying to sound calm, "did Bill say anything else?"

"Yes. He said if he told me anything more, it could put all of us in danger . . . including the children," she adds with her voice quivering.

"Mom, *please* try to calm down," Laurie says, while getting up to sit beside her on the sofa.

"Calm down? Calm *down*? How can I when my son says he's in trouble and we could be, too?"

"Mom," Roger interjects, "Bill was over here and told me about some trouble he had with a patient."

He casts a look at Laurie, who gives him a subtle nod.

"What kind of trouble?"

"Apparently this patient said something to Bill that could have serious legal implications. For the patient and possibly for Bill . . ."

Her hand goes over her mouth. "For *Bill*? What did he say?"

"Mom," Laurie says, "it's not clear, but . . ."

"But what?"

A moment of silence.

"Laurie, I know you and Bill talk all the time, and I also know you think you're doing me a favor by keeping me in the dark . . . but you're not. I have every right to know what's happening to my son, and to all of us."

The trembling in her voice is replaced by a defiant and angry tone.

Laurie knows Mom hates when her children treat her like a child, trying to shield her from something they think will be too upsetting for her to hear.

"For God's sake, tell me everything you know," her mother says.

Laurie sighs. Saying anything about the Albanians will only make Mom more hysterical and she'll run to the police. And that could complicate an already terrible situation.

"We don't really know if it's true," Laurie begins, "but this patient may have some sort of mob connection. Bill thinks some people might be worried he'll talk to the police."

"My God! This is *unbelievable*."

"Roger sent Bill to someone who may be able to help."

"Who?"

"Mom, Bill went to see a man named Rami. Roger has worked with him in the past to untangle messes like this one."

"Really? Like the stew Bill now finds himself in? I find that hard to believe."

Mom's voice seethes with hurt mixed with fear.

"Please, Mom, listen to me. Rami knows what he's doing," Laurie says even though she's in the dark about this mysterious man. "We have to follow his instructions."

"What instructions?"

"He said to keep quiet, to say nothing . . . that he's working on a solution." Laurie pauses, then says, "Now, tell me . . . how did you get here, and where did you come from?"

"Your brother's building, by taxi."

Mom's aggrieved tone is replaced by one of resignation.

Laurie goes to the window overlooking West End Avenue. She sees a man standing on the sidewalk across the street. He looks to be in his thirties, is unshaven, and wears a dark sports jacket and jeans. Standing casually at the curb, he looks like he's loitering.

Laurie turns from the window. "Mom, was anyone behind you?"

"Was anyone *behind* me? How should I know? There are people on the street everywhere."

Laurie returns to the window, looks down to the street.

The man is still there.

Is he waiting for someone or is he watching for Mom?

With her thoughts spinning, she goes to the intercom and presses the button.

"Yes?" says the doorman.

"Walter, after my mother came in, did anyone show up and ask about her?"

"No."

"Well, if anyone does come into the building and asks for any of us, just say we're not home."

"Sure enough, Mrs. Price."

Laurie turns to her mother and Roger. "Mom, you'll have dinner here, and stay over tonight."

"I'd love to have dinner, but why sleep here?"

"It's just a precaution, because I'm worried you may've been followed from Bill's building."

CHAPTER 34

As the day drags on toward early evening, Bill has finally stopped pacing.

What can he do about his mother? She'll only grow more agitated as time go by. He has to depend on Laurie and Roger to calm her.

If she or Laurie goes to the police, it will only pour gasoline on an already blazing fire. Maybe he *should* get the hell out of town. Just slip under the radar and live underground—somewhere—for as long as possible. At least until he hears from Rami.

Trying to burn off tension, he goes upstairs to the gym, lifts a few weights, heads back down to the den, and turns on the television. Daytime television's always sucked with its soap operas, talk shows, and judge fiascos. He turns off the TV, takes a few books down from their shelves, thumbs through them, knowing there's no way he'll be able to concentrate.

He's never appreciated how even the most ordinary day has a million little variations compared to the stultifying sameness of being confined to this house.

Trying to occupy his mind, he goes to Greg's computer and plays game after game of solitaire. He draws one shitty hand after another, and following eight or nine losses, he gives up and again turns on the television. But there's nothing that holds his interest or gets his mind away from Alex Bronzi and the Albanians.

Despite knowing what to expect, he telephones the office. The answering machine has recorded two more hang-ups.

*　*　*

Feeling calmer by six p.m., he makes certain the front door is locked and deactivates the house alarm.

Using the pantry stairway, he heads down to Elena's apartment. The thought of the evening ahead seems to have taken his mind off the shitshow his life has become.

In her kitchen, Elena greets him with a glass of sauvignon blanc. "I stopped by D'Agostino's on the way home," she says. "I hope you're a fan of veal piccata."

"I love it. But you don't have to make a fuss."

"Don't be silly," she says, sipping her wine. "My mother's recipe's the best in the world. And it's easy to make."

He feels even more relaxed now; the tension in his shoulders subsides.

He notices the finesse with which Elena uses kitchen utensils, how her fingers move deftly, as she prepares their dinner. And he's completely comfortable standing with her in this kitchen, making small talk while watching her cook.

He suddenly realizes that for the last two years, he's eaten at restaurants virtually every night, mostly alone. He occasionally stops by a Sichuan place on Third Avenue and brings takeout back to the apartment—chicken with garlic sauce or General Tso's chicken—and with his own plastic chopsticks, shovels it into his mouth right out of the white cartons. Why bother cleaning dishes? The only times he's had home-cooked meals have been when he visits Laurie or Mom.

It strikes him as he's standing in the kitchen near Elena, that when he's with this woman, he's not feeling that inner tension, nor are his thoughts preoccupied with Albanians and being on the run. The sauvignon blanc tastes crisp and herbaceous and is working it's magic, creating a pleasant buzz in his head.

Although true familiarity takes time to develop, it feels as though he and Elena have known each other for a long time. There's a sense of domesticity bordering on intimacy just being in her company. He feels the beginnings of a connection, something he's missed for a long time.

The aroma of the food grows more enticing with each step of the meal's preparation.

While she plates the veal, he carries the salad bowl to the table.

At first, their dinner conversation focuses on work. She's been offered a position heading up the comparative literature collection at Columbia University's library. "I'm pretty sure I'll accept it," she says. "If I do, I'll move uptown to be closer to work."

He finds himself regretting the possibility of her moving from this cozy apartment.

Am I crazy? We've only just met. It's absurd to think of anything beyond tonight.

Maybe he feels this way because of the disastrous turn his life has taken. It's as though he's sighted land while thrashing around in an ocean of danger. These feelings of closeness can't be trusted, not while he's running for his life.

After dinner, back in the living room, she asks, "And what about *your* work?"

He describes how it's difficult to be a solo practitioner in today's medical environment. "Between the insurance companies, Medicare, and Medicaid you spend tons of time on paperwork. It's almost impossible to have a practice without secretarial help. And most physicians today, including psychiatrists, are part of a large group practice."

The conversation feels natural, unforced, and he's not faking his way through it the way he's felt with other women since Olivia's death.

Of course, there's no mention of the Albanians, and surprisingly, he's had only a few fleeting thoughts about them since coming down to her apartment.

"Is there anyone special in your life?" he asks.

"Just a few dates here and there . . . you know, something arranged by a friend or someone Greg and Linda know. But there's no one special . . ."

Her eyes meet his, and a subtle smile forms at the edges of her lips.

"Yes, setups can be tricky," she says.

"You mean the way Greg and Linda set us up?" he jokes. "By causing the flood in my apartment?"

They both laugh.

"Ah yes, that leak," he says. "It's brought us to this moment."

"I'm glad for the leak," she says, raising her glass.

"To the *leak*," he adds, lifting his glass.

The laughter feels good. There's something natural, even intimate, in their joking together after having shared a home-cooked meal.

Before long, the bottle of sauvignon blanc is empty.

"How about a digestif?" Elena asks.

From a tall, clear bottle, she pours a small amount of a spirit into two cordial glasses.

"This is delicious," he says. "What is it?"

"It's Macchu Pisco," Elena explains. "It's Peruvian cognac. Can you taste the vanilla, lime, and lemongrass?"

"Yes. It's different from anything I've ever had."

Siting on the sofa, she slides her lower legs beneath herself, sits facing him, and he's again aware of how supple, how athletic her movements are.

They talk about so many things. She describes what it's like working in a public library, then again about the prospect of her new job at Columbia. It all seems so natural, so comfortable, as though they've known each other for a long time.

She mentions two good friends. "We meet twice a week," she says, "at a martial arts class. Then we'll have dinner at a restaurant or go somewhere for a drink. We go to the movies and sometimes we'll go to the MoMA or visit some of the galleries on Madison Avenue."

He hasn't had this kind of easy conversation with a woman in two years. In fact, he's faked his way through most social encounters. But he isn't faking now. There's an openness to Elena, a willingness to share, and he's genuinely interested in what she says.

Even though they met only a short while ago, he finds himself thinking the crazy thought that maybe there's a future with this woman.

Am I crazy to think this way?

But he feels so comfortable with her, and she's undeniably attractive.

And wasn't that the kind of instant attraction that drew him to Olivia?

Bill realizes the thought of his fiancée makes him feel neither sad nor disloyal.

Is this what moving on feels like?

He's not at all certain how it's happening, but it's as if Elena has opened a door, which is freeing him from the shroud of emptiness that has enveloped him for so long.

And for that moment, while looking at this beautiful woman and feeling very much at peace, he's forgotten the cruel reality that his own future is uncertain.

*   *   *

He and Elena have moved closer to each other and he's aware of the fragrance of her hair. Her scent is arousing, and in a moment of stunning awareness he realizes if not for Alex Bronzi, Elena and he wouldn't be sitting together in this comfortable apartment.

Then, as though he's dreaming, he hears her whisper, "I'm so glad you needed the key for the upstairs house."

And the words slip past his lips: "I am, too. Very glad."

"I really like being with you," she says, drawing closer.

"I haven't enjoyed being with anyone this way for a long time . . ."

"A moment ago we sort of laughed about that leak in your apartment . . ."

"Yes . . . ?"

"Do you sometimes wonder about how random things can be?" she asks. A smile plays at the corners of her lips. "Or have our destinies been preordained?"

"I think, in retrospect, almost everything can seem preordained. But how can we know?"

"I mean, that leak in your apartment began a chain of events. You called Greg and Linda, but they happened to be in Aruba, so they told you to ring my bell because I have the key . . . and now, here we are. If one little thing, that leak, hadn't happened, we wouldn't be where we are now."

"Ah, the butterfly effect."

"Yes," she replies. "A small thing can set off a series of events that changes everything."

But there was no leak, and Elena's belief is based on my lie. But it's still all random.

"Maybe . . ." she says, "we were brought together by something other than chance."

"I have no answer for that."

It's all so strange, Bill thinks.

I'll never really understand it.

One person meeting another because of a confluence of circumstance; maybe it's just the random spinning of the universe.

"Random or preordained, I'm glad we met," she says, drawing closer.

When they kiss, it's gentle, yet deep, and the taste of her is delicious, perfect.

"Do you want to spend the night?" she whispers.

"I'd love to . . ."

It seems the most natural thing in the world.

"I have to grab a few things from upstairs. I'll be right back."

"You don't have far to go . . ." she whispers, as she draws him closer and envelops him in an embrace.

They kiss again. Her lips move gently, like butterfly wings, flitting from Bill's mouth to his cheeks, then to his eyelids.

He's transported to somewhere he's never been.

If he could freeze one moment in time, this would be it.

"Get what you'll need and hurry back," Elena whispers, breaking the spell, but Bill knows far greater pleasures await him, soon.

"And when you set the house alarm, don't use the back stairs to get down here. If either the pantry door or the one to my kitchen opens, the alarm will go off and the security company will notify the police. So, after you set the alarm, leave the house by the front door . . . I'll leave my door unlocked. And hurry back," she adds, planting another wisp of a kiss on his lips.

CHAPTER 35

Bill feels a rush of anticipation, the likes of which he hasn't had since Olivia's passing.

As had happened minutes ago downstairs, thinking of her brings neither a twinge of guilt nor a hint of sadness. He knows it's a crazy idea, but Bill feels as if Olivia's encouraging him to move on with his life.

Move on with life . . . that is, if I'll even have a life.

With that thought permeating his awareness, Bill reminds himself to be especially cautious when he sets the alarm, locks up the house, and heads outside and down the front stairs to Elena's place.

His satchel is packed with a toothbrush, a change of underwear, and clean socks for the morning.

Should he take the Glock?

Yes, he'll slip it inside the satchel where Elena won't see it. He's gotta be armed in case they come for him.

Now it's time to head out.

With the alarm set and the door securely locked behind him, Bill stands at the top of the stairs leading to the street.

Peering left then right, he sees nothing that tickles his radar.

Traffic on Lexington is sparse and Park Avenue is quiet. At this hour, he doesn't see a single pedestrian on this quiet side street; and there's no sign of a car idling at a curb, or of anything even remotely suspicious.

What does strike him is the delectable scent of lilacs. It's odd how he never before this moment noticed the bush of lavender blossoms, growing next to Elena's front door.

With one last look up and down the street, Bill scrambles down the steps and opens Elena's unlocked front door.

CHAPTER 36

At the corner of Lexington and 70th Street, Luiza Murati sits at a window table in Neil's Coffee Shop.

This Bill Madrian fellow can't be far from here. For my own future, it's important to find him and let Besim know his location.

The man looking at her from across the table, Bruni Radaj, makes her uncomfortable. Her throat is dry, yet her armpits are moist. He reminds her of the men who kidnapped her ten years ago when she was seventeen. He's a hard-looking man with a narrow face and beady eyes. He looks like a lizard or some other repulsive reptile. She knows he's a hired assassin.

At eight in the evening, the coffee shop is nearly empty. She and Bruno are the only ones occupying a table on the glass-enclosed porch.

She's been here several times over the last few days, just waiting for Bill Madrian to either pass by or enter the place. For a diner, the food is decent, despite the smell of old fry grease hanging perpetually in the air.

The waitress approaches. "Will there be anything else, folks?"

Luiza glances at Bruno. He's clearly in charge of whether they stay a while longer, or leave.

"No, nothing else," Bruno says, sounding bored. "Just the check." His eyes remain lasered on Luiza.

The waitress tears the top page from her little pad and sets the bill on the table.

Bruno grabs it and drops a ten-dollar bill onto the table. In the coffee shop's lighting, his eyes glitter like slivers of crushed ice. His stare alone makes Luiza's heart batter her chest wall. Yes, his presence definitely brings back the horror of the past.

Keeping those eyes fixed on her, he says, "You've failed more times than anyone has a right to."

"Just because things didn't work out, doesn't mean I failed," she stammers, aware of a placating tone in her voice."

She must be careful not to offend or annoy Bruno because if he tells Besim she's being uncooperative, she'll be forced to go back to London. They'll throw her onto a private jet and she knows what awaits her. She'll be a prisoner and will be forced to service all those clients.

"At the bar in that place, Angelo's," he says in Albanian, "you could have enticed him to approach you, but from what Besim said, you blew the chance to drop a tablet into his drink."

"I did my best. I followed him from his apartment building the half-block to the restaurant. I sat at the bar, and though I could tell he was interested, he never made a move."

"It turns out your *best* wasn't good enough."

"Besides," she says, "his friend showed up and they went to the back room to have dinner."

"What about when you saw him at Starbucks."

"It wasn't my fault I lost him."

"Whose fault was it?"

"I did everything I could have done, and exactly what Besim told me to do. I stood at a distance and watched him walk out of that Starbucks; and when he hailed a cab, I got into one right behind his. I kept him in sight all the time. Even when my taxi got stuck at a red light, I never took my eyes off his cab, which was a block ahead of mine."

"So, what happened?"

"I saw him get out of his taxi at 70th Street, but moments later when I reached that street, he was nowhere in sight. He must have gone into one of the buildings on either side of 70th. I'm guessing that's where he's staying."

"You're *guessing*? There's no time left for guesswork."

"I did the best I could."

"And what happened when he went to that restaurant downtown?"

"Why is that *my* fault? I was standing on the corner of 70th Street but didn't see him come out of a house. I followed him walking south on Lexington. I watched him get into a taxi at 68th Street, so I got into one behind his. I followed him. When he got out of the taxi and went into that restaurant, I phoned it in; but Besim's men got there too late. That's not *my* fault!"

She realizes there's no sense in trying to justify herself to this man.

"I want you to do a better job patrolling the street, especially 70th. I don't care if you have to walk back and forth all day and night. And it's a good thing you've changed your look. Your glamorous one didn't do the job, did it?" His sneer sends a chill through her. "Just find him and call Besim."

Getting up from the table, Bruno walks out of the coffee shop.

* * *

On the street, Luiza inhales the night air. A cool breeze blows in off the East River, streaming westward on 70th Street. It's a refreshing change after breathing in that stale diner air.

She must find where this Bill Madrian is hiding. It could be the difference between life here in the States or being sent back to that brothel in London.

He must be staying somewhere on this block.

Poor bastard will surely die, but she can't worry about him.

It's herself she must save.

For sure, she'll be shipped off to London, if she fails Besim. She'd rather kill herself than submit again to servicing those filthy johns.

Midway along the street, Luiza detects a lovely fragrance. It's coming from a bush, planted on a little patch of grass outside one of the townhouses. She loves its cluster of delicate lavender-colored blossoms, and wishes she knew what it was called. She can't remember seeing anything like it back home in Petkaj.

But she quickly reminds herself not to allow her mind to wander.

Luiza resumes her slow pace, stopping every few steps to look in the opposite direction from which she's walking.

With a white wig covered by a babushka-like scarf, and wearing a drab brown raincoat and old-looking, laced-up shoes, she would appear to anyone noticing her halting gait to be just an elderly woman struggling to make her way along the street.

Suddenly, she hears something. It sounds like the thud of a heavy door closing.

Seeking the shadow of a thick-trunked sycamore tree, Luiza slowly turns around. She's confident she can't been seen by whomever just closed that door.

Yes, there's a man standing at the top of the flight of stairs at that townhouse she just passed.

It's *him*. Bill Madrian.

She doesn't have a single doubt about who it is.

She can't believe her good luck.

Her heart begins a drumbeat radiating to her ears.

She can see he's being very cautious. Before heading down those steps, he scans the street in each direction several times.

Luiza remains well-hidden by the tree, but even if he should catch a glimpse of her, she looks like a poor old soul, pausing to catch her breath before continuing on.

Madrian clambers down the staircase and disappears into an unlocked door beneath the staircase and located next to that fragrant bush.

More good luck. She doesn't have to trail him.

All she needs to do is phone the address of the townhouse to Besim, and keep an eye on the place until she's told she's free to leave.

CHAPTER 37

After hustling down the stairway, Bill opens the unlocked door to Elena's apartment.

She's waiting in the living room, holding two more glasses of Macchu Pisco.

He tosses the satchel onto a sofa and takes a glass.

They toast, wordlessly, take small sips and set the glasses on the coffee table.

Facing each other, they move closer.

Her hands reach around behind his neck and she draws him closer. "Do you want any more to drink?" she asks.

"Not now."

"Me neither."

"Who needs drinks when we have this?" he says.

They kiss on the lips, lightly.

His hands cup her face; his thumbs gently stroke her cheeks. For a few moments, he holds her that way, then they kiss again. This time, their tongues roll over each other. He delights in the feel and taste of her mouth.

Taking his hand, she leads him to the bedroom.

Buttons and zippers are undone as their lips wander over each other. There's nothing tentative about it; it's thrillingly new, yet feels so natural, and it's gentle, gradual, and true.

He's lost in the sound, the feel, the soaking heat, and scent of her, and it feels as familiar as the beat of his heart. It's as though they've done this many times before. Their joining is so powerful that, at its climax, he's no longer conscious of his surroundings.

He's lost in the exquisite lessening of awareness as he sinks into *la petite mort*.

The little death.

CHAPTER 38

Kosta Bronzi can barely sit still, even in his own living room. It's nine in the morning and Edonia is busy in the kitchen, baking for tonight's dinner guests. Kosta can't stop thinking about Alex. As much as he loves his son, he feels a swell of resentment toward the boy. His immaturity has endured well beyond his childhood and now, it's endangering everything Kosta has worked for all these years.

Alex isn't cut out to be a Kyre or even a captain like Besim. By now it's sickeningly clear: Kosta's son will never command the respect of the men in his faction, much less those of the entire Malotta clan. It's a shame because only through a son does one's legacy live on in the clan.

Yet, Kosta must make provisions for him in the clan's hierarchy, even though he'll never become an authority figure in the chain of command. It's through marriage, children, and family—solid blood ties—that power goes from father to son.

But right now, thanks to Alex, Kosta finds himself worrying about this headshrinker, a man who by mentioning a single word to anyone could endanger not only Kosta's people, but the entire Malotta clan. And if the government finds out who was behind the Levenko murder, trouble will come quickly. The Brooklyn

DA is an aggressive woman and won't hesitate to investigate, summon a grand jury, and indict. Complications could come from another clan or even from within the Malotta clan because the Levenko hit was unauthorized. Or, God forbid, if the Odessa mafia learns who orchestrated their pakhan's demise, they would surely seek revenge.

His encrypted cell phone trills.

"Hello, Besim."

"Good morning, Kosta."

"What have you got for me?"

"I didn't want to disturb you last night, so I'm calling now. When it rains, it pours. I'd already talked with a new skip tracer, but the good news is this: we don't need him or *any* skip tracer. We've located the target and we know *exactly* where he's staying."

"Good, good. Where's that?" Kosta feels his heartbeat ramp up.

"In Manhattan, in a townhouse on East 70th Street. He's either staying in the main house or in an apartment below it. I'll contact Bruno and he'll take care of it."

"Who spotted him?"

"One of my operatives. A very capable woman."

"Does she know why we want him?"

"No, she has no idea. She's the one who's been following him from the beginning."

"Who lives at this place on 70th Street?"

"Our IT expert scoured the database. It says the house is owned by Gregory and Linda Jeffries, and the downstairs tenant is a woman named Elena Lauria. We have the place under surveillance and no one has left yet. Now Bruno will take care of this headshrinker."

"It must be a silent kill."

"Don't worry, Kosta. Bruno will make quick work of it. He's an expert with a blade."

"Excellent. Once again, Besim, you've done a fine job."

"Thank you, Kosta. Your trust means a great deal."

"One other thing. I know I'm repeating myself, but this must be kept quiet. The only people who know why we want this man dead are you, me, and Alex. Is that clear?"

"Of course. It'll never come out."

CHAPTER 39

In the morning, they luxuriate in bed.

Bill's surprised and delighted: there's no morning-after awkwardness. It feels natural, as though the comfort of being together is something they should have expected. And yet, there's also the excitement that comes with having a new lover.

"Did you think it would be like this?" he asks as they lie next to each other.

"I think I knew," she says, nestling her head in the space between his neck and shoulder.

"How could you have known?"

She shrugs. "Some things are just intuitive."

They shower together, and he realizes this is the first time he's thought about the Albanians since they've been awake.

"I've decided to take the day off," Elena says as she scrambles eggs.

"I'm glad you did. I've taken a few days off, too."

"How come?"

"I need some time away from the office. And when that leak happened, I decided to take a short vacation."

It's lie after lie after lie. When will it stop?

"You know what? I'm glad your sink sprang that leak."

"So am I."
How long do I have to live a life of lies?

* * *

Two hours later, while Elena is food shopping, Bill goes outside, looks up and down the street, climbs the staircase, unlocks the front door, and enters the townhouse. He deactivates the alarm system. Retrieving his burner phone, he dials Rami's number. The outgoing voicemail says, "Leave a message."

"It's me," Bill says. "Have you learned anything?"

He hangs up hoping he hasn't said or done anything to reveal his location. After all, if the Albanians have enough IT skills, they may be able to hack into his burner. But not being a techie, he doesn't really know if that's possible.

A few minutes later, his burner trills.

"Hello?"

"It's me," he hears Rami say. "We're close to finding something out."

"Like what?"

"Which faction of the Malotta clan is after you . . . the people involved."

"Who are they?"

Silence hangs heavily in the air.

"Rami?"

"Yes?"

"Who are they?"

"I can't say."

"Is it Bronzi's people?"

"I can't talk now."

"Why not?"

"It wouldn't be safe."

"But we're using burners."

"You can never be too careful. Just stay off the grid while we work on it."

"But—"

"Are you someplace safe?" Rami asks.

"Yes, but—"

"Where are you? Don't say the location."

"In a townhouse."

"Are you staying with anyone?"

"No, I'm alone."

"Is it a house belonging to someone connected to you by a digital trail?"

"No."

"No details. Does anyone else know you're there?"

"No, only the couple who owns the place."

"Can they be trusted?"

"Yes. And they're away right now."

"Don't be specific . . . *away* meaning out of the city or somewhere else?"

"Out of the country."

"When will they be back?"

"In about a week."

"Have you gone anywhere since you've been there?"

"No."

"Are you alone now?"

"Yes."

"Are you alone day-to-day?"

"Yes . . ." he lies, not wanting to involve Elena.

More secrets, more lies. I'm even lying to Rami.

"Just stay where you are. Don't telephone anyone. Do you have access to a computer?"

"Yes."

"Is it yours?"

"No."

"Don't take any chances. Don't email anyone. Don't use your cell phone . . . even though it's a burner. Just stay out of sight. I'll get back to you in a day . . . at most, in two days. You have to be patient."

"What'll you have by then?"

"Just stay where you are."

"But how do you—"

There's a click as Rami hangs up.

This is unreal.

Bill activates the house alarm and leaves for Elena's apartment through the townhouse's front door.

CHAPTER 40

By midafternoon, they've finished a small plate of antipasto Elena had bought at a gourmet food shop on Third Avenue.

Being with her seems to quiet the motor that's been humming in Bill's chest since this nightmare began.

"It's a lovely day. How about going for a stroll in Central Park?" Elena suggests, after they've finished eating.

"I'd rather stay here with you."

He's about to rustle up some piss-poor excuse for not wanting to leave the house when a nerve-jangling sound erupts. Bill nearly jumps from the sofa. It's Elena's cell phone.

She answers after the third ring. "Hello?"

A moment later, she glances at the phone, then presses the red icon. "It's a hang-up," she says.

"What does the Caller ID say?"

"It said 'Unknown Caller.'"

A kicking sensation begins in Bill's chest.

How would the Albanians know he's here?

And how would they get Elena's cell phone number?

But hang-ups, wrong numbers, and robocalls happen all the time on both cell phones and landlines.

I can't suspect every little thing. Rami said he's close to finding out something. Or am I reading too much into what he said? Am I so desperate for good news, I'm starting to believe in miracles?

As for going to Central Park, no way can he risk it. Even if he could slip Greg's gun into his waistband without Elena noticing, it's way too risky to be anywhere outside.

And foolishly, he'd set the alarm upstairs, which means he can't use the back way, should he need to go up to retrieve something. But if that happens, he'll be very careful when he goes up or down the front stairway; and at most, he'll only be visible from the street for a few seconds.

On such a lovely spring day, he's lucky Elena is content to stay indoors, rather than pushing him to take a walk.

While she busies herself looking for something on her bookshelves, Bill finds himself growing increasingly concerned by the number of lies he's leaving in his wake. First to Linda and Greg, then to Mom and Laurie, and now to Elena, who in a matter of only a handful of days, has become so completely enmeshed with him.

If he lives—and that's a big "if"—will she forgive him for being so deceitful?

And what if he has to begin life somewhere else, as an entirely different person? How can he even think she'd be willing to join him?

Ridiculous.

He feels a sinking sensation at the thought of losing her.

But he knows it's a very real possibility.

"Why do you look so sad?" Elena asks, as she sits next to him on the sofa.

"I'm not sad. I was just thinking about my patients . . ." Bill murmurs.

"You're really committed to them, aren't you?"

"Yes. You develop relationships with them, which can be pretty intense."

"Speaking of relationships, let me show you some pictures of my family," she says, as she opens up a well-worn photo album and places it on both their laps.

They leaf through it, page by page, beginning with snapshots from when she was a kid. One photo shows her on a bike; another was taken at a petting zoo, and another was taken while she was standing with her mother in front of a public school.

"That was my first day of kindergarten," she says.

"You were gorgeous even back then."

She slaps his shoulder playfully. "Stop it."

"Have I embarrassed you?"

"No. I'm just not used to being complimented . . . or flattered."

"I'm not flattering you. I'm serious."

After going through the album, she asks, "Do you have pictures of your family?"

"Back at my place."

"Not on your cell?"

"No, I'm old-fashioned," he lies. "I only use it for making calls. Once in a while, I'll text or send an email."

He realizes he can't keep piling lie on top of lie. It's just untenable. And what really matters is he can't have a relationship built on a latticework of deceit.

Not to this woman.

Not now.

"I have to tell you something," he says, aware he sounds tentative. "I don't have my cell phone anymore. I had to destroy it."

"Destroy it? Why?" Her eyebrows rise and she cants her head.

"Because something happened in my practice . . . with a patient I was treating. And . . . I owe you an explanation."

How much can I tell her? Am I going against Rami's instructions?

Despite Rami's warning, he tells her about Alex Bronzi's question and the chain of events leading up to this moment.

"Oh my God," she sputters as her eyebrows rise. "I can't imagine how that must feel . . . to hear what you did and then to be chased."

"I owe you the truth," he says. "It's clear they want to silence me. And I didn't think it through until your cell rang and it was a hang-up. What I want to say is . . . without meaning to, I may've put you in danger just by being here."

She gasps and her hand goes to her mouth.

"I'll understand if you tell me to leave right now because . . . I don't want you to be hurt. I guess the only way to put it is . . . you have a choice. You can tell me to get lost or . . . you can take a chance with my being here."

She takes a deep breath. "Is there anything you can do? Are you sure you shouldn't go to the police or the FBI."

"That's not an option. I have no proof of anything."

There's a brief silence during which Elena stares off into the distance.

I wouldn't blame her if she throws me out of here this second.

The doorbell rings.

An electric shock jolts him, reaching every nerve ending in his body.

"Are you expecting anyone?" he asks.

She shakes her head, goes to the front window, separates the slats of the Venetian blinds, and peers out to the street. "There's a white panel truck double-parked out there."

Making her way to the door, she looks through the peephole.

"Yes . . . ?" she says.

"Flower delivery . . ." answers a man with a Spanish accent.

"You've got the wrong address."

"This is 133 East 70th, right?" he asks in a voice muffled by the door's thickness.

"Yes, but we're not expecting flowers."

Bill gets up from the couch. "Don't open the door," he whispers. "It could be them . . . the Albanians."

She stares at him, wide-eyed, then turns back to the door. "Who're the flowers for?" she asks in a tremulous voice.

"They're for Mr. and Mrs. Jeffries."

"They live upstairs . . . the front door of the house," Elena says, visibly shaking.

"I rang the bell there, but there's no answer. Can I leave them with you?"

"No, you can't."

"But I need a sig—"

"Sorry, but we can't help you," Bill cuts in, standing beside her.

"Just leave," Elena says. "We're not opening the door."

"Let me have a look at this guy," Bill whispers.

Elena steps aside.

Peering through the peephole, Bill sees a man with a thin face and prominent cheekbones; he wears a red baseball cap and sports a mustache with a neatly trimmed Van Dyke.

"Just leave the flowers at the door," Bill says.

"I can't. They gotta be signed for."

"Sorry, we can't help you," Elena says, sounding both frightened and annoyed.

"C'mon, man, I got a family to support," whines the guy. "If I don't get a signature, the boss'll think I dumped 'em. That's how the last guy got fired. I *need* this job. C'mon, give a guy a break."

Bill glances at Elena. She shakes her head and her eyes widen. "Oh my *God*. I just realized . . . I didn't lock the door when I came back with the food."

As Bill reaches for the lock, the doorknob turns and the door swings inward. Violently.

CHAPTER 41

Flowers are thrust in his face.

The man bursts into the foyer and reaches into his jacket pocket.

Bill rushes him, but the guy spins and lands an elbow to the side of Bill's head.

Bill sees a burst of pinpoint lights.

The gun . . . in the satchel . . . can I get to it? No, there's no time.

Recovering from the blow, he turns to the intruder and hears a clicking sound as a blade snaps out of a knife handle.

Bill lunges forward, rams into the guy just as the knife starts to rise. It's a full body blow that sends the man staggering backwards toward the sofa. He sprawls onto it, looking stunned. The side table and knickknacks tumble to the floor.

Bill leaps at him, but the guy twists away, and Bill's shoulder impacts the man's left arm. The knife is in his right hand. The guy leaps to his feet, whirls, and begins raising the knife.

A spike of fear-fueled fury bursts from Bill and without thinking, his right leg sends a kick toward the man. It lands on the attacker's left thigh. He grunts and pulls back.

A half-second later, Elena lands a vicious punch to the back of the guy's neck. He half turns and her elbow batters his face. Blood spurts from a gash on his cheek as he totters backwards. The knife clatters onto the floor. The intruder manages to remain on his feet, and begins raising his hands to ward off another blow.

In a kinetic burst of ferocity, Elena steps forward and her right leg is airborne as her body twists and she sends a roundhouse kick to the side of the man's head.

He flops to the floor in a heap.

Bill grabs the knife and stands over him.

The guy moans softly as his right leg quivers. His neural circuits are scrambled.

Elena sinks to her knees. Her chest heaves like a bellows. She sucks air desperately. "Oh my God, my God," she croaks as her hands go to her chest. "I can't breathe."

Bill turns from the man and clasps her shoulders. "Are you all right?"

"I can't get air," she gasps.

Raucous wheezes come from deep within her chest. She coughs, then gags; her shoulders are shaking as her hand goes to her mouth and she coughs repeatedly. She's wide-eyed with fear and her fingers tremble.

The intruder begins to stir.

"I can't believe this," Elena sputters. Tears pour from her eyes. Her entire body shakes.

"Call the police . . ." she says in a quivering voice.

The attacker opens his eyes. They look glassy, unfocused. He groans and peers up at Bill.

"Who sent you?" Bill shouts, crouching over the man.

The guy's eyes dart left and right. He says nothing.

Bill clutches the man's jacket and holds the knife to his neck. For an insane instant, he feels like slashing the bastard's throat.

"I'm calling the police," Elena cries and begins crawling toward the sofa, searching frantically for her cell phone.

Jesus, I've dragged her into this horror show. What a fuck-up.

The thug stares up at Bill, saying nothing.

This guy won't talk. He's a hit man. A pro.

"Where's my cell?" Elena gasps.

Bill notices her phone lying on the floor with the overturned side table on top of it.

Picking up the phone, Elena presses a few keys, but nothing happens. "Oh no," she rasps, "It's broken."

Bill can see the phone's glass face is cracked.

He pulls the attacker to his feet.

The man is only partly conscious.

"Bill, what are you doing?" Elena asks.

"I'm getting him outta here."

"Why?"

"We have to go and we can't leave him here. He'll go through your stuff and learn where your family is."

The guy's legs are rubbery. He staggers as Bill pushes him toward the door.

"We have to call the *police*," Elena cries.

"Do you have a landline?" he asks.

"No. See if he has a cell."

Bill rummages through the guy's pockets. "He's not carrying anything."

The attacker stumbles as Bill pushes him toward the door.

"This is unreal . . ." Elena cries.

"I never meant to get you into this mess."

"We have to call the police," she repeats.

"Elena, we're *both* in danger. They could be coming right now. We have to get out of here."

She stares at him, wide-eyed with her mouth agape. "This is insane. I can't believe this."

Bill hauls the attacker to the door and shoves the guy outside.

The intruder wobbles toward the gate, gets to the sidewalk, crosses it, and opens the van's door. He nearly flops into the vehicle. A few moments later, he starts the engine and drives away.

"Elena, we have to leave. Now."

"And go *where*?"

"We'll find someplace."

"But . . . but I *live* here."

Her chest heaves as she desperately sucks in air.

"They'll want to silence you, too. We have to leave. *Now*."

Elena shakes her head. Her eyes are wide and she looks confused. "But . . ."

"Please, Elena. We *both* have to get outta here. And I'm so sorry I dragged you into this."

"I can't believe this," she mutters.

"We have no choice. Let's go."

Bill retrieves the Mets jacket, feels the money-stuffed envelope. He grabs the satchel, knowing the pistol is inside.

Elena's hands are shaking and her face is chalk white.

Bill realizes she's terrified and must almost feel like he's taking her hostage. She must hate that he's put her in danger.

What if there are more goons waiting outside?

He has Greg's gun. If he must, he'll use it. There's no other choice.

He makes certain he has the burner.

"Where are we going?" she asks.

"We have to get outta here, now."

As they leave Elena's place, Bill realizes the Albanians will probably track him no matter where they go.

Is it all hopeless?

CHAPTER 42

Luiza Murati sits behind the wheel of a Subaru Forester.

Relieving Amar, who had watched the townhouse for hours, she pulled into the parking spot he'd occupied, directly across the street from the building.

Besim was clear in his instructions: "Wait until Bruno gets there. You'll stay until he leaves the house and drives away."

She watched as Bruno pulled the panel truck up to the house, double parked, and got out of the van holding an arrangement of flowers.

She saw him climb the stairway, ring the upstairs bell, and when no one answered, head back down, making his way to the downstairs apartment.

A few moments later, he was talking with someone inside. It looked like he was trying to convince whoever it was to open the door.

Not even a minute later, Bruno pushed his way into the apartment.

Luiza waits, as instructed.

It now seems Bruno is taking a long time to do what he must do. Maybe she should call his cell.

Suddenly, the downstairs door opens. Bruno is pushed from the apartment and stumbles onto the pathway. He nearly falls, then sways from side to side. He looks like he's been beaten. Yes, there's blood on his face. He's wobbly, but manages to make his way unsteadily to the low gate, opens it, then crosses the sidewalk, climbs into the van, and sits behind the wheel.

Luiza watches as Bruno starts the engine and drives slowly to the corner. The light is green, and he makes a right turn onto Lexington Avenue, heading downtown.

This is all wrong.

She hesitates for a while, not knowing what to do.

She decides to call Besim's cell, but before she can do it, this Bill Madrian fellow opens the door, looks around, and steps outside. A woman, who looks as pale as milk, is with him.

Luiza watches them make their way past the gate and get to the sidewalk. Madrian looks both ways; then, they walk quickly toward Lexington Avenue.

Using the car's Bluetooth, she calls Besim's cell, as she simultaneously starts up the Subaru and pulls away from the curb.

Reaching Besim's voicemail, she describes what she's just seen.

She pushes the Forester's starter button, pulls out of the parking space, and inches the Forrester toward Lexington Avenue.

Luiza never takes her eyes off the couple as they make their way to the corner.

They hail a taxi, get in, and head south on Lexington.

Luiza is a skilled driver, knows how to maneuver a car for surveillance purposes, and has timed things perfectly.

She turns onto Lexington and keeps the taxi in view from two car lengths behind. Thankfully, the driver doesn't weave in and out; he stays with the wave of green lights heading downtown.

A few blocks south, the traffic thickens. Luiza loses sight of the taxi when a box truck cuts in front of her. It's impossible to see around the thing and she's certain she'll lose them.

I have to make a move.

Glancing in her side-view mirror, she realizes she has room, so she swerves into the left lane and hits the gas pedal. Pulling ahead of the truck, she's again two cars behind the taxi.

I don't want to lose sight of them again. I'll get even closer.

She pulls out to the left again, steps on the gas, and slips back into the middle lane.

She's now directly behind the taxi.

The traffic light at East 50th and Lexington turns red.

Luiza hits the brake pedal as the taxi slips past the light and comes to a stop behind a glut of traffic on the far side of 50th.

If cars turn onto Lexington from 50th Street, they'll block my view of the taxi.

Waiting at the light, Luiza throws the gear shift into PARK, grabs her cell phone from the passenger's seat, and snaps a picture of the taxi's license plate. Glancing at her watch, she makes a mental note of the approximate time Madrian and the woman got into the taxi.

Even though I'll never keep up with them in traffic, there may be a way of finding out where that taxi goes.

CHAPTER 43

As the taxi heads downtown, Elena tries to control her trembling.

My God, this is unbelievable. What just happened? This is a nightmare.

She knows her body is in overdrive. Her heart drubs furiously and she's trying to catch her breath.

I actually beat that man unconscious. It wasn't like kicking dummies in the martial arts class. This is unreal. Bill wasn't kidding when he told me about that mob.

She closes her eyes, gulps desperately for air, then tries to slow her shuddering breathing.

Easy in, easy out. Stay calm, think of what Master Chang would say: Clear your mind. Find that inner calm.

She turns to Bill as the streets rush by in a blur. "Where are we going?"

Bill glances at the driver. Though there's a Plexiglass barrier between them, he speaks barely above a whisper. "I'm so sorry this involves you. Believe me, I'm—"

"Enough apologies, Bill," she gasps. "We almost got killed. Where are we going and what do we do?"

Now, it feels like an ice floe sits in her chest, surrounding her heart.

He clasps her hand. Despite the warmth of his flesh, her fingers feel like icicles.

This is unbelievable. What have I gotten into with this man?

Amid the blare of horns and the sound of the taxi's tires clopping on the roadway, she does her best to understand what's going on. Yes, he's been in danger and now, she is, too.

After what has just happened, those Albanians must think Bill has told her everything.

She's now every bit as much a target as he's been.

Despite her heart's rampaging beat, coupled with the jumbled emotions of fear mixed with growing anger, Elena does her best to focus her thoughts. She must think clearly and map out a plan, at least a viable one for herself.

This man sitting next to her, whom she scarcely knows, has not only put her life in danger, but likely has brought these thugs to her family's doorstep.

My God . . . what can I do?

"I'm so sorry . . ." he says. "If I'd known this could've happened, I'd never have involved you," Bill stammers, as she quickly withdraws her hand from his.

"We have to go to the police, right now," she says, as desperation threatens to overwhelm her.

"Elena, we can't—involving the police will only make things worse. It'll—"

"*Worse?*" she interrupts. "How much worse can it get than *this*?"

The taxi slows to a stop at a red light.

Elena reaches for the rear-door handle. "Bill, if you're not willing to save yourself, I'm getting out here and going to the police. Doing anything else is just crazy," she says, as her voice grows more strident. Her hand tightens on the door handle.

"Please, Elena, let me tell you about this guy, Rami, and why we have to follow his advice. Just give me a little time to explain things."

"So begin explaining," she says, aware she's struggling to keep from telling the driver to pull the taxi over to the curb so she can get out.

"The police can't do a thing. The guy who attacked us is gone and we have no evidence to show them. They'd file a report and then what happens? Absolutely nothing. They can't protect us. That's a fantasy. There's nobody they can arrest and they're not gonna give us twenty-four-hour protection. And if we *do* go to the cops, we'll wind up in even worse danger."

She shakes her head, trying to think of the best thing to do now that her home has been invaded.

"Listen, Elena . . . we're safe for the time being. We got away from the house and we're in no danger here, in this cab. We'll find a safe place to stay at least for a short while."

"How long is that going to be?"

"We can stay somewhere for a day or a day and a half. There are plenty of hotels near Grand Central. We can check into one and I'll call Rami."

"What can he do?"

"I promise I'll tell you everything about him after we check in. He needs a little more time to figure out the best way to handle this. Let's give it *one* day, and if nothing develops, we'll go to the police if that's what you want to do."

Elena withdraws her hand from the door handle, and without saying a word, looks straight ahead as the taxi proceeds down the avenue.

This is horrifying. Is this what my life has turned into?

CHAPTER 44

Bill sees what looks like a good place to hole up for a while.
The Kenilworth Hotel, a modern-looking building, is situated on the east side of Lexington between 40th and 39th Streets.

"Pull over to the left," Bill tells the driver. "We'll get out here."

He slips a few bills through the Plexiglass aperture. "Keep the change."

The cabbie mumbles his thanks.

Out of the taxi, they scramble up the hotel's front steps. Pushing through the revolving door, they enter an Art Deco–styled lobby. The floor is highly polished marble. The walls have touches of silver, black, and pink with lots of mirrors, chrome, and glass. The place looks moderately high-end.

They approach the lacquered reception counter with Bill virtually pulling Elena across the lobby area.

"We'd like a room," Bill says to the pert-looking clerk, a blond woman whose hair is pulled into a ponytail. A plastic name tag on her blouse reads ANNETTE.

"Do you have a reservation, sir?" she asks.

"No. What do you have available?" he asks, trying to keep his voice from warbling.

I hope I don't sound like I'm on the run. And I hope Elena doesn't look too spooked; this receptionist's gonna think I've kidnapped her.

"We have a standard room with a queen-size bed," Annette says. "Wi-Fi is included. It's four hundred thirty dollars per night, not including tax."

"We'll take it," Bill says, pulling out his wallet. He counts out the bills. "Here's a thousand for two nights." He slips ten bills onto the counter. "That should include tax."

"Sir, may I see your credit card?"

"I don't have one."

"I'm sorry," Annette says with a semi-smile verging on a grimace, "but the law requires everyone who registers at a hotel to present identification. If you don't have a credit card, a driver's license or some other ID like a passport will do."

He has no choice. He can't ask Elena to show her ID; it'll spook her even more than she is right now. He can't even be sure she won't bolt and run to the police. He has to show some ID, so he'll have to risk breaking one of Rami's rules.

Don't go anywhere. Don't write a check or use a credit card. It's a cash only existence. They can get to you through any database.

Fishing in his wallet, Bill presents his driver's license.

The clerk examines it, then begins tapping away on her keyboard. She's entering the license number into the hotel's database. This is bad news. If the Albanians have a skip tracer working for them, they'll locate him through the DMV data bank. He's toast, and Elena is, too.

A maelstrom of thoughts swirls through his head. How were they able to track him to Greg and Linda's building?

And then to Elena's apartment?

They've managed to find him no matter where he is. They must have a guy like Rami who sits at a computer and comes up with information about anything or anyone. How do we get out of this bind?

Why did I ever drag Elena into this nightmare? Jesus, I'm such a fool. I should have known better than to involve her and now she's stuck in this insanity, too.

After a few more keystrokes, the clerk gives Bill a printed receipt, then hands him his change, in cash, along with two key-cards for room 608.

Waiting for the elevator, Bill's certain the clerk is watching him.

She must suspect me of something, but so what? I'm too deep into this madness to worry about it.

His foot begins tapping a staccato beat on the floor. He can't wait to get to the room, away from the lobby or the street, far from anyplace where they can be seen.

What kind of life is this? We'll have to stay locked away in a hotel room. How long will that be? At this rate, I'll run out of cash soon. And my only link to the outside world is this burner for calling Rami.

For now, he has to wait. Rami said they might know more in a day, maybe two.

They? Who the hell are *they?*

And what happens then?

What's in store for Elena?

And how long will she be willing to stay locked away from the world?

He can't get his head around the possibility that he might have to vanish for good. Give up everything and everyone he's known his entire life.

How will he ever explain to Elena that, because of him, she might have to do the same thing?

CHAPTER 45

Trying to stifle her fear, Elena enters room 608 with Bill.

This is so insane. If I didn't know what happened at the apartment, I'd think Bill is paranoid. But that man was going to kill him, and no doubt, me, too. Now, they'll be coming for both of us. What on earth can I do? Master Chang would tell me to find that inner calm. Don't let your mind wander to negative things, that's what he'd say.

Tossing her tote bag onto the luggage rack, she sits on the bed while fighting back tears.

He plops down beside her. "Elena, don't use your cell phone. I have a burner you can use."

She gets up and begins pacing. "Bill, this is unbelievable. We nearly got killed and we're running for our lives . . . and . . . and we're in the middle of . . . this nightmare. And we're just going to sit here in this *hotel room*?"

Master Chang's words notwithstanding, she can't stop the trembling sensation inside her body. Her mouth feels dry; her tongue virtually sticks to the roof of her mouth. She's awash in fear. "I'm . . . I'm doing my best to deal with this, but it's just . . . I don't know . . . it's beyond the pale."

"Elena, I'm so sorry I got you—"

"Stop *apologizing*," she says, and without a thought, slaps his shoulder. "I'm not an idiot. I know you didn't want this to happen. But it *has* happened. And now, those people are after us . . ."

"Only for the time being."

"Meaning what?"

"Rami said he'll know more in a day or two."

"This man Rami . . . who is he and what's he going to do? You said you'd tell me more about him."

Bill tells her what he knows about Rami, which as best she can tell, isn't very much.

Now this seems even more insane.

"Is that it? He's a skip tracer? What can he do?"

"He'll find out who's after me and try to resolve this."

"*Resolve* this? What does that mean?"

He shakes his head. "I'm not sure. I should have left the city. I was a fool to involve you . . . or Linda and Greg."

This is all so unbelievable. Nothing like this was even imaginable an hour ago. And now I'm chin deep in this horror.

"What do I do about work?" she asks.

"For the time being, you have to call in sick."

"You know what? I *feel* sick."

"I know . . . I do, too."

"I could never have imagined anything like this. Do you think they can find us here?"

"I had to show my license to the clerk downstairs. They must have IT people working for them. Or a skip tracer like this guy, Rami."

"What sort of name is *Rami*?"

"I don't know. But he might have some advice that'll help. In fact, I'll call him."

He grabs the burner and dials Rami's number. After hearing the terse outgoing message, Bill says, "Rami, it's me. It's an emergency." He recites the burner's number.

Setting the phone on the bedside table, he turns to her and tries to embrace her.

She pushes him away.

They sit in silence.

Elena struggles to catch her breath. Here they are, hiding in a hotel room in the middle of Manhattan and they can't even leave the room. And her life is circling the drain, all because she met this man, Bill.

Shaking her head, she says, "I don't see a way out of this."

CHAPTER 46

A few minutes later, Bill's burner trills.

"Yes, Rami . . . ?" he says with the phone at his ear.

"Are you safe?"

"Yes."

"Are you in the same place?"

"No."

"Why not."

"A guy came to where I was staying and tried to kill me."

"When?"

"An hour ago."

"What happened?"

He tells Rami about the attack. He doesn't mention Elena's name. "But we got away, took a taxi to another place. We're there now."

"*We?* So you're with someone . . ."

"Yes."

"Who? No names."

"The person I was staying with. The downstairs tenant where I was staying."

"That complicates things."

Elena, sitting next to him, can hear every word Rami says. She shakes her head; she's obviously upset and exasperated.

"I had no choice," Bill says. "By now, there's a good chance they're coming after her, too."

"Again, where are you?"

"At a hotel."

"Did you pay cash?"

"Yes."

"Did you show ID?"

"I had to. I showed the receptionist my driver's license," Bill says, feeling more vulnerable than ever. A hollow feeling pervades him as he realizes the depth of the trouble he and Elena are now facing.

"Understood. But it's not safe. I'll call you in a while and direct you to a safe place, one where you won't be found."

"A safe place? What's going on?"

"I can't say."

"Listen, Rami, I can't—"

"No names."

"Sorry. I don't know how long we can go on like this."

"You have no choice. Nor does your friend. For all we know, they could be coming for you in the next twenty-four hours."

"How can they find us?"

"There are ways. As you said, you showed your driver's license. That creates a trail."

"This is crazy. We're about to lose everything."

"Lose everything? What? *Material* things? They count for nothing. You don't want to lose your *life*. So let me do what I have to do."

*   *   *

With a panther-quick movement, Elena grabs the burner from Bill and puts it to her ear.

Enough of this mystery. I have to find out more.

"What can you do?" she says in a voice that's nearly breathless. "What can you *really* do to help us?"

There's a moment of silence.

"I understand how you feel, but you must have patience," Rami says.

"*Patience*? A man invaded my apartment and tried to kill us, and you can't tell us what you're doing to put an end to this? How are you going to stop them?"

"I'm making contacts."

"What kind of *contacts*?"

"I can't say."

"Why not?"

This is so absurd. And so frightening.

"Listen to me. I know you got dragged into this, but you have to trust me."

"How can we trust you when you don't answer questions?" she says, aware her voice is rising and she's becoming more annoyed. "Why are you so evasive and why won't you give us any details? Is it money you want?"

"I don't want money."

"How can you do this gratis? I can get some money and—"

"You have to be patient."

"But we need something more to go on," she says. "We need some details . . . anything that'll help get us through this. So far you've just said we need to be patient. This'll take more than making contacts. I have a few thousand dollars in my bank account and—"

"That's not necessary. Right now, I need you to be smart. Don't even *think* about going anywhere until you hear from me. Very soon, I'll be able to direct you to a safe place."

"What *safe* place."

There's no response.

This is maddening.

"Are you going to hide us for the rest of our lives?"

"I'll have something for you by tomorrow . . . no later than noon."

"What'll you have by then?"

She turns to Bill and with the phone to her ear, shakes her head.

"I can't say," Rami says. "But until then, I need you to keep a clear head and stay where you are so we can get you out of this alive."

"*We*? Who's we?"

"My contacts."

"Who're they?"

"You don't want to know."

"Yes, I do. I very much want to know because my life's tipping over the edge."

"You're better off not knowing."

"Why?"

"It's not important for you to know."

"Knowing who your contacts are *is* important."

"The less said, the better."

"This is absolutely insane."

"I know. The world's an insane place. We'll do what we can to make it sane for you again. Just stay calm and stay put."

"But—"

The line goes dead.

Elena glances at the phone, then hits the END CALL button.

"I get the feeling there's no way out of this," she says. "This guy Rami is just treading water and we're in lockdown waiting for these criminals to catch up with us."

"Right now, we have no choice."

"There are always choices, Bill. Life is a series of choices and we have to make one. Do we stay here or get out of this place. Do we go to the police and hope for the best, or maybe do something else. One thing's certain: this Rami's a complete unknown. He's a computer geek who taps away at a keyboard. What else can he do?"

Bill shakes his head. "I wish I knew . . ."

"This is absurd," she says as a deep sense of unease shivers through her.

"I know . . ."

"What do you think this Rami guy is *really* doing?" Elena asks. "Aside from sitting at a computer."

"He says he's making contacts."

"Who's he contacting?"

"I don't know. But he said he'll find us a safe place."

"A safe place? Where? Here in the city or someplace in Wisconsin or Idaho where we'll have to start over, and everything in our lives before this is washed down the drain."

"I know as much as you do. Rami said we have to hold on until noon tomorrow."

"Why until then? What's going to *happen* then? What kind of magic is he going to pull?"

"Whatever it is, he can't say."

"Why do you think he's so vague?"

"The only thing I can think of is he's in the secrecy business."

"What on earth does that mean?"

"I don't know."

"This is the definition of stupidity," she says as a sense of helplessness infiltrates her. "We're just sitting here and waiting to hear from a guy about whom we know nothing, a guy who's supposedly making contacts while these criminals are hunting us."

"Let's wait until tomorrow . . . noon at the latest."

"Why? What's going to happen then?"

CHAPTER 47

Kosta Bronzi's encrypted cell phone sends out its ringtone. A quick glance tells him who it is.

"Yes, Besim."

"Kosta, it didn't work out as planned."

"What happened?"

"Our man got to them but they overpowered him."

"Who's *they*?"

"Madrian and this woman—according to our IT man her name is Elena Lauria. She lives in a downstairs apartment in that townhouse owned by the Jeffries people. It seems he was staying with her. Bruno said she's well-versed in the martial arts. They beat him and threw him out of the apartment. He called and told me what happened."

"Do you think they contacted the police?"

"We don't know, but there's good news . . ."

"Tell me."

"As a precaution, I had one of our people posted outside the house. She saw the couple leave, get into a taxi, and head downtown."

"And . . . ?"

"She followed the cab and took a picture of its license plate, then emailed it to me. I'll take it from there."

"We should be using a new skip tracer."

"The one I contacted isn't available," Besim replies, "but we don't need one now. I'm sure we can locate them."

"How?"

"Through the taxi license plate."

"You're sure of that?"

"Yes, I'm sure."

"Okay. Have it done and keep me posted."

"I will. Now, it's only a matter of time. One other thing, Kosta..."

"Yes?"

"That woman he was staying with ... we know who she is. A simple computer search showed us that her family lives in the Boston area. We can take one of her relatives as a hostage. That'll flush her out, and then we'll probably be able to get to Madrian."

"Good. But, right now, locate them, and we'll kill two birds with one stone."

*　*　*

Besim usually calls their IT guy for a job like this, but it won't be necessary.

He'll take care of this on his own. The fewer people who know anything, the better. Kosta has insisted on secrecy again and again. And Besim has just as much at stake in this as Kosta does. None of this can come to light. Because if Kasim Malotta finds out what's been going on, they'll all go down and it won't be pretty.

Besides, if Besim locates and takes care of Madrian and this Lauria woman, Kosta will be supremely grateful. It can only bode well for Besim's future in the clan. Who knows? Someday he might become a Kyre himself. After all, that idiot Alex isn't fit for the job. Why shouldn't Besim have ambition? Sheer will and competence is what got Kosta where he is today. The same will go for Besim.

Information is what's needed right now. And this is so simple he doesn't need an IT expert. Or a skip tracer. Watching Kosta operate over the years has taught Besim to use ingenuity, to think outside the box.

He can do this one himself. Once you have the intelligence, you put boots on the ground. Ultimately it comes down to foot soldiers in close combat. Not pencil-necked geeks sitting at computer terminals.

Now that he's got the taxi's license plate number, he'll track down Madrian and this Elena Lauria. It should be as easy as going online.

He boots up his laptop and gets on the internet. He goes to the NYC Taxi & Limousine Commission website. On the home page, he clicks on the box labeled LICENSE STATUS, then clicks on the link saying, CHECK LICENSE STATUS.

He goes to the sub-link, ACTIVE FOR-HIRE VEHICLES.

The page opens to a table showing all taxis currently operating within the five boroughs of New York City.

Yes, these days, almost everything is part of a huge database. And much of it is available for anyone in the public to access. There's no doubt about it: technology makes finding people easier than ever.

Besim scrolls down the list of vehicles for hire, hoping to find a matching license plate of the taxi Madrian and this Elena Lauria took. The site lists, among other things, the name of the garage where each vehicle is based. It also provides a description of a vehicle—whether it's a yellow cab, a livery car, or a limo—along with other relevant information.

But all Besim really needs is the location of the garage where this taxi is based.

He plugs the taxi's license plate number into the search box and hits ENTER on the keyboard.

Ah, there it is. The license plate number, as clear as daylight.

Luiza did a fine job. He'll make sure to tell Kosta about her. She's proving to be a valuable asset here in the States; they won't need her in London anymore.

According to the website, the taxi is garaged and operates out of the Riverside Taxi Company at 51st Street and Twelfth Avenue.

Only a few more steps and he'll be able to do what must be done.

This should be easy.

*   *   *

At nearly eight that same evening, Besim and his assistant, Valmir, a brute of a man—all six feet, six-inches and 280 pounds of him—get out of a Lincoln Navigator and walk toward the garage. Besim's parked the SUV a half-block away from Twelfth Avenue and 51st Street.

It's an eerie-looking industrial area with chain-link fences and parking depots for 18-wheel semis and triple-axle dump trucks. Twelfth Avenue runs along the elevated West Side Highway, which parallels the Hudson River. The water ripples in reflected light from New Jersey on the far shore. A cool breeze wafts in from the river. Traffic whooshes by on the highway; streaming headlights cast an eerie wash of beams across the nightscape.

*　*　*

Riverside Taxi Company is housed in an old brick building situated between a UPS depot and a place called Larry Flynt's Hustler Club, a titty bar Besim never realized existed. He might pay a visit one night, and find out if it's mob connected. Is it controlled by the Russians, the Italians, or another Albanian clan?

The Malotta clan could always use another place to launder money—locally, not overseas. Kosta will be pleased if Besim brings him that information. It might mean another bonus or, more importantly, could land him an opportunity to manage a club. There's lots of money to be skimmed in that kind of an operation.

But that's for another time. Right now, he needs to locate Bill Madrian and Elena Lauria. Quickly and with as little trouble as possible.

The depot is huge. Its interior is poorly illuminated by low-wattage light bulbs caged in wire enclosures. At least thirty taxis are parked in the place. Some are being serviced, while others are ready to begin their rounds throughout the city. A group of cabbies hangs around smoking and drinking coffee from diner containers while waiting to begin their shifts.

Approaching the dispatcher's booth, Besim introduces himself and Valmir to the dispatcher, a pudgy guy with a shaved scalp and a goatee. Besim makes certain he speaks without an accent and purposely garbles his and Valmir's names while flashing a detective's badge.

The badge is authentic because it was bought from a retired New York City detective. It's good to have all kinds of people on the payroll. Judges and politicians aren't enough. You need city inspectors and police officers. Especially detectives; they can streamline a manhunt or pave the way for you to accomplish things you'd otherwise never be able to do.

Any more cops on the payroll and Kosta could start his own precinct. That's where the Kyre's a genius. He knows how to work every aspect of government—knows who to massage and who to play hardball with—whether they're local or national. The banks and financial institutions, too. And he has a vast network of connections in Europe and the Middle East.

"We're tracking a perpetrator and need to see today's trip sheet for this taxi," Besim says, showing the dispatcher a cell phone photo of the taxi's license plate number.

"That'll take a couple of minutes, Detective," says the dispatcher. "Today's sheets haven't been entered into the system yet."

It's a simple proposition. Besim knows that any cabbie driving for a transportation company is required to jot down the location of every pickup and drop-off point during a shift. He must also note the time of each pickup and drop-off. Otherwise, the cabbie could haul people around without activating the meter, keeping the cash for himself. If a driver doesn't fill out an accurate trip sheet compatible with the odometer mileage and gasoline usage, he's history. In a few years, the companies will be using GPS technology to track the routes of all fleet taxis.

The dispatcher paws through a pile of documents, finally comes up with two sheets of paper, slips them onto his clipboard, and says, "The driver's a guy by the name of Carlos Cabrera. Whaddaya wanna know, Detective?" the dispatcher asks, holding Cabrera's trip sheet in his hand.

"I'm looking for a fare registered by this taxi. The pickup was at three thirty this afternoon, give or take a minute or two. It was at Lexington and 70th Street. We need to know the perp's drop-off point."

The dispatcher runs his index finger down the list of fares. "Here it is," he says. "I've got the pickup at three thirty-one at Lex and 70th . . . and the drop-off was at Lex and 40th, fifteen minutes later."

"Lemme use your computer for a second," Besim says.

"Okay, but make it quick, Detective. I got cabs I gotta dispatch."

Besim sits in the dispatcher's chair facing the computer and clicks on the Google icon.

He goes to Google Maps and types *Lexington Avenue & 40th Street, NYC* in the search box.

A map appears on the screen with an upside-down teardrop demarcating the intersection. He clicks on it and a photo of the intersection appears on a side panel.

Clicking on the picture, he brings up the Street View of the area.

He moves the cursor along Lexington Avenue: a Chase bank, a Bank of America, a Bagel Express joint, and then sees the Kenilworth Hotel.

He scans up and down Lexington, one block in each direction. There's no other hotel on the avenue within that range. So far, so good.

Still on Google's Street View, he moves the cursor along 40th Street one block east and one west of the intersection of 40th and

Lexington. There are only two hotels on 40th within a block of Lexington: the Seton and the Renwick, both small, out-of-the-way places you'd have to know exist to even *think* about taking a room in either one.

They must be in one of these three places. He grabs a piece of paper and jots down the names of the three hotels.

This headshrinker's life will soon be over.

And the bitch he's with will be gone, too.

"Thanks," Besim says to the dispatcher. "You've been a great help."

"No sweat, Detective."

He and Valmir leave the garage and head back to the Navigator.

"Is all good, boss?" Valmir asks as they walk back toward the SUV.

"Yes. It's good. We'll get them soon."

Besim thinks about the botch job Bruno did. One man isn't enough, especially when you want both of them taken out. And the woman has mastered some sort of marital arts routine. That wasn't expected. But he can count on the element of surprise, which is a powerful weapon.

"The *Kyre* wants a quiet kill," says Besim. "Knives and garrots will do the job. I want to make sure it happens. So, Valmir, you and I will do it."

CHAPTER 48

Opening her eyes, Elena gazes up at the ceiling.

She must have drifted off for a while, but now she's wide awake. Looking at the bedside clock, she realizes it's 8:40 in the evening. She dropped off out of sheer exhaustion and was asleep for maybe fifteen minutes.

It feels so strange to be in a hotel room lying next to a man she met only a few days before this. And it was just a few hours ago when that thug burst into her apartment and tried to kill them. And now, they're both on the run from mobsters.

This is all so unbelievable. I don't know if I'll ever be able to wrap my head around it. Where do we go from here?

She glances to her left. Bill is sleeping so deeply, if she didn't know better, she'd think he hasn't got a care in the world. It's nearly impossible to understand how this could be happening. It's what you see in movies or read in novels. It doesn't happen in real life, at least not in hers.

Her thoughts turn to how it all began.

When Linda called to say Bill Madrian, the couple's friend, would stop by for the house key, she hadn't given it a second thought. His apartment was flooded and he needed a place to stay for a few days.

Elena only knew what Linda had said about Bill over the previous few months. It'd seemed obvious: Linda wanted to get them together. "He's a great guy," she said, and mentioned the death of his fiancée. "It's been two years since she's been gone, and I think he's over it. I'm sure you'd like him."

After hearing about his fiancée, Elena wasn't sure she'd be interested. Why get involved with a man whose future wife had died a couple of years earlier? That kind of thing is sure to leave him scarred, maybe even permanently damaged.

There'd been enough complications with Eric and she knows better than to get involved with a man whose life was steeped in tragedy, a man needing to be rescued. Like Eric had been after both his parents had died in an accident when he was twelve. He'd grown up in a series of foster homes barely surviving emotional and physical abuse. Their marriage went down amid the flames of his cocaine and sex addictions. There's no doubt about it: the "rescue" scenario is one of the oldest traps in the book.

But when she saw Bill, she was instantly attracted to him. It was based on some primal kind of allure—and she'll never fathom it in a coherent way. Some people refer to it as chemistry, but whatever it is or was, she invited him in for a drink.

And until that monster invaded her apartment, she'd been re-creating in her mind that moment when she first laid eyes on Bill Madrian, and was beginning to feel nostalgia for it. There was something deliciously sweet in the memory.

But it now feels as though poison has infiltrated the bond that was beginning to form.

Thinking back now, when that intruder burst into the apartment, she didn't hesitate to use her martial arts training. It was pure muscle memory—she didn't have to think about it for a second—and her response was derived from countless kicks and punches to the heavy bag.

But when she really thinks about it, her reaction was based more on the need to survive. On instinct.

Is her instinct now telling her to go to the police?

Maybe not, because Bill was probably right. There's not much they can do.

Will they put a patrol car in front of the townhouse twenty-four hours a day?

Of course not.

Will they arrest this Alex Bronzi?

For something he said to a psychiatrist?

Not a chance.

They might even think both she and Bill are kooks.

Is instinct now telling her to disappear? At least for a while?

Maybe.

Is she going to disappear permanently, the way Bill described what this Rami fellow told him might have to happen?

How on earth do you do that?

How do you forsake the people you know and love, as though you have no mother, no father, no brothers, no aunts, uncles, nieces, nephews, or friends?

How do you live a life where you never went to high school in Boston, where there was no college at Tufts, no graduate degree in Library Science, where you have to work at some low-level job—probably as a waitress in some greasy spoon diner in a town called Nowheresville—where the money you've accrued in your pension plan can never be collected?

How do you live a life as though Elena Lauria, the person you've been your entire life, never existed? As though she's evaporated.

There's no way she can connect that distant version of herself to who she really is.

And now, she's just waiting for some guy named Rami to somehow get them out of this mess.

One thing is certain: for the next fifteen hours—until twelve noon tomorrow, she'll have to deal with the world from the confines of this hotel room. And she has to hope this guy Rami is legitimately trying to help them.

When she was younger—in her late teens and through her early twenties—reading a good book helped get her through some rough patches. Even when things erupted with Eric, she could escape reality by reading a novel.

But now, there isn't a book in the world that will provide an outlet from this horror because she can only think about one thing: survival.

Bill mentioned that she should call in sick to the library. At least for tomorrow.

What if this goes on beyond tomorrow?

She and Ann White—her best friend in the city—speak nearly every day. If this continues beyond the next day and Ann can't reach her, she'll show up at the apartment. Ann has a spare key and if she rings the bell and gets no answer, she'll let herself in. The place is a mess after what happened with that animal who broke in. For sure, Ann will realize something awful has happened and she'll call the police.

And there are Mom and Dad. If more than three days go by without a call to them, they'll telephone. They'll get her voice mail and leave a message. When there's no call back, they'll contact the library.

After learning she hasn't shown up for work, they'll get to Logan, hop on a plane, and head for New York. And when they see the mess at the apartment, they'll get in touch with the police.

And what about Greg and Linda?

When they get back from Aruba, Linda will stop by to say hello. She'll see the apartment is a wreck and will realize something dreadful happened.

But she's getting way ahead of herself. This Rami said he'll have some answers by noon tomorrow. They'll just have to wait it out and hope for the best.

God, this is awful.

As bad as things were with Eric, she'd never been terrorized like this.

She turns toward Bill and shakes him.

He awakens with a startle. "Huh?" he grunts, looking groggy. "How long have I been asleep?"

"Not long," she says. "I need to call the library, my family, and a few friends. I have to use your phone."

"Here," he says, reaching over to the bedside table and handing her the burner. "No one can track you if you use it."

She begins punching in a number.

It's absolutely stunning, Elena thinks, how the most trivial thing—a few words—*Do you wanna know who clipped Boris Levenko?*—can change your life.

And the lives of those around you.

CHAPTER 49

At nine thirty-five in the evening, Besim and Valmir are back at Besim's place on Fordham Road in the Bronx.

Using a burner, Besim calls the Seton Hotel.

"Good evening. Seton Hotel. May I help you?"

"Yes, Mr. William Madrian, please."

"One moment, sir."

There's a brief pause.

Besim waits as his heart rate ramps up. It's the fizz of pleasure he feels when he's closing in for a kill, that little prickle of antici-pation he so loves. It reminds him of his younger days when as a hit man, he took out some mid-level Dominicans in Washington Heights. It was the beginning of the Albanian takeover of the drug business.

"I'm sorry, sir, but we don't have a guest by that name."

"Maybe the room is under his wife's maiden name, Elena Lauria?"

"One moment."

Another short pause as Besim's foot begins tapping on the floor.

There are voices in the background. The receptionist is talking to someone while accessing the computer list of guests.

The receptionist is back on the line. "No, sir. There's no one by that name either. Are you sure you have the right hotel?"

"Thank you. Sorry to have bothered you."

He's not disappointed because he's now pretty sure they're at the Kenilworth on Lexington Avenue. And he'll soon find out.

He dials the Renwick Hotel, asks for William Madrian, then Elena Lauria.

He gets the same response from the desk clerk. There's no William Madrian or Elena Lauria registered there.

Keyed up even more, he calls the Kenilworth Hotel. "May I please speak to William Madrian or Elena Lauria."

Besim's fingers are tingling. He hears his blood rushing through his neck, pounding behind his eyes.

There's a three-second pause.

"One moment, sir. I'll connect you."

Besim hits END CALL.

His heart jackrabbits in his chest.

Yes, this is it. He's located them.

He turns to Valmir. "We know where they are. At the Kenilworth Hotel on Lexington near 40th Street in Manhattan."

"How do we get to them?"

"We use our badges at the front desk."

Now Besim feels that surge of excitement even more intensely. It's a strange kind of euphoria, a sickly but delectable high.

"Are you sure you don't want to contact the man you hired, that killer," Valmir asks.

"No, Valmir. You and I will take care of this. We'll do it my way. It has to be silent because they're in a public place. Knives will be best."

CHAPTER 50

Besim and Valmir enter the Kenilworth Hotel at ten fifteen in the evening.

They flash their badges to the clerk at the reception desk, a boyish-looking man with fleshy features and a swarm of freckles on his face.

"I'm Detective Lowry," Besim says, speaking in a voice barely above a whisper to hide any discernible accent. "We have reason to believe you have a guest registered in your hotel who we have to apprehend. In what room is William Madrian staying?"

Obviously intimidated by the two detectives, the clerk runs his fingers over the computer's keyboard. "Mr. Madrian's in Room 608."

"We don't want to create a disturbance so we'll wait here in the lobby."

"I understand."

"How long will you be on duty?" Besim asks the clerk.

"Until eleven o'clock, Detective."

"We'll do what we have to do as quickly and quietly as possible. "Please tell the receptionist taking over at eleven what the situation is."

"I certainly will, Detective."

"Do you know what Madrian looks like?"

"No, Detective."

Besim shows him a cell phone photo of Bill Madrian that was taken off an internet site for physician referrals. "Take a good look," he says. "Let us know if you see him."

"Will do."

"If Madrian or his companion, Ms. Lauria, comes down from their room, call me on this number," Besim says and writes his cell number on a hotel registration card. "We'll be waiting over there." He points to two leather couches near the main entrance. "One other thing."

"Yes, sir?"

"Let us know if anyone from room 608 calls for room service. We'll take it from there."

"Certainly, Detective. I'll let the kitchen know to call me if they order anything from room service."

"And tell no one else other than the person relieving you at eleven."

"Yes, Detective."

CHAPTER 51

At ten forty-five p.m., Bill wakes up after another fitful nap. His arms and legs feel leaden and his throat is dry. He knows he won't sleep tonight. Instead, he'll lie awake ruminating about the Albanians, about Rami, and whatever may come next. Right now, it seems there's a strong possibility Rami will have to create new identities for both of them. And they'll have to move somewhere far away. It's an appalling reality that's impossible to ignore.

How will we live for the rest of our lives?

"You've been napping," Elena says.

"I'm way too jacked. I'm never gonna sleep tonight."

"It's exhausting, isn't it?"

"I don't know how much longer this can go on," he says.

"I used the burner and left a message for Linda and Greg," she says. "I told them I'm away in Boston so they won't worry when they get back from Aruba. I also called my parents, and left a message at the library."

"Is there anyone else you need to call?"

"No. Not now. Besides, it's too late in the evening."

She sits on the bed beside him. "I want to apologize for being so angry with you before."

"There's nothing to apologize for. I was stupid to get you involved in this."

"You didn't know . . ."

"I should've known."

"Anyway," she says, "I said some things I regret."

Bill reaches for her and they embrace.

CHAPTER 52

"You think we should order up something to eat before room service shuts down for the night?" Elena asks.

Bill picks up the hotel phone.

"What's your preference?" he asks.

"Just some muffins—corn bread, oatmeal-raisin, anything—and a container of coffee. I won't be able to sleep anyway."

"Same here," he says, picking up the hotel phone.

They're in luck. The hotel kitchen is still open. He places their orders.

"I'm thirsty," he says.

"There's an alcove near the elevator," she says. "I saw vending machines in there, one for ice and the other has sodas and bottled water. Why don't I get something while we wait for room service? If we take anything from the minibar, they'll charge a fortune."

"I guess there's no problem going down the hall," he says.

"How 'bout some non-chlorinated water?" she asks, as a smile spreads across her lips. It's her first one since the invasion at the apartment.

"Sounds good."

Elena removes a ten-dollar bill from her purse. "I'll be right back."

She opens the door a crack, leaving the security chain latched in place. She peeks through the narrow space.

The hallway is empty.

There's nothing but silence.

She closes the door, unhooks the chain, then turns back to Bill. "Lock the door and use the latch. I'll knock three times when I'm back."

She steps into the corridor.

There's not a soul in sight.

After closing the door, she hears Bill turn the lock, then set the chain and latch back in place.

The carpeted hallway is illuminated with soft lighting. The alcove is down the hall, past the elevator bank, near the EXIT sign leading to a stairwell.

Walking along the corridor, the hallway seems eerily silent. Not even a housekeeper's cart is in sight.

Passing the elevators, she enters the alcove.

The vending machine is a huge thing, containing a variety of sodas and bottled waters. An ice machine stands next to it.

A twelve-ounce bottle of water goes for $5.00. What a rip-off, she thinks. But the hotel would probably hit them for $10 a bottle if they took one from the minibar.

A sign posted on the machine says it will make change for any denomination bill up to ten dollars.

She slips a ten-dollar bill into a slot. The bill is sucked in.

She pushes the button for Poland Spring water and a bottle rolls out into the bin.

She selects one more bottle.

A second bottle rolls out of the slot.

Elena hears a *ding* from the hallway; then, the service elevator door slides open. It's the first sound of activity she's heard since they've been here, but they've been squirreled away in the room since arriving at the hotel.

About to leave the alcove, she hears a knock on their door about fifty feet down the hallway.

"Room service," says a man's voice.

*   *   *

Room service is on the ball; they were quick getting here, Bill thinks.

He heads for the door, turns the lock, pushes the handle down, and opens the door a few inches; the security latch stays in place.

A man stands there.

He's huge, thuggish-looking with short hair, a prognathic chin, and jug ears. And he's wearing jeans and a leather jacket over a t-shirt. There's no way he's from room service. It's *them*, the Albanians.

Bill begins to slam the door shut when it's impacted so powerfully, the security chain snaps off the doorframe. Blasted inward, the door hits Bill with enough force to hurl him back into the room. He barely manages to stay on his feet.

A huge guy lumbers into the room.

A knife blade snaps open.

Bill backpedals, stumbles, nearly falls, but keeps his footing, gets to the far side of the bed. There's no way he can get to the pistol inside the satchel.

He hears a shout from the hallway. "Bill!"

"Elena!" he shouts. "Get outta here! *Run.*"

Another man, tall and slim, slips through the open door, passes the big one, and comes at Bill.

He, too, has a knife.

Bill is backed against the wall near the window.

The knife slices through the air, barely missing his neck.

Bill feints right, darts left.

The big guy turns and trudges out of the room; he's going after Elena.

The slim one advances, waving the knife left, right, and left again.

Bill dodges the slashing blade.

He's gotta get out to the hallway and to Elena.

But before he can get to the door, this guy'll be on him plunging the knife into him, so Bill grabs the desk chair. Using it lion tamer–style, he thrusts it at the guy's face.

The attacker steps back, feints left, then lunges at Bill.

The chair's legs block the thrust.

Jabbing the chair again and again, Bill keeps the attacker at a distance.

The thug backs off, tries to circle to his right, but the bed is in his way.

Bill raises the chair, swings it down.

The guy pulls back; the chair's legs miss his head by inches.

Bill keeps thrusting the chair.

The intruder backs off, tries circling again.

Still holding the chair, Bill leaps onto the bed, bounces across it; at the other side, he jumps off and heads for the door.

But the guy rushes around the bed and block's Bill's way.

I have to get to Elena.

The thug stays put, blocking the doorway.

It's a standoff.

A man with a knife.

A man with a chair.

Bill's thoughts spin.

How do I get past this guy?

He has to take a chance. Advancing with the chair as a shield, Bill lands a kick on the guy's shin.

The man howls.

Fuck this guy and his knife, I've gotta get to Elena.

Swinging the chair, he rushes headlong at the attacker.

He'll grab him by his jacket and slam him to the floor.

CHAPTER 53

Elena hears a bashing noise followed by a splintering sound.
It's the door smashing inward.

"Bill!" she shouts and dashes down the corridor.

"Elena! Get outta here! *Run.*"

He's in trouble. No, this can't be happening.

Suddenly, a man emerges from the room. He's seriously huge. Holding a knife in his right hand, he's headed toward her.

Without a thought, she hurls a bottle of water at him.

He averts his head as it flies past him and bounces on the carpet behind the man.

Never pausing, he advances.

"Help!" she shouts, hoping someone can hear her voice caroming through the corridor.

If he gets his hands on her, he'll stab her or crush the life out of her.

She rears back and flings the second bottle. It slams into his chest and drops to the floor.

Useless. Like a pebble bouncing off a stone wall.

Not even blinking, he closes in, holding the knife at his side, ready to thrust it up into her belly.

She'll never make it back to the room. There's not enough space in the corridor to get around this behemoth.

She turns, dashes toward the stairwell, flings the door open, and it slams against the wall.

He's behind her—snorting but moving quickly despite his size.

Two choices: she can run up or down the stairwell.

He's huge, has to move lots of mass. She has an advantage if she heads upstairs. She knows from her martial arts classes that unless he's a trained athlete, a man this ponderous will be short on stamina. Thankfully, she's in good shape and uses the StairMaster at the health club.

She pounds her way up the cement stairs, rushing past cinder-block walls. He's following. At the half-landing, she rips a fire extinguisher from the wall and flings it at his chest. It misses, bounces, and clangs its way to the bottom of the stairs.

She turns and races from the half-landing up to the seventh floor.

He's keeping up, snorting and huffing; maybe ten feet away, but gaining on her. She never imagined he'd be this quick, this agile. She stumbles, loses her footing, regains it, and turns on the afterburners and churns her way up the stairway.

It's a half-turn staircase—two parallel flights of stairs are linked by a half-landing midway between floors. She turns 180 degrees and heads toward the eighth-floor. The stairway segments are parallel; he's on the lower one; it's to her left as she races upward. The handrail and vertical bars are the only barriers separating them.

He thrusts his arm between the railings; the knife slashes up and down, missing her left leg by inches. She hugs the wall to her right; keeping away from the stairwell posts, she scrambles up to the next landing.

Don't stop, just keep going. Wear him out.

Another glance back.

Straining to keep up the pace, the man's face is crimson, engorged with blood, and his eyes are bulging.

She's outrunning him.

He's now a full flight below her.

She has to keep going, can't stop until he's tapped out and exhausted.

At the eighth-floor landing, despite the burn in her legs, she continues climbing. She increases the distance even more.

Fear pulses through her like a pile driver: powerful, relentless. She's so adrenalized it propels her higher, step by frantic step, as she powers herself upward so fast it feels like she's flying.

At the next landing, she stops and peers down.

At the half-landing, he pauses; his chest heaves. He begins trudging up the stairs; he's moving more slowly now but he keeps coming.

The knife is now in his left hand; his right clutches the wall railing as he partly pulls himself up the stairs.

But now, she's short of breath. There's just so much adrenaline the body can endure before collapse takes over.

But she has to survive.

Keep climbing.

She thumps her way upwards—more slowly now; her lungs are near-bursting and her legs feel so heavy she can barely move them.

Standing on the tenth-floor landing, her legs begin quivering.

God, they feel like rubber.

Her whole body feels as if it'll turn to liquid and her legs are wobbling.

Her lungs are on fire, and her heart beats quicksilver fast.

A gut-sick feeling rises from her stomach.

She hears him grunting and wheezing far below.

He's coming, slowly but steadily.

She's now light-headed and the stairwell looks bleached white—so she bends at the waist, sets her hands on her knees, sucks in air. Desperately. She remains stooped for a second, maybe two—or it could be longer—then straightens herself and watches as he reaches the half-landing below.

He stops to catch his breath. His chest heaves like a bellows and his mouth is open as he gulps air.

Peering up at her, the brute begins climbing the stairway.

Slowly.

One step at a time.

His left foot finds the next step, the right one follows and lands on that step; he's climbing the stairs like a three-year-old.

He won't stop, isn't giving up.

A frantic sense of inevitability washes over her.

No, I don't want to die. I want to live beyond this. I want to see my family and have a life.

Suddenly, she tastes death, can feel the world going dark. She has to do more than just wear this brute out.

The giant snorts, huffs, and gasps, making the climb step by step, his right foot following the left.

He stops, sucks in more air as she waits breathlessly at the top of the landing.

He's only four steps away, closing in on her.

He stops again.

My God, he's a bear of a man.

She knows when he's close enough he'll use an overhand thrust and plunge the knife into her belly and then rip the blade downwards, slicing through her bowels.

The man's left foot is now one step below where she stands.

She remains stock still.

Waiting for the inevitable.

She'll feel the blade plunge into her and her life's blood will leak everywhere and there'll be more thrusts into her guts, and she'll slip into nothingness.

He's so close she smells his sweat and his sour breath.

She can't let it happen, not now, and with blinding speed she lashes out with a Muay Thai *te chiang* kick as her right leg plunges upwards and slams into his ribs.

Breath explodes from his lungs and he topples backwards, arms pinwheeling in the air. Falling backwards, he tumbles down the stairs and lands on the half-turn landing below. The knife clatters onto the concrete platform where he lies on his back, unmoving.

On weak legs, she stumbles down the stairs.

The man doesn't move; his head has lolled to the side.

Is he dead?

No, he's breathing and blood leaks from his nose and mouth.

She leaps over his bulk, scampers down the stairway, nearly falls but regains her balance, and her strength has returned—adrenaline and cortisol are pouring out in a furious dump of hormones—and she keeps clambering lower, passes the eighth, then the seventh-floor landing in a whirling rush; at the sixth-floor, she flings open the stairwell door, and sprints down the corridor toward the room.

She turns sharply, bolts through the room's open door, and rushes inside.

Bill's face is bleached white. Blood spatters are on his shirt. He's been cut.

The intruder's back is to her as he raises his knife to thrust the blade into Bill's chest.

She bolts toward him and leaps into the air, driving her body forward. At the peak of her jump, she lands a flying knee kick to his upper back.

The attacker is slammed onto the bed, face down.

She lands a punch to the back of his neck, just below the base of his skull.

He lies face down on the bed, stone cold out.

Her body is shuddering and her chest is heaving.

She feels like vomiting.

But she has to see what's happened to Bill.

With her breath coming in honking gasps and her hands shaking, she turns to him.

He looks drained, as though he'll sag to the floor. His left shirtsleeve is soaked with blood.

"Thank God you're here," he whispers.

He clasps his left forearm, tries to stanch the blood flow.

She has to take control.

She rushes into the bathroom, grabs a towel from the rack, wraps it around Bill's forearm.

"Apply pressure, real hard," he says. "Keep it there."

She does it, and through parched lips says, "We have to get out of here before this guy comes to."

"Where's the other one?" he asks.

"On the stairs. He won't be coming for us."

"Press harder," he says.

A few minutes later, she lifts the towel.

Blood now oozes more slowly from Bill's arm. It's an ugly wound along his forearm, which he holds upright.

"It's a vein," he says. "Not an artery."

She tosses the blood-soaked towel onto the bathroom floor, snatches another from the rack, and wraps it tightly around his forearm. She grabs the edge of the bedsheet, rips off a strip, binds it around the towel and ties a tight knot, tears off another strip and ties it around the wrapping.

"Let's get outta here," she says.

She dashes into the bathroom, washes the blood from her hands, dries them on a bath towel then snags Bill's jacket from the closet and helps him into it. She clutches his burner phone and the satchel. "We have to get medical help," she sputters.

In the hallway, they move to the elevator, and she presses the button.

Calm down, just calm down. We'll get to a hospital.

The elevator lets out a ding as the door opens.

"Let's get that arm taken care of," she says. "Then, you'll call this guy, Rami."

The elevator ride seems like it takes forever.

Finally, the elevator door opens.

They're at the lobby.

Bill's wrapped arm is hidden by the jacket.

Elena rushes to the reception desk. "We're checking out," she says to the clerk. "There's a family emergency." She tosses both keycards onto the counter.

The clerk, a young woman, regards the keycards and peers at them. "Just wait a moment," she says. "This will only take a minute." She opens a door behind the counter and disappears.

Elena wonders what the receptionist is doing. The room has been paid for. They have the receipt. Nothing else needs to be done. And Bill's arm needs attention.

"The hell with this," Elena says. "Let's go."

She grabs Bill's shoulder, spins him around, and they race toward the front door.

Ahead of Bill, Elena scampers down the steps, and dashes across the sidewalk to the curb.

A taxi is discharging a woman in front of the hotel.

Elena grabs the door handle, holds the door open, and when the woman is out of the cab, she shoves Bill into the back seat and calls out, "New York Presbyterian Hospital, East 70th and York. The emergency room entrance. This man is injured, so please hurry."

CHAPTER 54

Bill must break another of Rami's rules if this wound is to be treated properly.

It's close to midnight when he shows his insurance card and driver's license to the registration clerk at New York Presbyterian's emergency room. She makes a photocopy of each, then hands them back to him.

Now my identity has been entered into two different databases. We're toast.

In a curtained-off cubicle, a fresh-faced young intern says, "That's a nasty cut. How'd it happen?"

"I was opening some boxes and the box cutter slipped, slashed me," Bill says, thinking once again he's a better bullshit artist than he'd ever thought possible.

"As bad as it looks, it's only venous blood; luckily, you didn't hit the radial artery," says the intern. "We'll disinfect it and stitch you up. Just to be sure, we'll also give you a tetanus shot."

As the intern places sutures into the skin on each side of the laceration, Bill sits calmly. He's not some squeamish wuss who can't watch himself being sewn up. When he was an intern at Roosevelt Hospital, he assisted in surgeries where frostbitten legs were amputated, spent time in General Surgery, and survived the horror of watching CPR being done on his father the night he died. Now it's his turn to be a patient.

* * *

Sitting in a corner of the treatment cubicle, Elena feels her heart drubbing. She tries ridding her mind of the image of that behemoth climbing the stairs and coming after her. Nearly shuddering, she wonders what they can do next.

Where can they go?

They can't return to the apartment.

The hotel is out of the question.

They're in limbo.

Somehow, these people manage to locate us no matter where we are.

Maybe New York's too dangerous.

They might have to get out of the city.

But go where?

And stay there for how long?

They can get to Penn Station, hop on the Acela, and leave for Boston. She knows some people who live in Lynn, Massachusetts. They might be able to stay there, wait this out until there's a solution.

But there *is* no solution. They'll be tracked down no matter where they go. And come to think of it, Lynn's too close to Charlestown and the family. They can't go *near* the Boston area.

And what can this Rami do?

What's going to happen by tomorrow at noon?

There's just something fishy about that guy.

* * *

A half hour later, with Bill's forearm stitched and bandaged, they sit at a table in a nearly empty all-night diner on the corner of First Avenue and 32nd Street.

They've ordered tea and muffins. The place smells of bacon and coffee.

Elena's hands have finally stopped shaking. But her heart is still thumping an arhythmic drumbeat. Never before has she felt so bleak, so helpless and uprooted as she does at this moment.

"You saved my life," he whispers. "Another few seconds, I'd have been a goner. I tried to get past that guy to get to you, but he cut me."

"I don't know how we get out of this mess," she says, as helplessness overwhelms her.

My God, I'm going to cry.

He reaches out and sets his hand on her cheek.

"This is so insane," she says. "I can't believe it's happening."

They clasp hands across the table.

She squints and looks out to the street. Manhattan's nightscape seems lurid and ominous. "How long do you think it'll take before they find us again?" she asks. "And what happens when the hotel discovers those two guys and they call the police. They'll be looking for us, too."

"I'll call Rami," he says.

"What can *he* do?"

"Right now, he's our only chance."

Using the burner, he dials the number.

She watches as he waits; he's obviously listening to a voicemail message.

"It's me," Bill says. "Call me ASAP. It's an emergency. They found us." He recites the burner's number.

* * *

Minutes later, Bill's burner rings.

Keeping his voice low, Bill tells Rami what happened. "What do we do? Where do we go?"

"Got a pen?"

"No."

"Get one and write this down."

Bill makes a scribbling motion.

Elena rummages through her purse, pulls out a pen, and hands it to him.

Bill grabs a napkin.

"Here's where you'll go," Rami says. "It's a safe house. I'd have given you the address before, but until late this afternoon, it was occupied. Get downtown to 247 Mulberry Street in the Village. Do you know where that is?"

"Yeah. Get to 247 Mulberry. Got it."

"It's a red brick building across the street from a restaurant called The Grey Dog. To the right of the door, you'll see an entry panel." He recites the entry code. "Press the code on the keypad and then hit the hashtag button. The door will open."

"Got it." Bill writes it down and repeats the code.

"Go to the third floor, to apartment 3-A. The place has its own keypad and code—write this down: one, eight, three, six followed by the star. Got it?"

"Yes." Bill repeats that code. "Who owns this place?"

"It's a studio apartment. Stay there until you hear from me."

"Whose place is it?"

"Just do as I say. It's a safe house."

"Meaning . . . ?"

"Meaning that no one will come for you. Just stay there. You'll be safe so long as you don't leave that apartment."

"How long will we have to stay?"

"I expect to have a solution no later than noon tomorrow."

"What'll you have?"

"I can't say."

"C'mon, Rami. What happens tomorrow?"

"I'll let you know then. Meanwhile, just get to the safe house. It's been cleaned up . . . fresh linens, the works. You'll find canned food in the pantry along with plastic dishes and forks. And there's food in the freezer . . . enough to last for weeks."

"*Weeks*?"

"It won't take that long."

"C'mon, man. What's going on?"

"Just go there and stay put. I'll have something for you tomorrow. I promise."

"I can't rely on anything with this shit going on. If not for Elena, I'd be dead. These guys manage to find us no matter where we are."

"That's because you didn't stay put in the beginning, like I told you to do."

There's a click.

The line is dead.

Frustrated, Bill presses END CALL.

They're on the hook to Rami.

And they're stuck in the midst of this insanity.

"So . . ." says Elena, "we go to this place?"

"What choice do we have?"

"None."

CHAPTER 55

In the taxi, Elena says, "What kind of a man has a safe house?"

"It must be where he hides people before they go off the grid."

"Go off the grid? I can't do that," she whispers. "I can't just disappear and never see my family again."

"We may not have a choice," he says, knowing he feels the same way she does.

"There are always choices," she says. "I can't give up my family, my friends, my job, my whole life. I can't do it."

"He said he'll have a solution by noon tomorrow," Bill says.

"What kind of solution?"

"He wouldn't say. But there's something about him . . ."

"What?"

"He's connected."

"Connected? To what? To whom?"

"I have no idea."

He wraps his good arm around her and she leans against him. "I don't know if I can do this," she murmurs.

"You're strong . . . stronger than I am," he says. "We'll get through this."

"There's something weird about all this," she whispers. "I can't put my finger on it."

She tries putting the sequence of events together, but there's no cohesive thread, at least none that makes sense.

At some point past midnight, the taxi drops them off in front of 247 Mulberry Street.

Bill removes the napkin from his pocket and hands it to Elena.

Looking at Bill's writing, she punches in the code on the keypad.

A clicking sound comes from the lock mechanism.

She presses the handle down and the door—a heavy metal one—opens to a small vestibule.

Tile floors.

Cement walls.

Dimly lit.

It looks creepy.

There's no elevator.

A narrow staircase is to their right.

"I'm not fond of stairs right now," Elena says, as an image of that giant on the stairway flares through her mind.

They trudge up to the third floor.

Her legs have that rubbery feeling. The stairwell reminds her of the chase back at the hotel.

At Apartment 3-A, holding the napkin, Elena presses the code numbers into the pad. The door—heavy and obviously reinforced with steel plating on the interior—groans as it opens.

She flips the light switch, and a lamp casts an orange glow through the room.

It's a studio apartment.

Furnished simply.

No frills.

No amenities.

No television or radio.

A small kitchen setup in one corner of the place.

Strictly utilitarian.

She notices there's no landline.

If they want to call anyone, they'll have to use the burner.

The room smells of Lysol.

Someone has recently cleaned the apartment.

Elena thinks, *Who is this man, Rami? Can he be trusted?*

She looks in the pantry closet; there are plenty of canned and packaged goods.

Opening the refrigerator's freezer door, she sees frozen foods: pizza, hamburger patties, bread, vegetables.

The bathroom is well-stocked with everything from toothpaste and toothbrushes in plastic wrappings to shampoos, aspirin, and deodorant.

"I don't like this setup," Elena says. "It makes me feel like a caged animal."

This is so strange . . . it almost feels like a dream.

"Rami said we'll be safe here," Bill says, though he doesn't sound terribly confident.

"Rami? You don't know a thing about him," she says, as the unsettling feeling she has about the man deepens.

*   *   *

Bill peers into the refrigerator and comments that there's enough food there to last for months.

"Months? Listen to you," she begins, feeling the mounting tension and frustration she's endured. "You're buying into doing whatever this guy tells you about how we get out of this. And when I asked what you actually know about him, your answer was basically that you know nothing."

Bill nods and plops down on a threadbare sofa.

"Both of us were almost killed this afternoon and again tonight," she goes on, "and that guy still won't answer a single question."

She begins pacing back and forth as her thoughts rush.

"You said he refused to take any money. Does that make sense? No one works for nothing, Bill. So, who's paying him? He wouldn't even tell you something as basic as that. This situation stinks, especially our being completely dependent on this guy."

"Maybe he owes my brother-in-law a favor," Bill says, with what sounds like a feeble explanation. "His firm probably has sent him a number of—"

"And speaking of your brother-in-law," Elena interrupts, "he didn't tell you anything about Rami other than he's presumably helped locate people on the run. Your brother-in-law's clients were criminal defendants, right? Those are the circles this guy Rami runs in, or maybe with a crowd that's even worse." She shakes her head. "For all we know, this Rami character could be hooked up with the *Albanians*."

"I don't see how. Roger wouldn't put me in harm's way."

"Okay, let's give Roger the benefit of the doubt, but keep in mind that he can't or won't tell you anything about Rami. Isn't there a chance that, without realizing it, he's led you deeper into this mess?"

Bill shakes his head but remains silent.

"And doesn't it seem strange that, ever since you've been speaking with Rami, you've been tracked everywhere you've gone?"

Elena paces back and forth. "What was Rami's office like?"

Bill describes the office setup and the receptionist.

"She was speaking in a *foreign language*?"

"Yes."

"Could the language have been *Albanian*?" Elena asks, aware of her heart kicking violently.

"I wouldn't know Albanian if I heard it."

"Let's think about it," she says. "Has Rami offered to get you a new identity?"

"No, not yet."

"Why not?"

"It hasn't come to that. He says he's working on things, that he'll have a solution by noon tomorrow."

"Let's look at it this way . . ." she says. "Rami's an expert when it comes to finding people, right?"

"Yes."

"So *he* could be tracking us and communicating with the Albanians."

"I don't buy it."

"And Rami directed us to this place."

"Yes . . . ?"

"For all we know, he sent us to this place so we can be picked off. Maybe a bunch of guys will show up *here* and we're dead."

"Elena, don't let your imagination take over."

"You said he's *found* people who were on the run. People like us. Maybe he's finding *us*. And he knows *exactly* where we are right now."

When she utters those words, Bill's face goes pale.

"I'm wondering . . ." she says. "Can a burner phone be hacked?"

"I don't know."

"What kind of name is *Rami*?" she asks.

"I have no idea. Roger thinks it's an alias."

"An alias? That's even *more* suspicious."

"Maybe we're both getting paranoid," he says.

"Or, maybe my gut's telling me something."

"I get it. But what can we do? Why not wait until tomorrow? If nothing happens by then, we get out of here."

"And go where?"

"I don't know," he says.

"We could be sitting ducks just waiting for these guys to show up."

"What choice do we have?"

"We have to *make* a choice," she says.

"And go where?"

"We can find a place . . . somewhere," she says.

"Let's wait 'till noon tomorrow."

"Maybe we should get out of here now because something is clear . . . each time you speak to this Rami guy, not long after that, the Albanians show up."

Bill's face turns milk white. "I get it, but let's wait it out," he says. "We don't leave this room. We don't open the door for anyone. If someone knocks, we call 911. I noticed the door's reinforced so we wait until the cops get here."

"Okay, Bill, I don't know about you, but if we don't hear from Rami by noon tomorrow, I'm out of here."

"And I'll be with you."

"And tonight . . . I can't imagine what it'll be like to sleep here just waiting for something else to happen."

CHAPTER 56

Bleary-eyed, Bill glances at his watch.

It's eight in the morning. He slept in restless segments.

"So, we're agreed about getting out of the city?" Elena whispers. "At least for a while."

"If we don't hear from Rami by noon, we leave for Penn Station."

But where will we go. We'll have to decide before then.

After showering, he makes coffee while she puts slices of bread in the toaster.

Setting their plates on the table, Elena says, "I've been thinking . . . there's no way we can seriously consider taking on new identities. Even if we change our names and take on new lives, if we become different people, they could come for our relatives and use them for leverage. If that happens, I'd have to let them take me."

"Then there's no way out of this," Bill says.

"It's hopeless."

"I can't tell you how sorry I am for having sucked you into this."

"You couldn't have known it would be this way."

As they embrace, Bill realizes how quickly their lives have dropped into a sinkhole.

Elena pulls away from him, looks into his eyes, and says, "I just don't trust this man, Rami."

CHAPTER 57

At nine fifteen that morning, Kosta Bronzi, with Alex tagging along behind him, walks into Kosova Delicatessen on Arthur Avenue in the Bronx.

Whenever he enters the store, he's reminded that the proprietors, Urtan and Lendina, came to America years earlier with little more than lint in their pockets. Though they took paths very different from the one he traveled, their story is not too dissimilar from his own. Aside from the death of their son, theirs has been a success story.

As he usually does, Kosta stops and examines the prepared food inside the glass-faced display counter. It's difficult to resist tasting and then ordering something, especially the Albanian *shendetlie*, the honey and nut cake he loves. It goes perfectly with a cup of tea, especially in the morning. Lendina, the gray-haired proprietor, makes the best *shendetlie* Kosta's ever tasted. Hers is even better than Edonia's, which is the highest compliment he can imagine conferring on anyone.

Urtan and Lendina greet him. "Good morning to you, Mr. Bronzi," says Lendina. "One of your associates is already upstairs waiting for you. Would you like us to send up some cake? The *shendetlie* will be out of the oven in a few minutes. I baked a larger batch than usual."

"That's so kind of you, Lendina. You know how I love your *shendetlie*. Please send some up along with five coffees and a container of tea. You know which tea I prefer."

"Of course, Mr. Bronzi. The Albanian tea. And with cream and sugar on the side as usual?"

"Yes, if you please."

Though he's about to go upstairs to the office, Kosta stops and turns to the couple. "You know my son, Alex, don't you?" he asks, clasping Alex's arm.

These poor people have suffered terribly since the loss of their son. How do you live beyond the death of your child, especially when that death resulted from senseless violence?

To help offset their grief, Kosta rents this retail space to them for a pittance and knows he'll never increase their rent, no matter what may happen in the future.

"Such a handsome young man," Lendina replies as she comes around from behind the counter.

Alex smiles, but remains silent.

Kosta has never known him to be capable of embarrassment, but it seems Alex doesn't quite know how to handle the compliment.

About to open the door leading to the stairway, Kosta again turns back. "By the way, how's business?"

"Excellent, Mr. Bronzi," replies Urtan. "Better than ever, thanks to you."

"And everything else?"

"We have wonderful news," Lendina says, approaching Kosta. "Our daughter, Leonora, is going to have a baby. Soon, we will be the grandparents of a little boy." Urtan and Lendina smile as they clasp each other's hands.

"Congratulations to you both. It's a cherished event that will tide you happily through this life."

Yes, for them, the child will take on the qualities of the son they lost. Though that loss can never be replaced, it's a fortunate turn of events. If only Alex could be half the son Lendina's and Urtan's was.

Wiping her hands on her apron, Lendina's tremulous voice betrays her nervousness when speaking to Kosta. If she only knew how plagued he is by his son's immaturity, she and Urtan would feel pity for him.

"No matter what has happened in our lives," Lendina says, "we have so much to be grateful for, Mr. Bronzi. We want you to know how much we appreciate what you do on our behalf. We wouldn't have this store if not for you. And we want you to know that our daughter is going to name the child Kostandin. And, of course, we will call him Kosta."

"I'm truly honored," he says, filled with a warm feeling.

Sometimes the good a man does can make up for the evil he has inflicted on others.

"I'm expecting three more men in addition to the one who is already here. That's why I've asked for so many coffees today, along with my tea. In fact, when they arrive, if the *shendetlie* is ready, have my associates bring it, and save yourself a trip up those stairs."

"It's no trouble at all," says Urtan. "Lendina will bring everything upstairs."

Kosta and Alex make their way to the stairway.

Climbing the stairs, Kosta recalls his own rise to power. As a young man, he was driving Agron Malotta, the nephew of Boss of

Bosses, Kazim Malotta, to an appointment. Suddenly, on a deserted street, two men from the Merko clan opened fire with semiautomatic weapons, intending to assassinate young Malotta.

Kosta steered the car toward the shooters and slammed one man against a wall, crushing his pelvis. Kosta leaped out of the sedan and pumped three bullets into the back of the other attacker who was fleeing. He finished off the injured man with a bullet to his skull. When Agron Malotta told his uncle Kazim what had happened, Kosta's future was assured and he rose through the ranks to become a Kyre.

Killing and intimidation have been his way of life since he left Albania. It seemed if he ever became Kyre, life would be beautiful. But now, it feels as ordinary as a cup of tea. He sometimes wonders why striving for what seems precious is so much better than achieving it.

But enough about wishes, dreams, or the past.

The present is most troubling.

His son has created a problem that must be solved.

As expected, the outer office door is already open and Jozif, the bodyguard, armed with a Heckler & Koch semiautomatic, is waiting at the top of the landing.

"Good morning, Jozif. How are you?" Kosta says.

"Fine, sir. And you?"

"Good, good. When Besim and Valmir get here, let them in. They'll have another man with them. Oh, Urtan and Lendina will be sending up honey and nut cake, along with coffee. There will be enough for you, too."

"Yes, sir. And thank you."

After Kosta and Alex enter the room, Jozif closes the outer door to stand guard outside the conference room.

The inner door is a heavily reinforced barrier and Kosta makes certain it's closed tightly. The rubber edging makes a sucking sound as it contacts the doorframe. No need for Jozif to hear what Kosta will say.

He and Alex sit at the table, across from each other.

"I'm going to tell you one more time, Alex. You're here today so you can see the trouble your carelessness has caused. I want you to listen to what's being said and say nothing. Not a single word. Is that understood?"

"Oh, Dad, I've told you, the guy doesn't know shit about anything."

"Watch your language, Alex. You don't speak that way to your father."

"Yeah, yeah. I know. I gotta show some *respect*." His lips spread into a forced grin.

"That's right, *respect*. And you'd better watch out because—"

"We're not the in the old country, Dad. This is America. We don't do that kind of crap anymore."

Something jumps in Kosta's chest, but he stifles the urge to reach across the table and give Alex a swift slap. Hitting Alex would only make the boy sulk and would derail the importance of what must be conveyed to his son. "This is so typical of you, Alex. You're reckless and immature."

Alex sighs and his eyes roll upward.

It's clear he's bored by Kosta's words.

"This headshrinker is dangerous," Kosta says. "And the woman he's with can't be trusted, either. Now, *two* people must be silenced. And eventually, there'll be three, and then more."

Shaking his head, Alex says, "I've told you a hundred times, the guy knows nothing."

Kosta feels stomach acid scorch the back of his throat. The boy is so irresponsible and, in his way, is stupid. He'll never be suited for life in the clan.

"You have to learn to be closed-mouthed," Kosta says. "You talk too much and you give yourself away. It's a child's way in the world."

Alex's lips spread into a smirk. He clearly has no tolerance for Kosta's warnings. It's maddening.

How is it that Edonia and I have been so cursed to have a son this arrogant and stupid?

"Listen to me," Kosta says, keeping his voice even, yet it's steely in line with his feelings. "And wipe that smirk off your face when I talk to you. A real man doesn't shoot his mouth off to others; he doesn't boast or let people know what he's thinking."

Alex gives him that I've-heard-it-all-before look; yet Kosta hopes he's making a small dent in the boy's stubbornness, hopes that *something* will penetrate his son's thick skull.

"When the others get here, I want you to act like a man who's taken the oath of *besa*, a serious man. If you don't live by the code, you'll bring shame on yourself and your family."

"The *code*? That's old-time nonsense."

"I asked if you understand."

'Yes, Dad," he replies in a jaded voice. "Whatever . . ."

Whatever . . . these kids use that word all the time. It signifies boredom. Don't tell me anything because I know it all.

"Don't use that tone of voice with me. You'll show respect."

"Yes, Dad." Another sigh.

Alex's cell phone lets out its ringtone. He reaches into his pocket, takes out the phone, and stares at the device.

Kosta can barely believe it. "Turn that thing *off*," he snaps.

Alex turns it off, then eyes Kosta with a look that says, *So what*?

"That's your regular phone. Have you had it on during this entire trip here . . . from Rye to the Bronx?"

Alex shrugs, then shakes his head, barely tolerating his father's concern.

"This is what I mean," Kosta says. "You should know better than to leave your phone on and bring it here. Besim gave you an encrypted phone. Where is it?"

"I left it home."

"My God, what is *wrong* with you?"

"Oh, stop making such a big deal out of everything," Alex says crossing his arms in front of his chest.

"I have news for you, Alex . . . your mother and I have decided it's time for you to get a place of your own. You must take on an adult's responsibility."

"Okay, okay. I'll move out if that's what you want."

"It has nothing to do with what *I* want. It's for your own good. You need to grow up."

"Yeah, yeah, yeah."

"I'm telling you, Alex, don't—"

Footsteps and voices can be heard coming from the stairway.

Kosta holds his tongue. There's no need for his family's troubles to be aired in front of his subordinates.

The outer door opens. Besim and his second in command, Valmir, exchange a few words with Jozif, then open the inner door and enter the room. Bruno Rudaj, the assassin, is with them.

It's as though an electric current interrupts the beating of Kosta's heart.

Besim and Valmir look like they've been in a brawl.

And came out on the losing end.

Besim is wearing a cervical collar. He walks stiffly as though he's in great pain.

And Valmir, an immense man, looks like he was run over by a truck. His face is swollen with black and blue circles around his eyes. His nose is flattened and bandaged; for sure it's been broken. And he walks with an obvious limp. And Bruno's face is bruised, too.

"What happened to you?" Kosta asks. "But before you tell me, close the door, Valmir. We don't want anyone to hear us."

Valmir limps to the inner door, closes it, then sits at the table next to Alex. Besim and Bruno sit on the other side of Alex. They all face Kosta across the table.

Besim describes the unsuccessful attempt to get Madrian and the woman at the hotel.

Kosta shakes his head. This has become far more complicated than he could have imagined.

Hearing Alex sigh, he shoots him a look cold enough to lower the room's temperature.

"We've lost too much time," Kosta says. "I'm sure Madrian will go to the authorities, if he hasn't done so already."

Another sigh erupts from Alex.

Kosta glares at him.

"Dad, I've told you a hundred times ... he doesn't know anything."

"But we know something very important," says Besim, straightening himself in the chair. "And it'll ensure we get to Madrian and this woman."

Alex lets out a deep sigh and shakes his head.

CHAPTER 58

Kosta stifles the urge to lash out at Alex. Physically.

But not in front of the other men.

And what's more, he must focus on the business at hand. This is too important to be sidetracked by his son's recklessness.

He turns to Besim. "What do we know?"

"We can get to the woman. We went online and learned she's from the Boston area. Her parents live in Charlestown and we have their address. We can hold one of them hostage until she gives herself up and tells us where Madrian is hiding."

"Very good, Besim. "

"Since we have a short window of time," Besim says, "I propose we send a team of men to Boston. We can get there today and take one of her parents, probably the mother. We have contacts in Boston and can keep her hidden away in case we need her as proof of life for the Lauria woman."

"Yes, that's best. And take Bruno with you. He has a score to settle with this Lauria woman."

"Dad, this is crazy," Alex blurts out. "Madrian knows nothing and you're gonna have these people clipped over nothing?"

Ignoring Alex's outburst, Kosta asks, "How will she learn her mother's been taken?"

"That's simple," says Besim. "We can leave a voicemail message on the home number. It'll instruct the daughter to call and give herself up. Once she learns her mother's been taken, I'm certain she'll cooperate. And then we'll be able to get Madrian."

Kosta nods. "Good, good. Besim, I want you to pick four good men and leave for Boston today. You'll call ahead and make arrangements for a place to hold the mother until we get the daughter. And, to make sure it's done right, you'll go with them and supervise."

"I anticipated this, Kosta. I informed Tomar that I'll be leaving for Boston within the next few hours."

"Ah, he's a trustworthy fellow," says Kosta. "I'm sure he'll oversee things capably while you're away."

"Yes he will. I'll have the men together by eleven, and we'll get to Penn Station by noon."

"And when you get your hands on this Lauria woman, you'll take care of her. *And* her mother. There can be no loose ends."

"It'll be taken care of."

Hearing footsteps on the stairs, Kosta says, "Here come *shen-detlie* and coffee. Lendina's is the best in the world." He's glad there will be a welcome break from all these worries.

Yes, Lendina always moves slowly so she won't spill the coffee and tea.

"Now, let's enjoy some cake, coffee, and tea," Kosta says anticipating that delicious cake along with Albanian raspberry tea.

CHAPTER 59

There's a soft thumping sound outside on the stairway.

Kosta realizes Lendina's dropped something. He hopes it isn't the *shendetlie.*

The inner door opens so forcefully it slams back against the wall. Two men burst into the room.

One holds a pistol fitted with a suppressor while the other has a short-barreled submachine gun. It too has a suppressor fixed to its muzzle.

Kosta hears the soft burp of muffled gunfire—it sounds like champagne corks popping—and he feels a percussive blast wave as blood bursts from Besim, Bruno, and Valmir, along with gouts of flesh as the bullets rake everywhere and the room fills with smoke. A pang of fear shoots through him, and getting to his feet, Kosta sees Alex blown apart in a spray of bullets and blood, and in the next half-second there's a thump in Kosta's chest—it hits with pile-driver force—and then comes another blow so powerful, he's hurled into the air and tumbles to the floor, landing on his back.

There's no feeling in his hands or feet; he tries to move but can't, and now he feels so cold he begins shivering as he gazes up through eyes clouding over and sees the ceiling pinwheel and a moment later, the room looks bleached white as though it's fading, then it all goes black.

*   *   *

The two men stand stock still amid the room now filled with smoke, plaster dust, and wood splinters.

Bullet holes are everywhere, in the walls, the floor, the furniture.

The bodies of the men are sprawled on the floor.

The room is eerily quiet.

Smoke curls from the ends of the suppressors, rises slowly in the air, and fills the room.

One man's silenced nine-millimeter Jericho pistol has an empty magazine—seventeen bullets have been spat out the muzzle end of his weapon.

He removes the empty magazine, pockets it, slaps another magazine into the pistol's handle, and fires a second burst at the dead men.

Their bodies buck and spasm as the bullets hit their targets.

The other man's silenced micro Uzi has fired thirty-two rounds in a matter of seconds. There's no need to slide another clip into the magazine. Still, just in case, he does it.

Shell casings lie scattered on the floor.

Chairs are toppled and broken, and the table is pockmarked with bullet holes.

The corpses are a tangled mass of torn flesh, bone, bowels, blood, and gore. The odor in the room is a mixture of burnt gunpowder, feces, and the coppery smell of blood.

The two men turn to each other. One nods, then points to the bodies.

The one calling himself Rami moves to where Kosta Bronzi lies on his back. He notices the Kyre's eyes are open and he's staring at the ceiling. His chest rises and falls ever so slightly as expelled air froths its way through the bloody holes in his chest. Despite the sucking chest wounds, he's still alive.

Using his pistol, Rami puts a bullet into Kosta Bronzi's head.

He then circles the table methodically and puts a round into each man's skull.

Saying nothing, the assassins tuck their weapons inside their outerwear, turn, leave the room with both doors still open, step over the guard's body on the landing, and head back down the stairs.

Passing the older man and woman behind the counter, they smile and nod goodbye.

The couple returns their greeting.

*   *   *

A minute later, Lendina begins climbing the stairs, and halfway up, smells something strange.

Is it smoke?

If so, it's mixed with something else.

It must be Mr. Nushi at the dry goods store burning trash again. He does it in the back of his place, only three doors down, and the odor of burning trash fills the street, gets into the delicatessen, and can be so overpowering it makes everyone cough. She's asked Mr. Nushi to stop burning garbage, but he's continued doing it.

It's strange, because there's no open window, so how come she smells it today?

She'll mention it to Mr. Bronzi when he leaves, and one of his men will talk to Mr. Nushi. That will stop the burning because, on the street, Mr. Bronzi's word is law. In a real way he's the king of Arthur Avenue.

Carrying a tray with a pot of coffee, a whole honey and nut cake, paper containers for the coffee, and a porcelain cup filled with tea for Mr. Bronzi, Lendina trudges upwards slowly so as not to spill the tea or drop anything. She's dropped it a few times in the past and proceeds slowly so it won't happen again.

At the top of the stairs, she comes upon Jozif's bloodied body sprawled on the floor just outside the office door. Gasping with horror, she drops the tray and its contents to the floor.

Both office doors are open.

Peering into the room, she sees the bullet-riddled bodies of Kosta Bronzi and his son and those of the other men, sprawled among overturned furniture and blood-spattered walls with gray-ish smoke still swirling in the air. The men lie in a grotesquely tangled heap of blood, gore, and guts. The stench of feces mixed with burnt gunpowder reaches her nostrils and brings on a feeling of queasiness.

With nausea rising from her belly, she scrambles down the stairway as vomit threatens to pour from her mouth. Stumbling, she nearly falls down the last few steps.

Reaching the bottom, she feels sick and clammy all over and recalls having heard a series of muted sounds soon after those last two men went upstairs. But she was preparing Mr. Bronzi's tea and the kettle had begun whistling and the brewing machine was grinding coffee beans. The counter-sounds were so loud she couldn't be sure of what she had heard. And Urtan, who's hard of hearing, never heard a thing.

Standing at the bottom of the stairway, she's frozen in place. She recalls those last two men coming into the shop: they had dark hair, penetrating eyes, and knew exactly where they were going.

They nodded politely when they walked past the counter toward the stairway.

And they nodded to her when they left. One man even smiled at her.

They were so polite, she didn't give it a moment's thought. Yes, she thought it was strange how they came late and left so soon, but she was concentrating on getting the coffee, tea, and *shendet-lie* ready to bring upstairs.

But they were killers, sent to put Mr. Bronzi in a grave.

How terrible this is.

It's awful for Urtan, for herself, and for the neighborhood. New people will take over. And a new landlord will raise the rent. They will never be as kind as Mr. Bronzi had been.

And once the rent goes up, she and Urtan will be put out of business.

That's the way thing are. Always.

Now, everything will change because Mr. Bronzi is dead.

CHAPTER 60

At ten fifteen that morning, Nikolai Golovkin sits in the conference room with the other Bratva commanders.

After the Q train passes on the elevated tracks, silence fills the room.

Nikolai's cell phone lets out a ringtone. "Excuse me, gentlemen," he says and picks up his device. He puts it to his ear and listens for a moment. "Send him in," he says.

Moments later, a knock sounds on the door.

It opens to one of the two bodyguards posted at the bottom of the stairway. The man enters the room, approaches Golovkin at the end of the table, bends down, and whispers a few words in the pakhan's ear.

Golovkin turns to him. "It's definite?" he asks in Russian.

The man nods.

"Thank you," Golovkin says.

The man leaves the conference room and closes the door.

Golovkin turns to the group. Speaking in English, he says, "I have good news. It was determined beyond a doubt who executed Boris Levenko. It was a faction of the Malotta clan, the one headed by Kosta Bronzi. The matter has been taken care of."

"The *Malotta* clan?" asks Dubov with an edge in his voice.

"The killing of Boris Levenko wasn't an approved operation," Golovkin says. "Kazim Malotta *himself* was contacted and denied knowing anything about it. In fact, he was appalled to hear that one of his Kyres, Kostandin Bronzi, was responsible for the death of Brother Levenko. Malotta knew nothing about it, absolutely *nothing.*

"And . . . though Bronzi has been dispatched, Malotta has gone out of his way to make a peace overture. He's offered to let us reclaim the distillery operations in New Jersey and Brooklyn. Above all, he emphasized that they have no wish to go to war."

"And the Bronzi faction . . . ?" asks Dubov. "What is to be done with those jackals?"

"Kosta Bronzi, his son, and underboss are dead, along with the other men who were present at a meeting in the Bronx. The matter has been taken care of."

"When did this happen?" asks Dubov.

"This morning, just a little while ago."

A chorus of approval resounds through the room.

Dubov asks, "Are you saying that Kazim Malotta *accepted* that the Bronzi faction was responsible?"

"Yes, he did."

"Why did he accept that as the truth?"

"Because there was proof of Bronzi's involvement."

"What proof?" Dubov asks as a truculent tone seeps into his voice.

"Our skip tracer tapped into his son's phone, the one used by Alex Bronzi. He overheard the son bragging to a friend about what the Bronzis did to Brother Levenko and his lieutenants. They'd outsourced the killings to some Serbs. And our skip tracer recorded the conversation."

"This skip tracer, have you used him before?" asks Dubov.

"Yes, and he's the best in the business."

"Who is he?"

"With us he goes by the name of Rami."

"How did this Rami fellow come to suspect the Bronzis?" asks Federov, the Atlanta pakhan.

"It came about in an unusual way," says Golovkin. "Apparently, there was a witness to the murder that Kosta Bronzi wanted tracked down and eliminated. The skip tracer Bronzi uses, a fellow named McMillan, wasn't available. He was on another job. So, Bronzi's underboss, a man named Besim Sukaj, approached *our* skip tracer, the man who calls himself Rami, though I'm certain he goes by other names as well.

"The Bronzis wanted to hire this Rami fellow to trace the witness to Brother Levenko's shooting. It was a random choice by this man, Besim Sukaj, when he approached our skip tracer."

"Who is this potential witness the Bronzis were tracking?" Dubov asks.

"Nobody important," says Golovkin. "And it's not our concern. The Bronzis have been taken care of."

"So this skip tracer arranged for the assassination?" asks Federov.

"Yes he did," replies Golovkin.

"Who did he use as a hit man?" asks Dubov.

"We don't know and it doesn't matter."

"What about the rest of the Bronzi faction? Why don't we take them down?" asks Dubov with a querulous tone in his voice.

"That won't be necessary. This Rami fellow learned that the hit on Brother Levenko was a secret operation arranged by Kostandin Bronzi. It wasn't approved by the Boss of Bosses, Kazim Malotta. When this man, Besim Sukaj, approached Rami, he said it was not to be discussed with anyone. Only Kostandin Bronzi, his son, and Bronzi's underboss, Besim Sukaj, knew they'd arranged the hit on Brother Levenko. Besim Sukaj emphasized the need for secrecy when he asked our skip tracer to track down the witness."

"Can this Rami be trusted . . . ?" asks Dubov.

"Yes, he's silent and untraceable. We don't know where he lives or if he has an affiliation of some kind. He may very well be a lone wolf operation. But that doesn't matter. What's done is done."

"You don't know *anything* about him?" Dubov asks as his eyebrows rise, nearly meeting his hairline.

"Only that he's ex-Mossad."

"Are you sure he's *ex*?"

"No, and it doesn't matter. I do know that the Israeli government is worried some Albanian factions have begun infiltrating their banking system and they might have wanted to send a message."

"What about the other Albanian factions?" asks Dubov. "There are four others in the Malotta clan."

"As I said, they want to keep the peace. Kazim Malotta himself made the overture of relinquishing the distillery operations."

"Tell us, Nikolai . . . you knew about these preparations in advance, yes?" asks Dubov.

"I did."

"And you told us nothing?"

"True."

"How come we weren't told about this *resolution* in advance?" Dubov asks.

"It had to be kept in the strictest confidence. We didn't want a possible leak."

"A *leak*?" asks Dubov. "So, again, it's a matter of trust, isn't it? Don't you trust us?"

"Yes, I trust every man in this room. But I long ago learned that two people can only keep a secret if one of them is dead."

Chortles resound around the table.

But Dubov doesn't laugh. He scours the table with his eyes, and turns to Golovkin. "You said the other Albanian clans want to keep the peace. How do we know that?"

"Once Kazim Malotta saw the proof of what Kostandin Bronzi arranged, he understood and accepted it."

"What proof?"

"This Rami fellow had a recording of the son bragging on his phone," says Golovkin. "And he secretly recorded Besim when he approached him with the request to track down this witness. It's ironclad evidence of the Bronzis' involvement. Most important, the problem has been taken care of. Brother Levenko's murder has been avenged, and we've regained control of the distillery operation."

"After this meeting we'll celebrate," says Anton Sakharov who, sensing dissension, sounds like he wants to change the subject. "Nikolai, I'm sure you know a fine restaurant right here in Brighton Beach."

"I do. The place is called Nadia's. Brother Levenko owned it. It's been taken over by his cousin Filip. And, gentlemen, after appropriate security arrangements are made, we'll go there tonight for dinner."

"Yes, it's important to celebrate good things," says Sakharov. "As the Bible says, 'Man lives not by bread alone.' Fellowship and goodwill are important."

Golovkin says, "Now that we've agreed on that, let's get back to why we should learn more about the advantages of cryptocurrency before the expert gets here."

CHAPTER 61

y ten fifteen, Bill feels more on edge than before.

What's going on with this guy, Rami?

Can he be trusted?

Is Elena's speculation correct?

Could it be that Rami's working for or with the Albanians?

Will some hit men invade this so-called safehouse, and waste us?

Elena's worries aren't frivolous. She's smart and thinks things through. And her doubts about Rami are magnifying with each passing minute.

And because of my stupidity, I've brought all this down on her.

"Why wait until noon?" Elena says interrupting Bill's chain of thoughts. "I think it's time to go. Now." She reaches for her purse.

Just as Bill turns to grab the satchel, his burner chimes.

He picks it up. "Yes, Rami . . . ?"

"It's over. You're free."

Bill suddenly feels light-headed. It's such a powerful feeling, the room seems to sway.

Steadying himself, he turns to Elena and nods. "Rami, can I put you on speakerphone? I need Elena to hear this. We're at the safe house."

"Okay."

On speakerphone, Rami's voice sounds tinny, but the transmission is clear.

"What happened?" Bill asks.

"I can't tell you everything, but your troubles are over. You can go back to your lives."

He and Elena hold hands. She squeezes his.

"We're listening," Bill says.

"Not long after you and I met, I got a call from someone in one of the Albanian factions. An underboss contacted me. His name was Besim . . . Besim Sukaj. He was acting on behalf of Kostandin Bronzi, the head of the Bronzi faction and the father of your former patient."

Bill says, "What made him come to you?"

"The skip tracer they use wasn't available; he was away in Europe, so this Besim fellow was looking to hire a new one."

"Yes . . . ?"

"Of all things, he wanted me to track down a man by the name of Dr. William Madrian."

"You're kidding."

"He gave me your home and office addresses and showed me a photo of you he took off the internet. They wanted you found, and he emphasized that the job had to be done quickly."

Elena's eyes widen.

"And what happened then . . . ?"

"Of course, I didn't tell Besim I knew you. I was also recording our talk. I asked him why he wanted you found. Of all things, he said, 'I can't tell you more, but the Odessa mafia could become a problem if this isn't taken care of.' Of course, I knew why he wanted you tracked. At that point, he said he'd get back to finalize the arrangement."

"So what happened?" Bill asks.

"He never called back. They must have decided they didn't need a skip tracer. Obviously, they'd located you at that hotel. But knowing what I did, I contacted some people who were very interested in the recording."

"What people?"

"I can't tell you."

"What then?"

"Your former patient was a very careless fellow. I hacked into his cell phone. He was texting and bragging, to a friend, about what the Bronzi faction did to Boris Levenko. You *do* know that a cell phone can also be a GPS location finder. Always remember . . . your smartphone is a spy."

"And . . . ?"

"This morning, Alex Bronzi and his father went to a location in the Bronx. I already knew that Kosta Bronzi holds meetings in an office above a store on Arthur Avenue. Sometimes, things happen very quickly."

"What do you mean?"

"The problem was solved."

"How?"

"Turn on the TV and watch the local news."

"So, Rami, you knew yesterday who was coming after us?"

"Yes, but I couldn't say anything until certain arrangements were made."

"What arrangements?"

"I'm not at liberty to say."

"Why not?"

"Unlike Alex Bronzi, I always assume my communications are being hacked."

"What about the other Albanians?"

"This man Besim was emphatic. He said finding Bill Madrian was urgent and had to be kept secret. It's clear the Levenko murder was a rogue operation undertaken by Kostandin Bronzi's faction. It wasn't sanctioned by the Albanian Boss of Bosses, Kazim Malotta, who was presented with the recording of my conversation with Besim."

"How did you get it to him?"

"The internet has many uses. You can transmit photos, recordings, almost anything."

"So the Albanians assassinated Bronzi for what he did to Levenko?"

"It's quite likely that's what happened. The Malotta clan probably had to demonstrate good faith to the Odessa mafia by taking care of Bronzi for what he did to Boris Levenko. They probably outsourced the assassination to avoid being implicated."

There's a pause. Bill feels his pulse slowing. His grip on the burner phone loosens.

"You're sure we're safe?" He glances at Elena whose eyes are wet.

"No one else knows Bronzi was after you," Rami says. "Or why he wanted me to find you."

Bill's flooded with both relief and disbelief.

It's over. Really over.

"This is such a strange coincidence," Bill says. "How did this man, Besim, know to contact you?"

"It was a random thing, but that's not your concern."

Gathering his thoughts, Bill says, "I . . . *we* can't thank you enough, Rami."

"Don't thank me . . . thank the people who got rid of Kostandin Bronzi."

"But, you were responsible for what happened."

"Hardly."

"Rami, aside from our lives, how much do I owe you?"

"You owe me nothing. It's over and done."

Bill's eyes find Elena's. She stares at him with raised eyebrows.

"I don't understand. Who paid you?"

"Also, not your concern."

"Rami, what can we do to show our gratitude?"

"Just go back to your lives."

"I . . . I . . . we'll never forget this."

"You both deserve better than what you've been through these last few days."

Elena's lips curl into a smile.

"I meant to ask you," Rami says. "What made you go to Elena's place? Were you friends?"

"No. We were total strangers."

"So how did you end up together?"

"She's a tenant in a house where I stayed the first few nights; the house is owned by friends of mine. We didn't know each other but we do now."

"Uh-huh."

From the sound of Rami's voice, Bill can picture his smile.

"It was a random thing," Bill says. "Like the way Alex Bronzi found me."

"Life is filled with random events, isn't it?" Rami says.

There's a brief pause. Bill wants to cling to this moment, not let it pass.

"Now, I'll say goodbye," Rami says. "I hope things work out for both of you."

"Rami, you've given us back our lives. If we can't pay you, let us send you something. We'll drop it off at your office."

"Not necessary. Just give my regards to your brother-in-law."

"Did *he* pay you?"

Rami laughs. "No, he didn't."

There's a moment of silence.

"So this is it?" Bill says. "We won't hear from you again?"

"That's right."

"We can't thank you enough." Bill's throat thickens.

"I wish you both well. And with that, I must say *shalom*."

There's a click and the line goes dead.

Bill and Elena stare at each other, wide-eyed.

"Bill, I think you should call your mother and sister to let them know you're okay."

"I'll do it now. And you can call your family and friends."

"Yes, I'll make some calls, too."

"But first things first," he says. They kiss gently and embrace.

CHAPTER 62

By one in the afternoon, they've returned to Elena's apartment and set everything back in place, leaving no sign of the struggle that had taken place.

Elena turns on the television. The lead story on New York 1 News is about a mass shooting that occurred in the Belmont section of the Bronx.

As the newscaster talks, there's an outside camera shot of Kosova Deli. Police cars are parked in front of the store. The area is cordoned off by yellow and black crime scene tape fluttering in a brisk breeze. A crowd of people stands behind the tape. Police light bars create a surreal flash of red, white, and blue colors washing over the building. Two ambulances and a coroner's van are parked at the curb. An Eyewitness News panel truck stands near the other vehicles.

There's a shot of EMT personnel wheeling gurneys with black body bags out to the vehicles.

A photograph of Kostandin Bronzi appears on the screen.

"His son, Alex, was a younger version of him," Bill says.

The camera shifts back to the on-site reporter.

The newscaster rattles off the names of the other victims; Alex Bronzi is one of them.

Bill and Elena exchange glances.

"I wonder if two of the bodies were the same guys who came to the hotel?" Bill says.

"If they show a picture of that big one, I'll know for sure," Elena says. "I'll never forget that face."

The reporter continues. *Police suspect the shootings were related to an organized crime feud. This is the second mob-related killing within the last week, and police are concerned there may be a revival of the gang wars of the seventies and eighties.*

"It's hard to believe," Bill says. "Alex Bronzi's dead."

"He didn't do you any favors," Elena replies with a sigh. "He put you in terrible danger."

"And I put *you* in danger."

"But we found each other."

CHAPTER 63

Two days later, Bill and Elena are in a taxi going downtown on Park Avenue.

"I'm glad I decided to take a few sick days," Elena says. "I need the time to settle down, but it'll be good to get back to the library."

"I know the feeling. And my patients are glad I'm back."

Bill now appreciates freedom in a way he's never considered. To be in a taxi and not fear they're being followed; to be able to visit Mom, Laurie, Roger, and the kids without worrying about their safety; to walk down a street and not feel exposed; to approach his apartment building or go to a restaurant or bar or a movie theater—are all ordinary activities that now seem like luxuries.

The taxi stops at a red light.

"I'm going to call a broker and put my place on the market," Bill says.

"I just wonder if it might be wise to wait a while, you know, maybe another month."

"Why? Are you thinking we might not work out?"

"No, it's just that everything happened so quickly; it seems too soon . . ."

"Elena, I'm ready to move on. It's been two years. I've already called the Salvation Army. They're coming on Monday to pick up Olivia's clothes. I'll be putting the furniture in storage."

* * *

The lobby of One Grand Central Place is as hectic as it was the day Bill first came to see Rami.

The receptionist, a woman with peroxide hair, peers at them inquiringly as they approach her desk.

"We're here for Rami Associates," Bill says.

"One moment," she replies and begins tapping on a keyboard while looking at the monitor.

"Sir, we have no listing for Rami Associates."

Elena and Bill glance at each other. "Why am I not surprised," Bill says. "Did Mr. Rami leave a forwarding address?"

"No, sir," the receptionist says, again peering at the monitor. "There's no forwarding information. He may have rented a small suite for a day or half a day. We don't keep records of rentals taken for less than a month."

* * *

On 42nd Street, amid the roar of traffic, Elena says, "It *was* a fly-by-night operation."

"The only thing he had with him was that laptop. I still have the burner. I'll give him a call. I really want him to have this."

He slips his hand into his pocket. The Apple wristwatch is gift wrapped.

Bill presses CONNECT for Rami's number.

An otherworldly beep sounds in his ear. A robotic voice says, "The number you have reached is no longer in service."

He turns to Elena and says, "The line's dead. He's gone."

CHAPTER 64

I t's a short walk to Times Square where the offices of Scanlon, Abrams, Sullivan, Morrison & Franks are located.

Roger's is a corner office with a picture window looking south over downtown Manhattan. His massive desk looks large enough to be a helipad. Framed newspaper clippings adorn one wall; they describe civil and criminal cases in which Roger acted as defense counsel.

Bill introduces Elena and Roger to each other.

"What a lovely office," Elena comments.

"Once I became a partner, I was bumped up from criminal to white-collar defense. This office is designed to impress clients, especially the pharmaceutical people," he says with a chortle.

There's a pause.

"So," says Roger, "I'm glad things worked out with Rami."

"You know about it?"

"Yes, Rami called the office and left a message saying the problem's been solved."

Bill and Elena describe everything that's happened since Bill and Roger last spoke.

Though his face blanches when he hears the details, Roger manages a weak smile.

Bill adds, "Do me a favor, don't mention any of this to Mom. I don't want her to worry, even though it's all been taken care of."

Roger nods.

"Tell me something, Roger," Bill says. "How do you know Rami?"

"I can't really say I *know* him. When he's in New York, he calls and asks if I have a project for him. You know . . . someone who needs to be located or who wants to disappear. I've had less contact with him since my promotion to white-collar cases."

"He just pops up here and there?"

"Yeah. So far as I know, he has no fixed address."

"How'd you know he'd be around when I came to you?"

"It was strictly a coincidence. He'd checked in with me only a day before you came for dinner that night and told me about your patient. I'd told him if something came up, I'd give him a call. So, like he always does, he gave me his temporary phone number. I called him as soon as you told me about your situation."

"You've paid him in the past for work he's done."

"Of course. Cash only. With money given to me by a client."

"How about this time?"

"There was no fee."

"How come?"

"I don't know, but I know better than to question him. He made it perfectly clear there would be no charge."

"Those times when you *did* pay him, where was his office?"

"It was at a different place each time."

"And you met with him personally?"

"No. I met with an assistant and gave her the money."

"But not this time because no money was due?"

"Correct."

"So you've never seen him?"

"Also correct."

"Roger, we both know nobody works for nothing. The guy pops up here and there, has no permanent address, and he only accepts cash? Weren't you suspicious, or at least curious?"

"It's none of my business," Roger says in a flat tone.

"Do you know where he's from?"

"I know nothing about him."

"You think he could be Israeli?"

"What makes you ask?"

"The last thing he said to us was *shalom*. That's Hebrew, isn't it?"

Roger shrugs. "I guess that's a possibility. If he *is* Israeli . . . he could be with the Mossad."

"Why the hell would they go after Kosta Bronzi?"

"I'm not saying they did. I just don't know. There are some things that're best not knowing . . . like when a patient asks if you want to know who clipped Boris Levenko." A smirk begins forming at the edges of Roger's lips.

"Assuming he's Israeli, why would he go after the Albanians?" Elena asks.

"I'm just guessing here . . ." Roger says. "I *do* know this . . . the Albanians have operations in the Middle East. They've been trying to infiltrate Israeli banks to launder money, mostly from human trafficking and drugs . . . especially Ecstasy. They avoid using banks in Muslim countries because, being Muslims, the Albanians know those are the first places the authorities would begin looking for laundered money.

"They've recently begun using Israeli banks. Israel has a tight and very stable banking system. They won't let any dark money

ᅟ

ᅟᅟ

flow into the country. I'm just guessing, but I think that if it *was* the Israelis, they may've wanted to send a message."

"To the Albanians?"

"Sure, why not? And maybe to the Russians and their criminal oligarchs, too. The bottom line? I know nothing about Rami or where he's from, or his connections. I'm better off not knowing. And the same goes for you. It's no different than being told who killed Boris Levenko."

"But don't you want to know who you're dealing with?" asks Elena.

"No, I don't," Roger says. "Not with him. Now, if you'll excuse me, I have some important overseas calls to make."

CHAPTER 65

TWO WEEKS LATER

Bill is in the kitchen pouring a glass of wine for Elena.

His sister appears at his side. "She's lovely. I really like her. Mom does, too." She throws an arm around Bill's waist. "You're living together, right?"

"Yes. For nearly two weeks now."

"Is it too early to say it's serious?"

"Is what serious?" he asks, knowing he's being coy.

"The relationship, dummy. Is it for real?"

"It could be. It's a little early to tell."

"Oh, Bill, I really hope it works out."

"And I'm glad you like her."

She's about to turn and reenter the living room but stops. "Bill, that problem with those Albanians . . . it's really over, right?"

"Oh, yes."

"Roger said you misread what that patient said."

"Yes, I overreacted to it. I'm sorry I got you and Mom so worried. It turned out to be nothing important."

"Tell me, Bill," she whispers. "Did that patient have anything to do with what happened in the Bronx? Where those Albanians were killed?"

"I have no idea."

"The news stories are saying it may've been revenge for what happened to that Russian mobster in Brighton Beach. I forget his name."

"Boris Levenko."

"Was your patient one of the men who was killed?"

"My *former* patient. I don't know and I haven't paid attention to it."

"Would you tell me if that shooting in the Bronx was tied to him?"

"Laurie, have I ever lied to you?"

"No, but there's always a first time."

"What about that guy Roger sent you to? Rami. Did he tell you anything?"

"He just made some inquiries and said it was all a miscommunication."

"Well, whatever it was, I'm glad you're not involved."

"I never was."

"You had us all worried."

"I know and I'm sorry I got so worked up over such a small thing," he says. "It turns out I was never in any real danger."

She shrugs and smiles. "Anyway, what really matters is that Mom, Roger, and I really like Elena. I hope things work out between you two."

Heading back to the living room, Bill knows when it comes to Alex Bronzi and the Albanians, he'll have to live a life of lies.

CHAPTER 66

FOUR WEEKS LATER

Bill reaches for the top shelf and takes down the last few books.

He sets them into the carton, tapes the flaps, making sure the contents are secure.

Elena wraps dishes in newspaper, places them in cartons, and stuffs bubble wrap inside.

"It feels so strange," he says, shaking his head. "After a month and a half together."

"Yes, but I really feel we have to do it. You're sure you want to stay here?"

"Yes," he says. "It's a lovely apartment and it's only five blocks from the office." He pauses a beat. "And you're sure about the place on Claremont Avenue?"

"Yes. It's a short walk to Columbia. I won't have to commute."

He sighs, knowing he'll again be living alone.

"It's good you haven't had an offer for the condo yet," she says. "You may want to move back."

"No, that's not in the cards. If I decide to move from here, I'll find another place near the office, somewhere in the Seventies."

"I think this is the way to go," she says. "At least for the time being. We'll sort things out in a few months."

"You're sure . . . ?"

"Yes, I worry we could be staying together because of what happened . . . as though trying to survive forced us to cling to each other."

Bill has to acknowledge to himself that the danger they shared may have fostered a bond that could weaken over time.

"I know how strongly I feel about us," he says.

"I feel that way, too. But I think we need a little more time to make sure it'll work."

"Elena, I know what we have is worth keeping."

"I hope so, but some time apart will help us see things more clearly."

"If we'd met under different circumstances, do you think you'd be more certain?"

Elena remains silent.

His throat thickens. She looks more beautiful than ever, and there's something so soulful in those eyes, something that makes him certain he doesn't want to lose her.

"You saved my life," he says.

"And you changed mine. I'll never look at things the way I did before this happened. Let's just give ourselves some time and space."

He finishes taping the last of the boxes.

"So, it's dinner Friday night?" she asks.

"Yes, at that Italian place on Second Avenue. Lusardi's."

"I'm looking forward to it, Bill."

They fall silent.

Could it be that staying in this apartment is a way of trying to hold onto her? Just looking at the walls, the fireplace, the windows, or the bookshelves re-evokes her voice, the sight of her, even her scent.

Maybe living here is similar to the way he clung to the memory of Olivia by remaining in the apartment they'd shared.

But Elena is a reality, not a forlorn cache of memories.

When she said she'd be moving uptown, a hollow feeling had formed in the pit of his stomach. He knows that for the first time since he lost Olivia, he's felt tethered somewhere in the world because of Elena.

Moving on and anticipating new beginnings.

He's got to give another chance to living life.

That's why he's accepted the offer from New York Presbyterian Hospital to be the chief psychiatrist of an in-patient ward. There'll be contact with people—interns, residents, staff, and fellow faculty members. He'll be back in the world, not just sequestered away in his office seeing patients for counseling. He's decided to gradually cut back on his private practice; so he'll just see patients in the early evening.

And he'll never forget the question Alex Bronzi asked in that last session.

Hey, Doc . . . ya wanna know who clipped Boris Levenko?

As he finishes packing up the last box for Elena, Bill is struck by the fact that this causal utterance, spoken by a foolish, brash, and now-dead young man, has changed his life.

And Elena's, too.

For both of them, gone are the days of feeling alone and adrift.

Their shared nightmare and its loving aftermath have left them in a better place.

Will they inhabit that place together?

Only time will tell.

A NOTE FROM THE AUTHOR

The reader may have noticed certain inaccuracies about minor details of New York City. I've also taken liberties with descriptions of Russian Organized Crime and Albanian mob life.

While accuracy can be helpful in conveying fictional verisimilitude, it seems to me the essential elements of storytelling are those describing how people think, feel, and behave at the extremes of the human struggle. This is certainly true of crime fiction, which deals with universal themes of life, death, duplicity, loyalty, vengeance, guilt, and regret.

Or, as Cormack McCarthy put it so well, crime stories deal with "the fiction of mortal events."

These tales describe how people deal with powerful currents of fear, love, envy, temptation, grief, sorrow, or life-and-death challenges. Such stories are closest to the truth of the human condition.

As Camus once said, "Fiction is the lie that tells the truth."

And I would say: If you want to read lies, read autobiographies and memoirs.

I'm also fascinated by how a seemingly random event can bring about life-altering consequences, either good or bad.

It's always struck me as amazing how one's life can be forever changed by something that happens randomly in a single moment.

—**Mark Rubinstein**,
Connecticut, 2023

ACKNOWLEDGMENTS

I consider myself lucky to have the luxury of sitting down at my desk and telling stories.

As I've said before, though every novel I write feels like I'm on a solitary journey, it really is not. The truth is I never write alone. While it took time to realize this simple truism: my writing has benefited from the collective wisdom imparted by people who've been important in my life.

Among them are relatives, friends, teachers, and authors who've been instrumental in my life and who've influenced the person I've become.

I'm thankful to Patricia and Robert Gussin and the entire staff at Oceanview Publishing for believing in me.

I owe a special debt of gratitude to three teachers who influenced me deeply during my years of training to become a psychiatrist. They are Dr. Bill Console, along with Drs. Dick Simons and Warren Tanenbaum. They imparted to me a degree of insight into human behavior that has been central to my life as a reasonably sentient human being and writer. Dick and Warren remain treasured friends who have enriched my life enormously.

Certain authors are friends and have been important to my growth as a writer. I've shared lunches, dinners, telephone conversations, and emails with them and have read most of their novels. Foremost among them are Don Winslow and his wife, Jean; David Morrell; Simon Toyne; Jon Land; and Lisa Gardner. I can never thank them enough for having shared so many insights about the writing life, its challenges, disappointments, and the role it plays in our lives.

A small coterie of people has helped ease my way through the choppy waters of the publishing world. Foremost among them are Sharon Goldinger, Kristen Weber, Skye Wentworth, Fauzia Burke, John Burke, Victoria Colatta, Andrea Reider, and Penina Lopez. It's always been great to have these people on my team.

Relatives, friends, and associates of many kinds have been vitally important over the years. They include Claire and Dr. David Copen, Laura and Dr. Roger Rahtz, Bert and Joyce Serwitz, Alan Steinberg and Mindi Stark-Steinberg, Phil (Dog Man) Kaufman and Helen Kaufman, Dr. Jeff (the engineer) Ketchman and Niki (the artist) Ketchman, and Dr. Warren Tanenbaum and Nina Tanenbaum.

My gratitude also goes out to Dr. Joel Albert, Dr. Helen Farrell, Phil Lauria and Elaine Tai-Lauria, Jill Kotch, Lou LeJaq, Dr. Peter LeJaq, Dr. Barry Nathanson and Susan Nathanson, Jeannette Ross, Kimberly Simons-Patterson, Bruce Glaser, Harriet Senie, Joe Berland and Suzy Berland, Mark Kelley, Jeff Kelley, Bob Disabato, Gentra Curran, Chris Brubeck and Tish Brubeck, Martin Hirsh and Barbara Hirsh, Pam Smith-Barrett, Arnold Newman, Dr. Harold Sherrington, Tina Schwartz and Bob Schwartz, Scott Williams and Terry Williams, Harvey (HarvHog) Morgan and Valentina Belyanko Morgan, Ann (Rose on the go) White and Steve White, Ann Chernow and Martin

West, Judith Marks White, Laurie Uhl, and many others. It would be futile to try naming all the people who have provided kind words and encouragement over the years.

I owe a debt of gratitude to librarians Elaine Tai-Lauria, Cindy Bloom Lahey, Laura Woodward-Cavers, and Elizabeth Joseph who have provided me with opportunities for author talks at various times and in different venues. A special note of thanks is due to Amy Davenport and Megan Smith-Harris, brilliant people and superb interviewers.

Certain bookstores have been important in my writing life. They include the Elm Street Bookstore in New Canaan, Connecticut; R.J. Julia Bookstore in Madison Connecticut; the Bank Square Book Store in Mystic, Connecticut; and the Fairfield University Bookstore in Fairfield, Connecticut.

Connecticut libraries have supported me by hosting author talks and discussion groups as well as luncheons and special events. They include the Wilton Library, the New Canaan Library, the Bethel Library, the Ridgefield Library, the Stamford Library, the Westport Library, the Bridgeport Library, and the Yale University Library.

My heartfelt gratitude goes out to all the readers who have been loyal fans and given over their precious time to read my books. Time is the greatest gift, and I appreciate the generosity of readers in devoting some of it to my writings. Without readers, a novel is merely a story untold. Fortunately, this tale has been told and, hopefully, has been enjoyed by others.

Many readers have virtually begged for a continuation of the Mad Dog trilogy with Roddy Dolan and Danny Burns, but I must leave Roddy to his peaceful life without my muck-racking intrusions. We must all move on, including Roddy. In a sense, the guy has become a part of me, and thus lives on. I wish him well far into the future. So, I'll leave him alone.

And, of course, there are more stories to tell.

My deepest thanks to Sidney, Billy, Maggie, Hannah, Hank, Jenny, and Jake.

My wife, Linda, has been a source of creative inspiration, selfless input, and boundless encouragement. Aside from being CEO of my life, she's my first reader, a top-flight grammarian and editor, conceptually and in many other ways. The truth is she's rescued every novel I've written. Above all, she's given me the love that makes my life worthwhile.

Website: www.markrubinstein-author.com
Twitter: @mrubinsteinCT

NOTE FROM THE PUBLISHER

We hope that you enjoyed *A Lethal Question* by Mark Rubinstein and that you will read his prior novel, *Downfall*, another psychological thriller. As a psychiatrist, an award-winning novelist, and the author of several nonfiction books related to psychiatry, he is in the perfect position to write dark thrillers with all the elements of authenticity.

Here's a brief synopsis of *Downfall*.

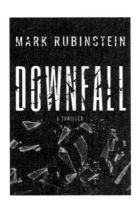

Dr. Rick Shepherd switches on the evening news and sees his own face on the television—except it isn't him, it's a man who looks exactly like him and who was killed on the doorstep of Rick's office. Two nights later, his father is killed, and Rick senses a growing target on his back. Rick needs to learn what's behind these macabre events—before it's too late.

"Downfall is a compelling psychological thriller enriched with a superb (eighties New York) sense of time and place. A page-turner that doesn't sacrifice depth of understanding of the human condition."

—Jonathan Kellerman,
New York Times best-selling author

We hope that you will enjoy reading *Downfall,* Mark Rubinstein's prior novel, and that you will look forward to more to come.

For more information, please visit
www.markrubinstein-author.com.

If you liked *A Lethal Question,* we would be very appreciative if you would consider leaving a review. As you probably already know, book reviews are important to authors and they are very grateful when a reader makes the special effort to write a review, however brief.

Happy Reading,
Oceanview Publishing
Your Home for Mystery, Thriller, and Suspense